# TRANSITION

The Next Evolution Book 1

VERED EHSANI
AVERY BLAKE

STERLING & STONE

## Chapter One

ALIENS DIDN'T EXIST, SO IT MUST BE A BATCH OF crap drugs.

That was Caleb's brilliant conclusion as he numbly watched the creature materialize before him. Except it wasn't really there, just a bad trip on low-grade pharmaceuticals adulterated with some other equally low-grade garbage.

After all, what would an alien be doing in the middle of the largest slum in sub-Saharan Africa?

He gazed at the statuesque alien towering above him and frowned. Could weed rot? Was there even such a thing as *bad* cannabis? Caleb forgot the questions a second after he thought them.

Exhaling slowly, he grinned as the smoke rings enveloped the alien's head. "Wah! Me, I'm gonna tell Samuel a thing or three. What was he thinking? Greedy bastard, sellin' me this junk. The mkundu."

Yellow eyes unblinking, the tall, ridiculously muscular alien tipped his bald head at Caleb. Despite the dim lighting in the one-room tin shack, the alien glowed. His hairless skin was whiter than any of the tourists who flocked to Kenya.

Caleb waved the joint at the strange apparition and decided to call him Sam. "Eh, Sam. Get a tan. You're worse than the mzungus. I thought they were white, but you. Wah! Sammy boy, you redefine white skin. Am I right?"

Sam's colorless lips lifted in a suggestion of a smile, polite and disinterested.

"Eh, wewe, you." Caleb flicked bits of ash over his bare chest. "The strong and silent type. That makes one of us." His cackling laugh echoed against the sheet metal that made up the walls of his house.

The whore next door slammed a fist against their shared wall. "Caleb, you no-brain loser, keep it down. I'm trying to sleep."

Rolling over, he punched his side. "And me, I'm trying to have a chat with my new friend Sam!"

He sank back onto his mattress. "I'm telling you, Sammy. Women. Am I right? Sam?"

The silent alien was gone.

That suited Caleb just fine. Drifting into a dreamless sleep, he forgot about powder-white, statuesque aliens and bad weed.

When Caleb woke late the next day, the world had changed forever.

## Chapter Two

BY THE TIME TRISHA COLLAPSED IN THE BACK OF
THE belching Land Cruiser, she was ready to cry. It had been a day
of firsts: the first day in their new home after living for three months
in a serviced apartment; the first day she had to manage house staff
because, according to Jake, living in Nairobi meant she had to have
staff; and the first day of school.

The only thing that wasn't new about this day was how she felt.
Like every morning since landing in Kenya's capital, Trisha had
woken up and mentally declared how much she hated the city and
everything about it. Three months was long enough to consider a
city, and as judge and jury, she'd made her verdict.

She hated Nairobi.

Even as she slumped in the back seat and wallowed in the ooze of
her self-pity, she recognized how unfair her attitude was. If it was
possible to discriminate against an entire city, she definitely was. Her
unhappiness began long before they moved to Kenya. If she was
being honest — and what a drag *that* was — it had started even
before Geneva.

Tugging at her ponytail, Trisha swiveled in her seat and gazed at

Celine. As expected, her daughter didn't look around; she stared straight ahead, her unearthly pale blue eyes unfocused as they gazed through everything and everyone into a world from which Trisha was barred.

In her lap was a box of crayons, the only thing that really interested Celine. Most kids her age had their own personal, hand-held juke pre-loaded with parent-approved music, books and videos. But not Celine.

Then again, Celine wasn't like most kids.

Forcing a cheer she didn't feel, Trisha stretched her arms. "Let's put on our seatbelt now. Okay, Celine?"

The six-year-old flinched when Trisha's fingers brushed over her to grasp the seatbelt.

Trisha's smile wilted. *After six years, you'd think I'd be used to this. Well, I* am *used to this. I am.*

Even as she told herself these reassuring affirmations, the lie was bleeding through to the core of her being. The same drowning sensation she felt every time she told someone her daughter was fine: *She's just a bit shy and introverted.*

The maid shuffled up to the passenger side and peered through the window at Celine. Trisha immediately bristled at the curiosity in the woman's too-intelligent brown eyes. For a moment she was tempted to tell Mama Noah to stay at home, to inform her that she, Trisha Walker, was Celine's mother and would stay with her child, at least for that critical first day at the new school.

Even as she opened her mouth, Trisha felt a familiar sense of defeat roll over her. There was *no way* she could spend four hours in a room with other children like Celine. It was exhausting enough with one child. And now a school catering to such difficulties?

Trisha snapped her mouth closed and yanked at the seatbelt.

At the same time, Mama Noah opened the door and pressed her body against Celine's booster seat, her smile bright against her dark skin. "Now, mtoto, you must wear your seatbelt."

With utter disregard for Celine's reaction, the maid snatched the seatbelt from Trisha, yanked it across Celine's frail body and snapped it into place.

Celine tipped her head up and stared at Mama Noah. Trisha waited for the inevitable explosion of nonverbal protest. Celine wasn't as far along the autism spectrum as other children, but still enough to fray Trisha's last nerve.

But instead of silently screaming, flailing her arms or jerking her body away, Celine continued to stare at Mama Noah.

"Good, mtoto. Now, let's go to school. Yes?"

Trisha laid her arm across the top of the booster seat. "Her name isn't mtoto. It's Celine."

Mama Noah's confident pose receded. Keeping her eyes averted, she ran her weathered, calloused hands down the red kikoi she had wrapped over her skirt. She mumbled, "Mtoto is Swahili for child."

Pulling her own seatbelt over her, Trisha gritted her teeth. "Her name is Celine."

A large man opened the driver's door. The vehicle leaned slightly forward and to one side as Simba sat in the seat.

*Oh, yes. Add* that *to the list of things reminding me I'm no longer in Kansas. Except there's no yellow brick road leading to the mighty Wizard of Oz, that's for sure.*

She had a personal driver. Since when was she the type to have a driver? Only the super wealthy were supposed to have chauffeurs.

"We're in Nairobi now," Jake had told her as he occupied himself with whatever was so fascinating on his juke.

*Probably that blasted Astral App. What a time suck.*

Sitting next to her husband while being worlds apart, she had stared out the living room window at the man standing at attention next to their vehicle. His strong stance, straight back and toned build didn't match the role of a driver. "He looks ex-military."

Jake had laughed her comment off — his response to many of her statements, as if *she* was the unreliable one. Even after what happened in Geneva, he still dismissed her concerns. "Seriously, Trisha? Everybody here has a driver."

And while Trisha was pretty sure that wasn't true, she hadn't argued. The truth was, she couldn't drive the Land Cruiser. It was an antique, powered with a pre-2000 manual engine. Those old vehicles were banned in Western cities for failing to meet environmental and fuel economy standards, but not here in Kenya.

And of course, what did Jake have to buy? Not a newer model she could manage. He was obsessed with obsolete technology.

All the vehicles she'd ever used were either electric or hybrid, and had self-driving software. At most, she pressed the button to turn it on or change the temperature. But actually shift the gears and direct it through the chaos on these roads? To be responsible for her own safe arrival?

It was no wonder Nairobi had such a high rate of traffic accidents.

She tugged at her ponytail.

*Who, in this day and age, buys an antique? They're museum pieces, for Christ's sake.*

On the plus side, having a driver meant she didn't have to deal with the traffic and insanity that defined Nairobi. But with Jake away on a work trip, she did have to manage Simba.

Their gazes met in the rearview, Simba's penetrating dark brown eyes surrounded by skin that was almost as dark. Pretending to search for something in her purse, Trisha wondered who named their kid after a cartoon character.

Wordlessly, Simba started the engine, his wide shoulders blocking part of her view. Mama Noah slid into the front passenger seat and muttered something in Swahili, or perhaps it was one of the tribal languages. Trisha couldn't tell. Whatever the language, Simba nodded and said something back, his voice low and melodic.

Were they talking about her?

As Simba directed the vehicle onto the rough dirt road outside their new home, Trisha glanced compulsively down the narrow side road bordering their compound. She hadn't noticed it when they first visited the house, or perhaps the estate agent had distracted her so she wouldn't realize there was a poverty-stricken village on the other side of their garden wall.

She'd noticed the shanty buildings from one of their bedroom's windows when they arrived with the moving truck yesterday. Turning to Jake, she'd gestured to their view. "It's little more than a slum."

Focusing on his juke, he'd shrugged at her complaint. "They're just people, Trisha."

"Living in shacks right outside our wall."

After the movers had left, Trisha walked around to stare down the narrow, potholed side road. Several young men loitered outside a kiosk selling something edible, though they weren't eating anything. Their expressions were unreadable, and their eyes tracked her movements.

Momentarily frozen, she stared at the men, her breath catching, before twirling around and hurrying back into the walled compound. Only when she'd closed the automatic gates did she resume breathing in anything approaching normal.

*They're just people. But did they have to be living right next to her?*

Shaking off yesterday's memories, Trisha slouched into her seat and studied the high, concrete wall topped with electric fencing as they drove past their house.

"All part of security requirements," the estate agent had reassured her.

It felt more like a prison, but now, Trisha was grateful for the walls enclosing her new home. The village was overflowing with unemployed youth. The Walkers were wealthy by comparison, and those villagers knew it.

Turning away, she leaned her head back and stared at the ceiling. Despite everything that had happened, she missed Geneva and the order of it all. The cleanliness, the lack of dust, the smooth roads and self-driving vehicles.

"Is Simba your real name?"

The driver's eyes flicked upward and met hers in the rearview before looking quickly away. "A nickname." He eased his hands along the steering wheel and directed the vehicle away from a particularly large pothole.

Trisha smirked, then peered outside.

He cleared his throat. "Simba is Swahili for lion."

"Clearly," Trisha said, not bothering to hide her smile. "The main character in the *Lion King* is a lion."

Simba veered around a cow crossing the road and shrugged. "Members of my squad liked it."

Trisha froze, her smile wilting. "So you were in the army?"

Simba nodded. "Yes, madam."

"Don't call me madam."

"Of course, Mrs. Walker."

"And don't call me …" She shook her head. "Call me Trisha. Do you have guns? Do they let you keep them?"

This time, Simba stared straight ahead, but Trisha could see his eyes narrow, his jaw clenching.

"No, madam."

"Call me Trisha."

He said nothing.

"It's right here." She tapped on her window as if to emphasize the point.

Simba nodded twice, his chin dipping sharply each time, and pulled into the small cottage school driveway.

For a moment, they all sat there, waiting in stillness.

*They're waiting for you. This is new for all of us. They want to know what to do next.*

What if she didn't have the answer?

Snapping off her seatbelt, Trisha reached toward Celine. "You're going with Mama Noah to the school now, darling. Just like we talked about last night."

Talked about. That was a joke. Celine had never spoken. Last night, Trisha had done all the talking — babbling, actually — while

Celine stared into space, and Jake packed his bags. Typical. The house was full of boxes and clutter, and he was on his next trip. Missions, they called them. Working at the UN, he was always *on mission*.

More like a paid holiday with a bit of work here and there.

"Just like we talked about," Trisha repeated, hoping her words reached into Celine's mysterious world.

A car door slammed, and Trisha's heart pounded harder. Mama Noah stomped into view and yanked Celine's wide open. "Let's go, mtoto. It's school time."

Celine turned to face Trisha, reached into the pocket of her blue school uniform and pulled out a folded paper. Without looking up, she handed the paper to Trisha, then extended her arms toward the maid, who scooped her up and lowered her to the ground.

And despite watching another woman walk off with her child, Trisha felt a warm, gooey sensation in her chest, as if her heart had grown big enough to swallow her torso.

There were only three other times Celine had given her a drawing, and Trisha had kept them all tucked in an envelope inside her purse. Whenever life's events wore her thin, Trisha would remove that envelope, slide out the drawings one by one, and recall the heartwarming sensation of each unexpected gift.

Most of Celine's drawings showed the same image in red, yellow and blue. No matter how many times Trisha prompted her to draw something else, her daughter stubbornly drew dots and small circles scattered across the surface of the paper.

The first time she'd sketched this, Trisha had been thrilled that her child — then only two years old — had been able to do something as normal as using crayons. Even better, she'd done what most toddlers do by giving her mother a gift.

And then, for two solid years, the only drawings Celine had made were of those dots and circles scattered across the page. Over and over, reams of paper dedicated to red, yellow and blue. Dots and circles on repeat.

Finally, two years ago, Celine had made her a castle. Or at least, Trisha liked to think that's what it was. It looked different than every other castle she had ever seen, but four-year-olds were supposed to be creative and highly imaginative. Normal kids drew all sorts of fantastical things. Trisha had clung to the hope that this was the start of a new wave of creativity, but the next day, Celine returned to her dots and circles.

A year later, she had presented Trisha with a drawing of a mountain. She was amazed at Celine's level of detail.

*She must have seen it in a photo,* Trisha had thought as she studied the beautiful drawing. The mountain could be anywhere. A jagged structure capped with snow and covered by lush forest across its base.

And now, a fourth drawing.

Feeling it was a positive omen for the day, Trisha eagerly unfolded the paper and stared at the cluster of silver discs floating in a vast expanse of dark blue.

"Celine, how lovely! Can you tell me what it is?" Trisha looked up in time to see her daughter step away, her back to the vehicle.

Not that it mattered. She had received a new drawing from her daughter, like every normal mother who had a regular child. But other mothers didn't celebrate the occasion. They didn't appreciate how magical it was, nor did they treasure the gifts.

Trisha knew better.

She folded the paper with a smile and slipped it into the envelope with the other three masterpieces.

"Have fun, Celine."

But Mama Noah slammed the door before the words had left Trisha's mouth.

As she watched her daughter walk toward the school hand-in-hand with a stranger, Trisha blinked back the tears. She should be with Celine, not the woman they had only met a couple of days ago. Screw the anxiety twisting her stomach into knots at the thought — she should be in there with her daughter.

Surreptitiously wiping a tear from under her eye, she turned her head so Simba couldn't see her in the mirror.

*It's going to be okay. Everything is going to work out.*

All the way to the UN compound, she silently repeated these words like a mantra, even though a sinking weight at her center swore it wasn't true at all.

## Chapter Three

SIMBA WAITED FOR MRS. WALKER TO EXIT THE VEHICLE BEFORE reaching for his phone. Once he could no longer see her, he scanned the screen and reread the message from a young man he hoped never to see again.

*Life at risk. Need help. Only 25K. Please, bro.*

He didn't recognize the phone number, and it wasn't in his list of contacts already, but Simba knew who it was.

Twenty-five thousand Kenyan shillings wasn't much, but that wasn't the point.

*Please, bro.*

Huffing a laugh, he swiped the message off of his phone. The coward who sent it behaved less like a brother and more like the kind of scheming, distant relative no one wanted around. Besides, Simba wasn't one to get burned a second time.

Leaning an elbow on the window frame, he tapped the steering wheel with his fingers. There wasn't a day when he didn't thank his mother for leaving her cheating drunkard of a husband. He'd escaped that life thanks to her. But the adult who called himself his brother hadn't been as fortunate.

"Fortune belongs to the determined."

Simba spoke his words on a soft breath. He was proof of that. His half-brother could make whatever excuses he wanted, but he'd dug his own grave. He could toss himself into the hole, or climb out on his own.

Simba tilted the seat back, clutched the phone in one hand and crossed his arms over his chest. Staring up the path Mrs. Walker had taken to reach the UN gym, he wondered if he had time for a nap. He didn't know Mrs. Walker, but he was familiar with her type. She'd spend at least an hour purging her unhappiness and whatever scraps she had for breakfast while pretending it was all for her health. She'd sweat out her sins, then indulge in a high-calorie, overpriced coffee with women as equally skinny and unfulfilled.

Meanwhile, her husband paid him to sit and wait.

He scoffed at the foreigners. "Works for me."

It was only midmorning, but a gentle heat had enveloped the interior already. His eyes slid shut, and he didn't resist. He wasn't back in Somalia, where dozing on the job was a hazard. With al-Shabaab and several splinter groups targeting the Kenyan army and their allies, sleep had been a luxury.

Now he was paid to wait in peace.

Grunting, Simba closed his eyes, gliding from a relaxed wakefulness to sleep in a sequence of breaths.

In the darkness of his sleep, a figure strolled into view.

"Mom?" Simba squinted, struggling to decipher the landscape. "What are you doing here?"

She smiled, but her eyes held a familiar blend of worry and sorrow. "Simba, be careful."

"I'm always careful." Simba started to laugh, stepping toward her. But with every step, she drifted farther away. "Mom, where are you going? Come back with me."

Even in his dream state, Simba sensed this was not possible. There was an excellent reason why she couldn't stay with him, but he couldn't remember what it might be. Frowning, he wrestled with a memory that refused to reveal itself.

This couldn't be real.

But why not?

*Because she's dead.*

"Simba, my son." His mother's soft voice pulled him into the present, into this strange space they now occupied.

Simba glanced around, searching for any clue as to the time and place. A watery blue light glowed everywhere around him. He stared at his boots. Army issue, one of the few things he'd taken when he'd left, along with a collection of memories he no longer wanted.

The ground glowed blue as well. He lifted a boot and tapped it a few times against the strange surface. There was no bounce to it, no softness of earth or yielding of wood. And yet it wasn't concrete either.

"Simba, escape."

He lifted his chin and stared at his mother.

Except she was no longer there. The mute white child with the strange behavior stood there instead. Her unnaturally pale blue eyes peered at him, saw through his mask to the ugliness he showed no one else.

"What did you do with my mom?"

He finished the question and winced with his own stupidity. This was clearly a dream. An odd brew of memories and emotions which had been stirred over the last few days from the changing of jobs. Nothing more than that.

*They're coming.*

The words echoed in his head. A soft voice, light and childlike, but serious enough to convey an ominous message. He shuddered. "Who's coming?"

The child turned around and walked away. Before he could follow, the light engulfed her, leaving him alone in a sphere of blue. A screeching klaxon boomed from every direction. His hands snapped over his ears, and he flinched as the alarm continued to bray.

*They're coming.*

Jerking awake, Simba gasped and gulped his breath, as if he had been drowning rather than dreaming. His hands gripped the wheel, his knuckles an angry pale color. How long had he been asleep?

Blinking his eyes several times, he forced his hands to loosen, wincing at the painful buzz through his fingers.

He pulled his arms to his chest and stared out the windscreen.

There was no alarm, or sense of any disturbance. Yet the emotional vestiges of the dream clung to him, cold tentacles wrapping him tight and constricting his breath.

"It's only a dream."

His words rang false, but what else could it be?

Wiping a hand down his face, he felt around for his phone until he found it by his feet. Stretching his arm past the steering wheel, he patted the carpet until his fingers brushed the phone's cool surface.

He stared at the notification onscreen.

"What now?"

He pulled up the Astral App.

The image felt like the proverbial punch in the gut. His mouth went dry as he gawked at an impossible vision while the dream words echoed around him.

*They're coming.*

## Chapter Four

*AIR. WATER. AIR. WATER.*

She fell into the rhythm of her swim, arms and legs flowing in sync, vision alternating between the air touching the pool's surface and the water below.

*Inhale one, two, three. Exhale one, two, three, four, five.*

Jake always said her body was designed for swimming. That wasn't really true. But over the years, she had honed her skills, training rigorously on an almost daily basis. Living in Geneva had nearly killed her in more ways than one. She hadn't had easy access to a large public pool. That, and the birth of their unplanned child had thrown her for a loop. At least in Nairobi, she could use the UN facilities.

*Inhale one, two, three.*

As her head broke the surface, a mother walked along the far end of the pool, tugging a reluctant toddler behind her.

*Celine.*

How was she doing? Was the maid able to handle her? And the teachers. Were they really experienced with such children?

*Exhale one, two, three, four, five.*

Pushing away the tension which invariably surfaced at the

thought of her daughter, Trisha sunk below the ripples of her passage. A soothing silence surrounded her, inviting her to forget everything and everyone. She stayed under for several more strokes than usual.

As she breached the surface, Trisha blinked in time to see Joyce and Sheetal arrive from their yoga class, coffees and phones in hand, bodies embraced by formfitting spandex. Joyce waved at her.

Pretending she didn't see, Trisha plunged below the surface and into the calm lurking beneath, the soothing silence that only water could ever really provide.

After several more laps, she finally acquiesced to her body's need for caffeine. Climbing out, she wrapped herself in a towel, trotted up the stairs to the balcony overlooking the pool, and approached Sheetal and Joyce's small table.

Joyce raked Trisha with her gaze, assessing and judging, her lips twitching into a hint of a smile. "Oh my gosh, Trisha. Did you lose more weight? Again?"

That was how too many conversations started with Joyce: *body weight*. Had someone lost or gained anything worth mentioning? And if it wasn't the weight, it had to be the haircut or color, or was that a new shirt? Questions were never asked in a flattering manner or out of friendly curiosity.

Shrugging, Trisha dropped into a chair on the other side of the table.

Joyce kept babbling to Sheetal. Trisha hadn't realized how chatty Joyce really was until that moment. She talked the entire time, her mouth flapping with so many useless words, eyes glued to her phone, thumbs tapping out messages while her eyes fixed on whatever held her fascination for the next fleeting moment.

Trisha combed her fingers through her wet hair, eyes narrowing. Joyce reminded her of Jake, with his fixation on whatever was happening outside their conversation, on pretty much anything that wasn't the person directly in front of him.

Focusing on Joyce's mouth, Trisha sunk back in her chair. *How rude.*

"Have you heard about the new café at Westgate?" Joyce swiveled to face her, eyes wide with this riveting piece of news.

Eyebrows raised, Trisha stared back and wondered when they all had become so boring.

*Maybe when you agreed to quit your job and follow Jake all over the planet.*

Trisha wanted to gnash her teeth at the nasty tone of her inner voice. Yes, that had been a mistake. One of many. Her gaze drifted over Joyce's shoulder to a rock jutting out from the middle of a large concrete planter. A blue-headed lizard basked in the sun, eyes closed, tongue occasionally flicking into view as if tasting the air.

A waitress reluctantly walked over, her eyes half-lidded, her expression about as interested in them as the blue-headed lizard was. "Can I get you anything?"

No offer for a menu. Probably because she knew there was no point. The women would spend too long staring at the options, and end up ordering the same as they always did.

"Masala chai. Please." Trisha added the *please* as an afterthought.

Sheetal murmured a response to Joyce, encouraging her to continue babbling about the new café. Whatever it was, Trisha couldn't summon enough energy to care. But she smiled and nodded at the appropriate moments, trying to calculate when she could leave without appearing rude.

It was still early in the day, but the café overlooking the UN pool already had a number of patrons inhaling their caffeinated beverage of choice. As Joyce launched into yet another monologue about the executive director's wife's new dog or something equally insipid, beeps and blings began to bleat all around them.

Without pausing their conversations, people mindlessly reached for their phones. Arms crossed over her chest, Trisha watched Joyce and Sheetal both grab their phones and swipe the screen.

"Oh. My. Word," Joyce said. "Have you seen this?"

Trisha rolled her eyes to look up at the umbrella shielding them from the sun. "Of course we haven't seen it, Joyce. You just looked at it yourself."

"Oh, Trisha, stop being such a wet rag."

A chair fell over near the kitchen. Before Trisha could check what had happened, Joyce gasped. "This is crazy. The biggest news ever."

Of course Joyce was exaggerating. The biggest news ever? For her, that meant discovering she was pregnant on the same day Jake announced his promotion to the Geneva office. Yeah, those were both high up the *big news* category, and it was a toss-up as to which had changed her life more.

Sheetal leaned toward her and shoved her phone across the table. "You have to look at this." She moved around the table to sit beside Trisha as if to emphasize the occasion's importance. "It's not possible, right?"

Trisha obliged with a heavy exhale, her eyes sliding sideways to stare at Sheetal's screen. As her brain finally caught up with her eyes, she leaned forward so forcibly her chair scraped against the stone floor.

"What the hell is that?"

For once, Joyce was silent as she gawked at the image floating across the Astral App's newsfeed. Time tiptoed as Trisha zoomed in and out, trying to make sense of the photo.

Sheetal glanced between them, swallowed hard as she rubbed the side of her nose, barely avoiding the gold ring looped around a nostril. Her dark eyes, lined with that heavy black pencil preferred by Indians, widened even farther with the cousin to excitement and the sister to fear. "They're saying —"

Someone screamed from the far corner of the café. A man ran past them, a towel wrapped around his waist, phone shoved against his ear.

"It can't be true," the man stuttered. "It's a hoax."

Trisha glanced over her shoulder as an overweight woman waddled out of the café, her scream bleeding to a whimper. Most of the people on the balcony or around the pool stayed frozen in stunned silence, staring at their phones and trying to process how the universe had just shifted around them without any clue it might happen.

As minutes trickled, shock settled into denial. Yet how could any of them refute the photo the Astral App was displaying from its telescope on the dark side of the moon?

As terrifying as the images were, Trisha was frozen to her seat by the memory of Celine's drawing: silver discs against a dark blue background, a childish replica of the photo.

She had to keep telling herself it was impossible.

Sheetal pressed her shoulder against Trisha's, and they read the comments in silence. They surveyed the analysis and guesswork that was already flooding in from all over the world. The waitress never brought Trisha's tea, but it didn't matter. She'd lost her appetite.

"It's getting late."

Joyce's words cut through the numbness that had settled around them like a heavy cloak.

Trisha glanced at her watch and started. They'd been staring at the newsfeed for almost an hour. How had that happened?

Hands shaking, Sheetal retrieved her phone and continued to scroll through more of the ever-lengthening newsfeed.

Not sure what she was supposed to do next — and there was *something*, she could feel it — Trisha stared at the concrete planter. As if tasting her shift in emotions, the blue-headed lizard's eyes flicked from side to side before darting out of view.

Reaching for her bag, Trisha rummaged around. Her fingers brushed the envelope with the four drawings, and she almost pulled it out to look at the fourth one, the one that reminded her of the Astral photo.

*Coincidence.*

Because there was no other explanation for that drawing.

She patted around the inside of her bag until her hand found the reassuring solidity of her phone. There had to be a reasonable explanation. Because if the photo was real …

"It can't be," Trisha whispered to herself.

Pressing the screen, she stared at the notifications without reading them. Another blinked into view.

Shaking her head, Trisha focused on the bits of text. Several missed calls from Celine's new school. Her heart raced as she realized her phone had been on silent. Had Celine thrown a fit? Had something happened to her?

Scrolling down, she read a message sent more than half an hour earlier from the headmistress:

*Evacuation protocol. School closing, effective immediately. Please collect your child. Not a drill.*

Fingers quivering, she fumbled with the phone and punched at the digital keyboard several times before she clicked on the school's number.

No response.

Gasping around a wail of despair, Trisha jumped up, knocking her elbow against Sheetal's shoulder.

"I have to go."

Sheetal reached up and latched onto Trisha's arm, fingers digging in.

"What?" Trisha shrieked.

Was Celine still at the school? They wouldn't send her home alone, would they?

Trembling, Sheetal lifted her phone to show her the screen. "NASA has just confirmed it. And the media is saying —"

Trisha tugged her arm free. "What? What are they saying?"

Clutching a hand over her mouth, Sheetal squeezed her eyes shut and whimpered.

Joyce slumped in her seat and stared vacantly at the ceiling. "They're saying those are alien spaceships, and they're heading toward Earth."

## Chapter Five

"WHAT'S SO SPECIAL ABOUT THIS SCHOOL, ANYWAY?" MAMA NOAH ASKED the nanny sitting beside her.

The nanny, a young woman named Anne, shrugged, looking as bored as Mama Noah felt. "The fees are special, that's for sure."

The women cackled together, soft enough not to disturb the teacher, Miss Rita. Despite their caution, the plump Indian woman sitting in front of the class looked up from her book to frown at them.

Mama Noah lowered her head but kept smiling.

*Mzungus. What a funny lot of people these foreigners are.*

She watched the children. Half of them ignored Miss Rita's attempts to hold their attention. Mama Noah wondered why they were really here. If Mrs. Walker wanted a break from her child, she could have left Celine at the house and gone. Why this pretense at school?

Too much money; not enough sense.

Shifting in her seat, Mama Noah searched the room for the child. She was easy to spot. Many of the children were European, but Celine redefined pale. It looked as though she had never seen the sun.

Mama Noah scoffed to herself. Although she had only just met

Mrs. Walker, she could imagine the woman's mothering style. She probably never let her child outside for fear she'd catch a cold or skin her knees. As for the father …

Mama Noah had only met Mr. Walker on two occasions. The first was when the couple had visited the house with the real estate agent, and the second was on moving day. He showed up at the end of the day, grunted a greeting as he passed the kitchen, and that was it. The next morning, he'd left before Mama Noah entered the house.

But she'd heard the Walkers talk. More like shout. Although it had nothing to do with her, she was relieved to hear he'd be traveling. It made her job easier.

Mama Noah glanced at Celine, wondering how much she understood about her parents' relationship. The child didn't seem to react to the tension. She suspected that while the girl didn't talk, her brain worked just fine.

Celine looked up, as if sensing that she was being watched. Straight, blonde hair swirled around her face like a living curtain. The eyes staring back at Mama Noah were a washed-out blue with no emotion, interest, or anything else.

She smiled and waved at Celine to go to the other children, most of whom were now clustered around Miss Rita and listening to her story. Celine held her gaze for a moment longer, then turned her back and continued her coloring.

Mama Noah slumped in her chair. If it made the child happy, that was good enough for her. Crossing her arms, she wondered if anyone would notice her sleeping.

The classroom door swung open hard enough to slam against the wall and rattle the window beside it. A tall, wrinkled British woman strode into class, her eyes wide and startled as she searched the room.

Seeing the teacher, the headmistress scurried over and leaned in to whisper something.

The nannies' soft chatter drained into silence. Mama Noah

watched with mounting curiosity as Miss Rita blanched, and her mouth fell open.

"Are you sure?" Her voice jumped an octave.

The headmistress shushed her, eyes twitching upward toward the circle of children, then beyond them to the line of watching nannies. Her mouth moved, her words a whisper.

Fishing a phone from her pocket, Miss Rita swiped her fingers across the screen. Then a strangled squeak dribbled out of her gaping mouth. "What are we going to do?"

The headmistress stood and gazed over the children at the nannies, chin jutting out firmly while her hands clenched by her side.

"We are closing the school, effective immediately. I've already sent messages to your employers. Please gather your children and prepare to leave."

With no more explanation the headmistress left the room, her long skirt swirling in agitation at her ankles. Mama Noah and Anne traded knowing looks.

Clucking her tongue, Mama Noah shook her head and smiled. "Mzungus."

Despite the special nature of the children, the school's closure proceeded with efficiency and precision. In minutes, the headmistress had herded everyone outside where a lineup of cars was already forming.

Holding Celine's hand tightly, Mama Noah maneuvered through the cluster of children and nannies until she had a clear view. No sign of the blue Land Cruiser, Mrs. Walker or Simba.

Peering down at Celine, Mama Noah squeezed her hand reassuringly. "Your mom will be here soon. Don't worry, mtoto."

Celine tilted her chin up and stared past Mama Noah. She didn't look the least bit worried. Instead, she stared at the sky, her eyes flickering with the first indication of interest in anything beyond her crayons.

Mama Noah glanced up and squinted against the glare,

wondering what the child saw. "Nothing up there except sky and more sky."

As children departed, the hubbub in front of the school began to settle down. By the time Mama Noah realized that Simba wasn't coming, the other children had all been collected. Even the teachers were filing out of the school.

Clucking her tongue, Mama Noah turned and watched as the headmistress closed the school's front door with finality and twisted the key. In the silence, the click seemed strangely loud.

"I tried calling Mrs. Walker and I've left messages," the headmistress announced on her march to the roadside. Without looking at Mama Noah, the elderly woman patted Celine on the head. "I'm sure she'll be here any minute."

Mama Noah gawked at the headmistress. Was she actually leaving them?

The headmistress frowned at Mama Noah. "You haven't read the news, have you? I can't wait around for Mrs. Walker to show up when she feels like it. They're coming. Everything's changed, and I'm not a babysitter."

The headmistress hurried into the small parking lot and slid into her car. Then, as if having second thoughts, she rolled down her window and leaned out. "Can I give you a ride?"

Mama Noah stared down Kinanda Road. Even with her failing eyesight, she could still see the corner of their compound. No more than a ten-minute walk.

Straightening up, Mama Noah brushed a hand down the red kikoi around her waist and nodded at the headmistress. "The house is just there. We'll walk."

Satisfied by her response, the headmistress revved her car's engine and sped off in a plume of dust.

Mama Noah waited until the dust settled. "What news has the old bird so excited?" Fishing down the front of her shirt, she withdrew her phone from its hiding place in her bra. She flicked on the screen, but nothing happened. "Bad battery."

Sighing, she tucked the phone back in between her breasts. "A little walk won't hurt us, will it? Come along, mtoto. Maybe I can pick up some mandazis on the way. Have you ever tried a mandazi? Probably not. Your mother's too skinny. I'm sure you'll like them."

Tugging at the child, Mama Noah started at a leisurely stroll down the road. It was already late morning, and the day's heat had baked the clay soil into a hard, cracked surface. The road was pitted with holes and bumps, so they kept to the side, right above a clogged drainage ditch. A cow peeped at them through the wooden slats of a fence on the other side.

"It's not far, mtoto. You're a big, strong girl, right? No need to drive to school and back for such a short distance." Mama Noah clucked her tongue. "I used to walk for an hour each way to school when I was your age."

Celine kept staring straight ahead, as if she could see into the house and beyond. Her little shoes barely stirred the dust.

Mama Noah swung her schoolbag back and forth. "It's not easy, mtoto. Life, I mean. Not for anyone. You think it's hard for you? You have a big house, lots of food, parents who pay for your school fees. But not everyone has those things. God is my witness, and He knows life is never easy. It's not supposed to be. All these people running around and complaining, as if they have a right to the easy life. Fools, all of them. And the men. *Bah!* Don't get me started." She clucked her tongue and walked faster.

As they approached the house, Mama Noah continued past it, leading Celine down the narrow road along the side of the compound. "I promise you, mtoto, your mother isn't coming right now. So we're going to have mandazis for a treat. Look at you. Scrawny little thing. You need to eat more."

She continued down the side road to the village entrance where a rickety kiosk leaned against a wall. A young woman with a complicated braided hairdo crowning her head stood behind the rough, wooden counter.

Smiling in anticipation, Mama Noah stared at the large pan of boiling oil propped precariously on a small burner. "Jambo, Martha."

Martha nodded back, her face gleaming with sweat as she worked the pan. Squatting next to her sat a little girl in a spotless red dress.

"Celine, come. Meet a new friend. She's your age."

But she wasn't interested in the other girl. Tugging free of her hand, Celine wandered off instead.

Mama Noah ordered a small bag of the sweetened bread rolls. Chatting softly, Martha dropped several blobs of dough into the oil and scooped a few others that had already finished. The tantalizing scent of baked flour surrounded her.

As Mama Noah waited for her order, she watched Celine crouch in front of a nondescript brown dog owned by one of the village youth.

The dog sat on its haunches, eyes fixed on the mandazi kiosk, tongue poking out of its gaping mouth as it panted. Celine stroked the dog on its head.

And just like that, the scrawny beast forgot about the food. Standing, it licked the little girl's face.

Preparing to intervene, Mama Noah waited for the child to make a fuss and push the dog away. Instead, she wrapped her arms around its neck and nuzzled her face deep into the fur.

Mama Noah popped a mandazi in her mouth, savoring the crisp crust and gooey goodness beneath. She gestured toward the child with a smile. "Well, isn't that a sight?"

She handed a mandazi to the girl in the red dress and stuffed the remaining paper-wrapped treats into the schoolbag. Brushing crumbs off her skirt, Mama Noah called Celine, but the child ignored her.

"Okay, mtoto. But only one more minute, then we go home." She turned and lowered her nose over the open bag to inhale the warm, sweet aroma of the fried bread. "After all, the school called your mom, and you know —"

The dog snarled as a piercing scream shattered the air.

## Chapter Six

WAS IT JUST A COINCIDENCE THAT THE ALIENS ARRIVED THE DAY HER HUSBAND went on mission?

The thought almost made her laugh, but Trisha squeezed her eyes closed instead.

*Hurry up. Hurry up. Hurryuphurryup.*

That was all she could think of. She had to get to the school and find her daughter. But they had to go faster before that could happen.

Why was Simba driving so painfully slow?

The reasonable part of her brain — the part that hadn't melted upon reading the missed calls and the message from the school — attempted to reassure her. Celine would be fine. The teachers wouldn't abandon her at the school, just because her mother was a negligent, self-indulging, spoiled housewife. They would all be there, with Celine, waiting for Trisha, caring for her daughter. It didn't matter that she would most certainly be the last person to show up. They would still be there.

The other part of her brain screamed that she needed to hurry.

A panting filled her ears. Even if it was impossible, Trisha swore she could feel Simba's eyes flicking up to the rearview before looking away. Whatever he thought or felt about her reaction, his expression was impassive.

She didn't care.

Because the lizard part of her brain, the primitive and primordial beast lurking in the depths of everyone's soul, howled the same message: her child was in danger. Rational or not, nothing changed that.

"Can you drive any faster?"

The words gushed out before she realized it. Only when Trisha peered over the front seats at the road ahead did she realize how ridiculous her question really was. A lineup of cars, each containing at least one frantic human, stretched ahead to the red light at the intersection between UN Avenue and Limuru Road.

She pressed a hand to her forehead, willing her throbbing brain to think, think of some way to end this. "Isn't there another road? You know, so we can get there faster?"

Simba shifted in his seat. His fingers tapped along the top of the steering wheel for a moment as he seemed to mull over her question. "No, madam. This is the fastest way. We'll clear the light in a few minutes."

His voice was steady, too calm for her.

*A few minutes?*

So much could happen within a splinter of time. A few minutes might as well be a few hours. Didn't he know how precious every second was with a life in danger?

Except Celine wasn't in any danger.

She was at school with Mama Noah and the teachers. Surely, the school didn't expect people to be lurking around the corner, waiting to pick up their child at a moment's notice whenever the head-mistress issued an evacuation notice? They would wait until every child departed in the safety of a responsible adult. Everything would be fine.

But the rasping from her mouth suggested otherwise.

Staring at the line of cars didn't calm her nerves or make the lights change any faster, so Trisha pulled out her phone and opened the Astral App. Comments exploded in the newsfeed as more photos showed the same silver discs she'd seen at the gym.

No, not discs. *Spaceships.* An armada of spacecraft floated toward Earth, still hidden from unaided eyes by the moon. And despite the horror and the fear for her child, Trisha gazed in fascination at the photos. How was it possible? And did it really matter?

The Land Cruiser lurched forward and turned at the light.

"Finally," Trisha muttered, then frowned as the vehicle rolled to a halt. Staring up from the mesmerizing photos, she groaned, taunted by another line of cars. "Can't you drive on the side of the road? I've seen others do it."

Simba's deep, dark eyes stared in the mirror. The calm intensity, the penetrating strength, trapped her for a moment and caused her face to flush.

"Matatus do that, madam."

Her hands tightened around her phone as one of the minivans providing a privatized form of public transport eased by them, using the sidewalk as a passing lane.

"So?"

His eyes slid forward. "It's illegal, and there are police officers ahead."

Trisha pushed herself upright, straining against her seatbelt. Sure enough, farther down the road, the police had set up a roadblock. "Of all the days."

Simba said nothing. For some reason, his unflappable calm made her want to slap the man or shout at him — demand a reaction. He sat as if the world hadn't just changed forever. As if aliens weren't heading straight for Earth, as if her daughter wasn't abandoned at a school, alone and …

The line of cars crawled forward. The Land Cruiser's engine revved, cutting through her useless thoughts. Trisha tried to call the school again. No answer.

Leaning against the window, she studied the scenery. Jungly green growth lined the street, while on the thin strip of land between private property and public road, enterprising Kenyans had established various informal businesses from plant nurseries to home renovation suppliers. Colorful woven baskets hung above concrete paving slabs. Piles of compost and manure towered over fruit stands and pottery makers.

It was a chaotic jumble of businesses, yet she found it endearing, a quaint and delightful bit of culture to buffer the city's rapid development. Jake thought it was a waste of real estate and the source of criminal activity in the area.

Despite what her panicked heart insisted, they were stuck in the traffic for no more than a few minutes before the next traffic light allowed another wave of cars to pass. At the intersection, Simba veered the vehicle off the main road and onto Red Hill Road.

Trisha exhaled at the lack of congestion ahead. At least now, they were moving toward her daughter. As long as every minute moved them that much closer, she could hold it together long enough.

*And then what?*

Before marriage, pregnancy, and an international move, Trisha had been a woman who made critical decisions that others carried out. An entire department followed her lead. But the last few years, her biggest decisions had dimmed to designing the weekly menu.

She suspected all that was about to change, along with humanity's position in the universe.

Pulling out a pad and pen, she tapped the paper. "Simba, once we pick up Celine, I want you to do some shopping. A lot of it. And fuel up the car. If you can, also fill a canister with diesel, plus buy another cylinder of cooking fuel."

Trisha began to write out a list of groceries, just in case any of this was really necessary.

"I'm sure it's nothing. There must be some rational explanation for the photos. But it's always good to stock up. Right?"

Simba answered with a pair of precise nods.

Fumbling in her purse, she pulled out her wallet and fingered a wad of bills. She hesitated, holding more than Simba earned in a month. But did it matter if aliens were heading to the planet?

*It's a hoax. It has to be. Some elaborate, ridiculous hoax. Or asteroids. Shiny, silver-colored space rock.*

Either way, she wanted those groceries, before the city and everyone in it fell apart.

*Trust Jake to leave on the day the aliens arrive.*

Of course, they hadn't arrived yet, and Jake hadn't known what was going to happen. Still, his timing was impeccable, as usual, and Trisha suspected her husband would have gone even if he had known.

She sank into the morass of disappointed memories but was jolted into awareness when the road's structure changed. They were no longer driving along uneven tarmac; instead, they were on a rough dirt road. Despite the bumpy surface, someone still considered speed bumps important. The Land Cruiser took both them and the troughs with equal efficiency.

As the road dipped, rose and curved, their house came into view. The school was only another kilometer ahead.

"Oh, thank God." Trisha leaned forward, clutching at the front seat as if that could make them go any faster.

Simba maintained the same speed, regardless of terrain or her stressful presence behind him. They rolled past the house, took the elbow turn in a controlled swerve, then …

Trisha had her seatbelt off and the door open before the ancient vehicle came to a complete stop in front of the school. Stumbling out, she jogged to the front gate, her eyes grazing the grounds for Celine's blonde hair.

The school was empty.

Even before she reached the front door, she could feel the absence of childish energy and exuberance that every campus possessed when class was in session. There was nothing but the overly cheerful chorus of birds in a nearby thorn tree, twittering as if nothing had changed, as if it was just another normal day.

She banged on the front door, shouting, jiggling at the lock. Some part of her clung to the hope that she could change the emptiness, that her noisy efforts would summon a teacher and Celine from some hidden corner of the school. Their faces would appear in the window at any moment, astonished at her frantic expression. She'd laugh it off, hugging her daughter with a silent vow to never let go.

No one came.

Her heartbeat pounded in her ears, blood swishing to keep up with the urge to run, fight, find her child.

Twirling around, she ran back to the antique vehicle and snatched up her phone. This time, she called the headmistress' personal number. The woman had given strict instructions to all parents to use it only in case of an emergency.

If this didn't qualify as an emergency, nothing did.

She listened to a song in Swahili replace the ringtone.

"Pick up. Pick up." Her voice rasped harshly against her dry throat.

The old bat finally answered, and Trisha croaked out the words, "Where is she?"

There was a heavy pause, and Trisha could imagine the head-mistress trying to identify who was asking about whom, her heavily wrinkled face like a raisin of confusion.

"Mrs. Walker? We sent the children home a while ago. I tried to call you but—"

"Why would you close the school? Nothing has happened."

"What do you mean, nothing has happened?" she huffed. "Everything has changed, Mrs. Walker, and I felt it prudent to send the children home *before* the roads became impassable."

Slamming her finger on the button to end the call, Trisha gritted her teeth and willed herself not to hurl her phone onto the ground. She heaved herself back into the vehicle and slammed the door with more force than necessary. "Go home. They must be there."

She gripped the handhold as the Land Cruiser swerved in the

small parking lot, driving over stones bordering the footpath until they were finally facing the right direction.

Not waiting for the dust to settle, Simba swerved through the cloud of grit and dry clay soil, the view momentarily obstructed. Once they cleared it, he pressed down on the accelerator, both hands clasping the wheel.

Trisha willed him to go faster, despite the rough terrain. Instead, he maintained his irksome, steady speed. As they approached the turn to the house, Simba slowed and stopped in front of the narrow side road bordering their compound.

"What are you doing?" Trisha meant to sound assertive, but the words came out in a strangled scream.

Simba clicked off his seatbelt and opened the door with one hand while pointing through the windscreen with the other. By the time Trisha decided she had no idea what he wanted her to see, he was already outside and striding toward a small kiosk half a block away, near the entrance to Kinanda Village.

Throttling the frustration threatening to tear her apart, she jumped out and ran after him. As Trisha opened her mouth to lecture him and demand he take her back to the house, her eyes fell on a horrifying sight.

Her mouth finished opening wide, but a scream spilled out instead.

## Chapter Seven

THE THING WAS GOING TO KILL HER CHILD.

Ignoring Simba's shout and Mama Noah's open-mouthed stare, Trisha ran toward Celine and skidded to a halt several feet away.

"Celine, come here."

Her bland expression didn't flicker, although a twitch fluttered along her jaw. Celine remained still, one arm draped around the neck of a mangy-looking stray dog.

The beast probably had rabies.

Trisha straightened, trying to control her unsteady breathing. The woman operating the kiosk gawked at her while a little girl in a red dress snatched something off the table and stuffed it in her mouth.

Ignoring the audience, Trisha softened her voice. "Celine. Let's go home."

Her daughter was all kinds of difficult but not disobedient. Celine's chin slouched onto her chest while her arm dropped away from the dog. Eyes downcast, she patted its head and shuffled toward Trisha.

And while she felt a pang of remorse at her child's sorrow, fury consumed her even more. Her eyes burned with it until the world blurred around her.

She snatched up Celine's hand and glared at her maid. "She could have been killed."

Ignoring Mama Noah's incredulous expression, she dragged Celine back to the main road and her waiting driver. His gaze fell down and to the side as she passed him.

Only once they were safely inside the house did Trisha begin to breathe normally. What had she been thinking, leaving Celine with a total stranger?

She fumbled with the kettle while watching Celine for any sign of distress. Not that she would ever show any — Celine didn't express emotion the way other children did — but a mother could tell. The flicker of her eyelids, the twitch that always appeared at the hinge of her jaws. These small signs revealed her daughter's inner turmoil.

But there was none. Celine sat contentedly at the island counter, the dog forgotten, her head hovering over a blank page, crayons in both hands. Her tongue stuck out to the side in concentration. In that pose, she appeared like any normal six-year-old.

Mama Noah slinked into the kitchen. Averting her gaze and staying that way, she made preparations for dinner.

Staring at the woman's back, Trisha felt her face flush with irritation. "What were you thinking?"

"It was only a ten-minute walk, madam. She was safe."

Glowering at her maid, Trisha wished she would go away. "Ten minutes? That's long enough in this city. You should never have left the school."

Trisha slammed the cupboard door and gripped her mug until her knuckles were white all around it. "But I wasn't talking about the walk. I was referring to the stray dog. That thing might've bitten her. It probably has rabies. How could you allow her to touch it?"

Mama Noah peeled the potatoes, her downward strokes forceful yet confident.

Not for the first time, Trisha wondered if she really wanted a maid. Sure, it was the norm in Nairobi, but at what cost? If she couldn't trust the woman to follow basic common sense, why bother? She'd raised the issue once with Jake, a couple days before they'd moved.

Eyes glued to his juke, he shook his head before she'd finished her sentence. "It's not a big deal, Trisha. She comes with the house."

*How does a person 'come with the house'?* Trisha thought, not for the first time. *She's not an appliance.*

Gritting her teeth, Trisha turned her back to the maid and stared vacantly at the large juke imbedded in the wall above the counter, next to the fridge.

Like Mama Noah, the juke — a top-of-the-line version made by Kwan Glass — came with the house. Jake had selected Global News as the default home page, probably because he appreciated the various assets of the lead anchor, Greta San Lucas.

*Yeah, like most of the world's heterosexual male population.*

Nothing against Greta, but couldn't the woman wear a slightly less revealing blouse? The top half of the woman's cleavage was clearly on display. Wasn't there some minimum level of profession-alism required of a journalist? If there was, Global News didn't expect it from their reporters.

Trisha hadn't had time to reset the juke to *her* favorite channel. So now, Miss Greta San Lucas' delightful curves filled the screen along with chatter about the latest calamity and outrageous scandal. The news played in the background whenever the juke was on, which seemed to be most, if not all, of the time.

Jake had always insisted on having access to the news in whatever room he was in. Even when eating with the family, he liked to split his attention between the juke and them. She never understood Jake's obsession with knowing the latest in current events.

"Whatever is happening, it'll still be happening an hour from now" she'd once argued with Jake during breakfast while images of plague victims haunted the juke. "Ruining our mealtime with the most recent disaster won't make it go away or improve our appetites."

Jake had waived a milk-drenched spoon at her. "I need to know what's happening, for my work. Educate yourself, Trisha. No one wants an ignoramus."

And there it was. The not-so-subtle reminder that she was no longer in the workforce, and by extension, had allowed herself to slip into a swamp of ignorance.

Shedding the memories, Trisha sagged against the island counter. Suddenly exhausted even though it was only noon, she took her teapot and mug to the living room and set them on the coffee table.

A squeaky flutter caught Trisha's attention before she could sit.

Huffing, she turned around and drilled holes into Mama Noah's back. "Please make sure that damn back door is closed properly."

The maid gave a noncommittal grunt as she washed the dishes.

Raising her arms before letting them fall in disbelief, Trisha stormed down the small hallway between the living room and kitchen. The corridor connected the front of the house to the guest room, storage area and a study, and ended at a back door. Unlike any of the other doors or windows, the rear entrance had a screen door in addition to a heavy-duty metal one.

She couldn't understand why anyone had bothered to install a screen door if there was no mosquito netting over any of the other openings to the house. To cap her irritation, the screen door fluttered in the slightest breeze unless it was firmly closed and properly latched. It seemed she was the only person capable of doing that.

*Because it's such a difficult skill to master.*

Opening the metal door, Trisha yanked at the screen door until it clicked shut, then pulled the bolt.

"You're going to be a pain in my butt," she muttered at the screen. "I can just see it."

Leaving the metal door open to create a draft, Trisha returned to the living room and slumped onto the sofa. She poured her tea, staring through the archway into the kitchen where Mama Noah and Celine were chatting. Or rather, Mama Noah did all the talking. She nattered incessantly. Celine ignored her, crayons speaking on her behalf, sliding over the paper in a continuous sweep. But what were they saying?

Somehow comforted by her daughter's obsessive behavior, Trisha opened her juke and made a conscious decision *not* to look at the Astral App. Thinking about the photos made her squirm enough. Staring over the juke, she watched Celine hold up her newest drawing in triumph before letting it fall. The paper fluttered down, flashing black and white.

Once it hit the floor, the girl selected a clean piece of paper for her next piece of art, or rather a variation of the same thing, repeated over and over. It seemed she was taking a break from drawing dots and circles. Instead, it was silver discs set against a dark sky.

Trisha smiled at the intensity of her daughter's focus even as a niggling worry wormed its way forward. Surely, it was a coincidence that the drawings so closely matched the photo. Someone with a mind for paranoia and conspiracy would suggest a six-year-old had known about the aliens approaching Earth from the other side of the moon before the Astral App had announced it.

"Coincidence," Trisha murmured even as her breath hitched.

A phone icon buzzed across her juke, and she swiped to answer. "Hey, Jake."

"Everything okay?"

"Of course. Have you heard?"

Jake nodded, frowning, his gray eyes like storm clouds. He swept a hand through his dark hair and exhaled loudly. "Yeah. Do you want me to come home? I can try to catch a flight back to Nairobi. This evening or whenever they let us go. They've grounded all flights for now."

But Trisha wasn't paying attention. She looked past his shoulder at a familiar scene. "Where are you?"

"Geneva Airport." Jake grimaced self-consciously, as if anticipating her reaction.

The edges of her mouth tightened, her smile past its expiration date. "You're in Geneva. Really. Of all places, why Geneva?"

"Jesus, Trisha." Jake glanced down and to the side, jaw clenching, a small twitch forming at the hinge. "I'm transiting. I could've gone through Paris, Amsterdam or London. This was the easiest option."

She wanted to ask why he hadn't transited through those other cities. They were major hubs, and Geneva wasn't. How could he say that was the easiest option? *Easy in what way?*

Jake rubbed at the creases in his forehead and dodged the issue like always, changing the topic on his way. "How did things go today?"

"Great." Trisha nodded mechanically while staring at a larger-than-life hologram hovering behind Jake. A scantily dressed woman selling perfume in the airport's Duty Free. Apparently, it magically enhanced the user's breasts. Of course, Jake would be sitting right there. "Celine's first day went without a hitch, and she loved it. The teachers all adored her."

Jake smiled the megawatt smile that always caused women to take a second and third look. "That's fantastic. Can I see her?"

Trisha glanced up at the kitchen where Celine was furiously tapping a crayon against the paper. Without seeing the picture, Trisha knew what it was. The same image she'd been drawing for the past four years, since she first learned to grasp a crayon.

Dots and circles in a now-familiar pattern, over and over and —

"Trisha?"

*Guess she got tired of the discs.*

Trisha's gaze fell to the juke, and her husband, not in London or Amsterdam or Paris. No. It had to be in Geneva.

"It's been a long morning, Jake. Celine was exhausted after her first day, so she's taking a nap."

"Oh." His smile dimmed. "Well, give my sweet pea a hug and a kiss from me. Tell her how much Daddy loves her."

Her smile hardened. "Will do."

Trisha hung up and dropped the juke onto the sofa cushion.

Chin to knees, Trisha cradled her bent legs. Closing her eyes, she listened to the silence settling around the house and waited expectantly for Simba to arrive with the groceries.

Any minute now.

But there was no Land Cruiser's roar.

Had Simba taken off with the money? She'd been foolish, handing over a month's salary to the man. What did she know about him? He had a license, was hired by Jake and wanted everyone to use his weird, army nickname. That was it.

She didn't even know his real name.

For all she knew, he was driving out of Nairobi like the other panicking rats with her groceries.

But more importantly, and the thing she couldn't stop thinking about despite there supposedly being aliens on the way, *why had her husband transited through Geneva?*

## Chapter Eight

"YOU DON'T HAVE TO KILL HIM."

Caleb flinched as the words left his mouth. Why couldn't he ever keep it shut?

Then again, Madam Zahir the Rat Queen had just threatened his only living relative within a hundred-kilometer radius. Estranged as he and his family may be, blood was blood. Unless it was his blood getting spilled all over the place, in which case he'd have to rethink how attached he was to his half-brother.

Madam Zahir smiled.

That was never a good sign.

In morbid fascination, Caleb studied her wide mouth, fleshy lips, plump cheeks, and the double chin flapping under her heavy jaw. She reminded him of Jabba the Hutt — the grotesque, obese, slug-like alien from Star Wars — except Zahir was way less cuddly and a lot less forgiving.

Her smile widened, the crimson lipstick perfectly matching the red on her talon-like nails and closely cropped hair. She raised an index finger and made a wet-sounding click of her tongue against the roof of her mouth. "Tsk, tsk, tsk, Caleb."

With every *tsk*, she tilted her finger back and forth, like the pendulum rod on a metronome. Tick-tock, tick-tock, the long red nail marked the beat of his life's remaining seconds slinking away.

"My dear boy. You know better." Her voice oozed false compassion and maternal affection.

Caleb gulped. *Yep, I'm dead.*

Why had he bothered to wake up? And the day had started so well. After rising from a drug-induced dream involving an alien who morphed into a sex goddess of all things (not that he was complaining), he'd rolled out of bed into a puddle.

Spluttering, he'd twisted his head to the side. "Dammit."

The filthy water roused him completely, and he leaped to his feet to the sound of driving rain. While Kenyans usually referred to the rains as a blessing, it was never a good thing in the slums of Kibera. With the open drainage channels clogged with garbage and raw sewage, heavy rains collected in the narrow dirt roads and network of pathways. Water gathered the congested slum's waste and carried the filth into people's homes.

"It's May," he'd shouted at the low ceiling, his words drowned by the bombardment of fat drops pinging against the flimsy metal roof. "You're supposed to stop now."

The rain intensified its assault, mocking his irritation. Wiping grime off his chest, Caleb pushed his long dreadlocks off his face, yanked on a faded T-shirt and shrugged into a third-hand leather jacket.

Maybe it was time to consider moving.

The moment he stepped outside, Samuel and Timothy, the left and right hands of Madam Zahir, had been waiting for him.

So that had been his morning ruined.

This afternoon's agenda probably included torture and painful dismemberment, or if he was *really* lucky, a quick death.

Caleb doubted he was so lucky.

Madam Zahir lounged in her bright pink, plastic chair. At a glance, she looked like any of the neighborhood matriarchs, until you peered into her unnervingly dark eyes and witnessed the lack of humanity within. "And why shouldn't I kill him?"

Caleb wanted to look away, but felt compelled to meet her hard gaze with his own, although his gaze wasn't as hard, and was a lot more terrified.

While she might be a slum dweller, Madam Zahir was by no means impoverished. Ironically, a great deal of wealth existed in the slums for clever, enterprising individuals with street smarts and a total lack of morals.

What Caleb knew — granted, that wasn't a heckuva lot — was that Madam Zahir had her pudgy fingers in a number of mud pies. She might not flaunt it by buying a big house in the leafy, overpriced Nairobi suburbs, but she definitely owned both property and people.

"Caleb, Caleb, Caleb." She waved her index finger with every mention of his name. "What am I going to do with you, boy?"

It was probably a rhetorical question, but Caleb dared to stare into her cold, black eyes anyway, give her back his cockiest grin. "Let me go? Allow me to live to serve you for another day?"

"Why should I? Oh, I know. Because you're such a *faithful* servant." She chuckled and clapped slowly, sarcasm in every movement. Kenyans weren't particularly inclined to sarcasm, but Madam Zahir was different in almost every conceivable way.

He shifted his legs as much as he dared, trying to relieve the pressure caused by the grit poking into his knees. Instead, a pebble dug deeper through his jeans and into his skin.

Samuel scoffed and smacked the back of his head on one side. On the other, Timothy tightened his grip on Caleb's shoulder. Timothy was too dense to pick up on humor, but what he lacked in intelligence, he made up for in brute strength and total obedience to his boss. He pushed down, as if to remind Caleb about his place in this room and the world.

He needn't have bothered. Caleb knew exactly where it was, kneeling on the floor and groveling for his life.

*I can do groveling.*

Dying was the thing he couldn't do. And if Zahir ever figured out he'd stolen from her, death would be the least of his problems. He'd probably beg for a bullet to the brain before she was done with him. Her minions weren't roasting him over a fire or snipping off bits of his appendages, so she hadn't discovered his real betrayal. Not yet, anyway.

Caleb had used a shoelace to suspend the strange object around his neck, tucking it under his T-shirt. Maybe it was his guilt, but he swore the weight became heavier, its surface burning into his chest. Why had he given into his impulse and taken what obviously belonged to his unforgiving, tyrannical boss?

And then — dumb and dumber — he hadn't hidden the item away. That would be the *slightly* smart thing to do. Instead, he was wearing proof of his crime right in front of her. How stupid could he get?

There was no limit, in his experience.

*Yup. That's my superpower,* he thought, blinking as a dribble of sweat slid across an eyeball.

Then again, was it his fault Samuel had given him that particular van to use for the job? And could anyone really blame Caleb for possessing a natural curiosity, an inability to control his thieving impulse, and an inclination to sniff out trouble better than a lion sniffs out its prey?

They really should've known better.

The item buzzed against his skin, as if sensing its owner sitting immediately in front of him, reminding him of *Lord of the Rings*. If only this thing could make him invisible.

Off to one side, Hyena leered at him, exposing his blackened teeth. Yellowed eyes glittered with malice. If Samuel was the brains and Timothy the brawn among Zahir's personal bodyguards, Hyena was the vicious, sadistic soul. A crazy-eyed bastard who loved no one and feared only his boss.

Madam Zahir tapped her long nails on the armrest, the red

polish clashing with the sickly pink plastic. "And this brother of yours."

"Half-brother."

The grip on his shoulder tightened painfully, and Timothy grunted in disapproval.

Madam Zahir's thin eyebrows rose in genuine surprise at the interruption. "Very well. *Half*-brother. Does he have the means to pay your debt? Because I don't care for defaulters. You *do* know what I do to people who break their contract with me. Don't you, Caleb?"

*Like I need a reminder.*

But this time, his big mouth obeyed the wiser part of his brain and stayed shut. Instead, he just nodded.

Samuel kicked the back of his thigh. Gritting his teeth, Caleb looked down and to the side, glaring at the brown leather loafers. He had been there the night Samuel shot a man for those shoes. Yanked them off his twitching feet before he finished dying.

Hyena cackled.

"Excellent." Madam Zahir inspected her nails, picking invisible grime from beneath them.

They belonged to a Disney villain, not a real-life person. Yet there they were in the real world, ridiculously long and sharp without a single chip on the painted surface. He didn't know anyone who could keep their nails so maintained, especially not in a place like this.

"Caleb, I need to collect that debt now. That's the way the world works."

Pressing her hands on the flimsy armrests, she pushed herself upright and swaggered toward him. Her black skirt waved around her thick legs, a mesmerizing medallion hypnotizing its victim into a false sense of comfort.

She paced around him, a shark scenting her prey's weakness. "I've given you so many chances, my boy. Far too many by some reckoning." Raising an arm, she gestured vaguely over him toward the door. "Why, there might be people out there who believe I've gone soft. You don't think I'm getting soft in my old age, do you, Caleb?"

If he hadn't been on his knees with two thugs breathing down his neck and the Rat Queen looming above him, Caleb would have laughed. Madam Zahir, soft? The only soft thing about her was the pouches of fat she proudly carried on her waist, neck and cheeks. Everything else about the woman was uncompromising, rock hard and brutally efficient.

Again, he managed to keep his mouth shut and throttle his smirk. He shook his head.

"I'm so glad we understand each other. So, what does your brother, your *half*-brother, own that can cover your debt?"

Caleb opened his mouth, then closed it. What did that muscle-bound brute have that was worth anything? And should he be dragging an innocent relative into this mess?

*Of course you should,* whispered the devil on his left shoulder. *What has he ever done for you, apart from lecture and criticize?*

The angel on his right didn't even bother. Caleb suspected she had left the premises a long time ago, giving up on her charge as a lost cause.

Sweat glided into the other eye, but he didn't dare raise a hand to wipe it away. "He has a job. So he must have money. And a car. He drives, you know, so he must have the keys to a vehicle."

Madam Zahir stopped in front of him and stared down, her face a slate sheet of calculating hardness. "Do I look like someone who sells stolen vehicles?"

*That's exactly what you look like.*

Caleb involuntarily leaned away from her. His back pressed against Timothy's thick leg. He didn't know all the details of all her businesses, but was pretty sure selling vehicles was one of them, or at least their parts. "Maybe?"

The sound of Madam Zahir's laughter grated on his nerves. "You have forty-eight hours, Caleb. And by any standards, that is the height of magnanimity. Do you understand what that word means?"

He licked his lips. "Very generous. Thank you."

She looked over his head. "I like you, Caleb. That is to say, you've been useful to me. That's why I'm giving you this one last chance. Find your half-brother, get the money, and bring it to me. And if he doesn't have any, take his vehicle. If he has nothing to steal … you cease to be useful."

Five red-covered nails appeared in his vision and grasped him by the chin, their points drilling into his skin and tilting his head back until his neck was fully exposed. She stared directly into his eyes, her breath blending with his.

*Too close. Way too close.*

Caleb held his breath.

She licked her lips. "You're a skilled thief, Caleb. But if you are not back here in forty-eight hours with some means to repay me, you both will die."

## Chapter Nine

MADAM ZAHIR WATCHED CALEB SCUTTLE AWAY. THE YOUNG MAN ALWAYS reminded her of a beetle, cowering beneath its shell, keeping low to the ground as it dodged the world's many dangers.

*Except a dung beetle has more courage than Caleb*, Zahir mused and chuckled to herself.

One of her stooges, a hulking dolt named Timothy, glanced up as if expecting an order to maim or kill.

With a *tsk* and a wag of her finger, Zahir stopped him and resumed her reflections. Caleb was only one of many minions to manage. It was tiresome at times, but she didn't mind. It was a sign of how far she'd risen in the food chain. She could now eat while others worked for her.

Not bad, for a slum rat.

Oh, yes. Zahir knew what people called her when they didn't think she would hear about it: Queen of the street rats, or Rat Queen for short.

"Ain't you insulted, Madam Zahir?" Timothy had once asked, his thick head crunched in confusion.

Zahir had eyed the man, tempted to tell him to keep his mouth shut. But she'd been in an indulgent mood that day. "Not at all, my dear boy. Rats are survivors. If anyone drops a nuclear bomb, the rats will still be skittering across the planet."

Timothy had scratched his shaved head and studied his fingernails.

If Zahir wanted intelligent conversation, she had to talk with herself. Ignoring Timothy, she had continued. "Not many creatures can successfully inhabit and thrive in underground sewers and mountaintops, or any place in between. Rats are everywhere, and unlike other species, they are in no danger of extinction."

Just like Madam Zahir the Rat Queen.

Come hell, high water, or anything else the world threw her way, she would survive and thrive every time.

Rubbing her ample belly, Zahir grinned. She worked hard to maintain such a girth. Westerners were always starving themselves, prizing frailty as if hunger were a virtue. In Kenya, thinness suggested you were either impoverished or deathly ill. But if you carried extra weight, you clearly ate well, the ultimate proof of prosperity in a region where famine lurked in the shadows, waiting for an opportunity to attack.

"Enough of that." She picked up her chair to set it behind a battered, wooden desk.

Timothy lumbered to her side, a towering mass of muscle without any brain. Cackling softly to himself, Hyena stood at her other side.

Samuel, the third bodyguard in her personal retinue, took a bit longer to find his attention, and not because he was naturally slower. Quite the opposite. His eyes were sharply intelligent, always searching for danger and opportunity.

As Zahir strode past him, she surreptitiously watched for any sign of a blade in Samuel's hands. She didn't expect him to attack her, at least not yet, but it was a compulsive habit born from years of brutal survival. No one lived as long as she had, and under these conditions, without developing a healthy dose of paranoia.

He held no weapon, although his eventual betrayal was inevitable, as was her decision. One day, she would have to dispose of Samuel. While he was one of her smartest employees and definitely more than capable of protecting her, there was a downside to having an intelligent minion. You really had to watch your back. Of all her crew, he was the one most likely to stick a knife in her ribs to advance in the ranks.

*And I've lived too long and fought too hard for that.*

But for now, Samuel behaved, and he could live so long as he continued to do so.

Swaggering out of the small brick hut, Zahir hitched her thumbs over the waistband of her skirt and surveyed her kingdom. Kibera, the largest slum in sub-Saharan Africa, sprawled before her in all its stinking, chaotic glory.

Most people, especially the pale-faced charity workers, wrinkled their noses at such a view. They saw poverty, burning garbage and open sewers.

Madam Zahir saw an entrepreneurial labor force, buyers for her products, and opportunity — *endless* opportunity — unlimited by burdensome regulations. The law of the nation extended to the slum's borders and didn't dare penetrate much farther. Another set of laws governed this city within the city, and people like Zahir created and enforced those laws.

Rubbing a hand down the front of her neck, Zahir turned her head slightly to the side and nodded.

Samuel veered away and jogged down the narrow dirt track between two mounds of compacted garbage.

As she waited for her bidding to be done, Zahir scanned the neighborhood. She spotted Caleb running for his life, ducking around ramshackle structures made of sheet metal and scraps of wood. Dreadlocks stuck up from the boy's head like a beacon.

Zahir smirked. Could he be any more obvious? If he was smart, he'd shave those hairy protrusions and take on the appearance of someone who *wasn't* a drug user and scoundrel. But no one had ever accused Caleb of being overly smart.

Samuel returned with another hired thug. A scrawny, nameless man struggled between them. Upon seeing Zahir standing above like a monarch before her throne, the man began to snivel and beg, though any human with a functioning brain cell knew it was too late.

Zahir beckoned him forward with an indulgent smile. "Knife, gun or fire. Choices, choices."

He pleaded for mercy while tears and snot soiled his face.

She could afford to be benevolent, but only to a point. In this corner of Kibera, people looked to her for guidance and control. She was judge, jury and executioner. Court was always in session. Without her firm hand, the place would erupt into chaos and confusion. That was always bad for business.

Her subjects occasionally required a reminder of these facts. This was one of those times.

"Knife," she decided.

Flicking open a switchblade, Madam Zahir the Rat Queen rendered her verdict.

## Chapter Ten

LONG AFTER CELINE HAD GONE TO BED, AND MAMA NOAH had returned to the staff quarters, Trisha was still awake, staring out her living room window.

She'd made a big mistake. And now she'd given away her vehicle and all her cash. They didn't have a lot of groceries in the house. What was she going to do?

*Inhale one, two, three.*

She paced the living room, cursing herself and her stupidity. Although she hadn't told Jake, she could imagine exactly what he would say.

"What did you think would happen? You hand a wad of cash and the keys to freedom over to a man you don't know, and then expect him to come back with your bread and milk?"

"Yeah, well, you hired him," she muttered to the imaginary Jake.

*Exhale one, two, three, four, five.*

And just as she was about to give up on ever seeing her groceries, money, or the Land Cruiser again, a screech shredded the air. At the end of the driveway, the two halves of the black gate opened, and the Land Cruiser's bulk rumbled up the slight slope and rolled to a stop a few meters from the front of the house.

Trisha watched in disbelief as Simba pressed the button to close the automatic gate and then sat back, an unmoving shadow, his features hidden by darkness.

*What's wrong with him?*

But really, she should be asking what was wrong with her.

Still shaking from the overturning of her absolute certainty that she'd made a *really* big mistake, Trisha opened the front door.

As light spilled out, Simba's head jerked upward, and their eyes met. He looked weary, as if the effort to pick up a few groceries had been overwhelming.

Dropping his gaze, Simba slid out of the vehicle and slammed the door. The sound ricocheted like a gunshot all around her. She swore he swayed, but before she could ask if he was okay, he straightened and marched toward her, each step precise and solid.

*I hope he hasn't been drinking.*

She frowned at her cynical inner voice. He had returned with the vehicle and hopefully groceries. How much more could she expect?

"Did you have any problem finding everything?"

Simba lurched to a halt in front of her, and his eyes flicked up, his expression guarded. "No. No problem, madam."

"Please don't call me that." She gave him a once-over. "Is everything okay?"

A splattering of dark splotches on his left hand and forearm caught her attention, reminding her of the spots and circles on her daughter's drawings. She leaned forward slightly and squinted her eyes.

Hands behind his back, Simba looked over her shoulder and nodded. "It's fine, Mrs. Walker."

Trisha gasped. "Was that blood? Are you hurt? Let me see." She held out a hand, palm up.

Simba kept his hands hidden, the hint of a smile softening an otherwise stern face. "Hakuna matata."

Trisha almost laughed — *The Lion King* was one of Celine's favorite films — but she held it in. Not only was the situation lacking in humor, she could feel the hysteria bubbling through her. She would sound crazy if she laughed.

Then again, the entire day could be described with that word.

As Trisha studied Simba for any additional hint of injury, she mentally reviewed her first-aid supplies. Apart from a few Band-Aids and an expired tube of antiseptic ointment, the first-aid kit was useless. Anything more than a paper cut and she wouldn't be able to help.

From the number and size of the brownish-red splotches she'd glimpsed before he hid his arm, Trisha suspected he had something more than a small scratch.

Restocking the kit was one of those things she had been planning on doing for a while, along with throwing out expired products and buying replacements. But there was always something higher on the list, more important, worthier of her attention.

She crossed one arm over her waist and rested the elbow of the other on it. Her hand fluttered around her mouth, as if trying to lure the words.

He returned her inquisitive gaze with disinterested calm. There was nothing in his eyes, his expression, or the slight quirk of his otherwise straight mouth to suggest pain or discomfort. He portrayed only stoic patience as he awaited her decision.

What did he expect from her?

"And fuel? Were you able to fill up the car?"

*What a way to show compassion, Trisha. And it's not a car. It's an SUV.*

Simba nodded a couple of times, his movements sharp. "And the spare canister."

"Great. That's great."

The silence between them stretched out, filled with the chirping of insects and the flutter of bat wings as the creatures dipped and swirled above them. Jake would have gone inside already. He'd never admit to being scared of bats, but Trisha knew he was. She found them fascinating to watch, the way they flitted around obstacles without ever crashing into anything.

She peered around Simba at the Land Cruiser. He had stacked boxes behind the front seats, filling the entire back of the vehicle nearly to the ceiling.

"Wow. That's a lot of boxes." Inwardly, she grimaced. *A lot of boxes?*

Simba said nothing.

Chewing on her cheek, Trisha stared up at Simba and marveled at his calm expression. Only patience and an unexpected weariness.

Narrowing her eyes, she tried another tactic. "Why did it take almost all day?"

He met her stare with one of his own. "The lines were long."

A bird hooted from a clump of trees just outside the gate, and another responded, sounding like it was on top of the house. From the nearby village, a dog barked, reminding Trisha of her scare earlier in the day when Celine was stroking the mangy stray.

Staring past Simba, she saw an elongated shape squatting behind the antique Land Cruiser. "What is … Is that a horse trailer?"

"Yes, Mrs. Walker."

"I told you to call me Trisha. Why do you have a horse trailer? Oh, God. You didn't buy a horse, did you? I'm not eating horse meat. I don't care how much looting there is. Alien invasion or not, we are *not* eating a horse."

"There's no horse." As if anticipating Trisha's next comment, Simba added, "No other animals. Only groceries. I'm going to move them into the horse trailer along with other supplies."

Trisha looked at Simba, wondering why he would bother, and where had he found a horse trailer? How had he paid for it? *Or had he?*

Shivering, she crossed her arms over her chest and wondered how well Jake had investigated this man's past. For all she knew, he could have been in a terrorist army.

Feeling slow, she frowned. "Why do you want to put our groceries in a horse trailer? That can't be hygienic."

"For when you leave, so there's enough room in the Land Cruiser." Simba met her gaze, although his eyes seemed lost in shadow. "There are too many groceries. You'll need room to sit. You'll also need to pack camping gear. Tents. Blankets. Survival gear."

*He said* you, *not* we. *Does he think I'll leave him here?*

*Maybe I should.*

*But who will drive?*

Trisha rubbed her arms, wishing Simba would return to his room so she could go back inside. "Survival gear. Like what? Matches? God, I have no idea how to make a campfire."

Simba watched her, his expression neutral. Somehow, that felt more judgmental than if he commented on her incompetence. Who didn't know how to make a fire?

Exhaling heavily, she stared at the horse trailer. "We're not going anywhere."

Simba's poker face finally cracked, his eyebrows rising. "Mrs. Walker. Trisha. You should get out of the city. It's going to get dangerous."

She laughed, a brittle sound clashing with the soft nocturnal calls all around them. "Too late. It's going to get dangerous everywhere. The roads will be a mess. We're safest here. I'm staying. Feel free to leave."

Simba said nothing, his mask slipping back into place as he waited for her.

What did he want? She'd already thanked him, hadn't she? Did she have to dismiss him, or give him permission to return to his small room in the staff quarters at the side of the house?

Trisha shivered. Nairobi was at altitude, so the temperature dropped the second the sun set. They may be close to the equator, but it was still cool enough to feel the night on her skin.

She eyed the boxes. "Well, I suppose the groceries can wait until tomorrow."

Simba's exhale was barely audible.

Trisha swallowed hard.

*So he* was *waiting for me to let him go.*

Backing up until she crossed the threshold and was back inside the house, she stared at his face but didn't meet his gaze.

"Good night. And thank you."

Before the awkwardness could stretch any further, before she could wonder why he had blood on his arm, Trisha closed and locked the door.

## Chapter Eleven

THE DYING HAPPENS IN MOGADISHU, IN A WAR WITHOUT A beginning or an end.

Simba recognizes the location. It's hard not to. Their superiors had dropped his team into the middle of the disaster zone to clean up the mess and to push the al-Shabaab terrorist group out of the Somali capital.

Even in the dream, he scoffs at the notion of a capital. There's not much of a government to fight for. It's an open secret that no one wants to admit. The combined efforts of the African Union and their Western allies fail to do more than prop up a few self-appointed government officials overseeing what is essentially a failed state.

But it isn't his job to analyze the asinine politics of the situation. His job is to lead the team and complete their mission.

He glances around, half-expecting his fallen companions to appear at his side. Hope surges through him at the prospect of seeing them again, even if it's only in his mind.

No one arrives.

So why is he back here now?

Dark, oily smoke mixes with a clammy mist and billows through abandoned buildings and carcasses of burned-out vehicles as he walks the empty street.

He flinches at the sounds of people fighting and dying, bombs exploding, and bullets winging through the air. But they are muted, as if everything is happening behind distant hills instead of in this part of the city.

The cloud of smoke and mist surrounds him, swirls around his legs, stings his nostrils, and smothers everything except the sound of his harsh breathing and the crunch of his boots over rubble and bones.

Involuntarily, his fingers tap the comms button on his wristband. Static buzzes in his ear, then dies. Compulsively he pats himself down, searching for a weapon, but there is none.

"What the hell?" His voice echoes back at him, mocking his weaknesses.

Something crashes in the building to his right. Automatically, he lowers himself into a crouch and hides behind a demolished tank.

Something feels off.

This is a memory, yes, but there are elements that don't make sense. There were no tanks in Mogadishu that time, and no mist. Only dust and death. The sting of ozone is new. His skin itches from its heavy presence, and his lungs burn as he inhales the toxic air.

Next to the tank, he spots a twisted length of metal rebar. Picking up the rod, he clutches it like a bat, comforted by its hefty weight. At least now, he has some means of defense, as rudimentary as it is. He peers around the front of the destroyed tank, searching for the source of the noise.

A loud, raspy inhale echoes from inside the hollowed-out building on the other side of the street. It sounds like a giant animal.

But there are no animals in Mogadishu, apart from men and their ambitions. Maybe a few stray dogs, although almost anything remotely edible has been eaten.

Pressing his body against the reassuring hulk of the tank, he dares to expose himself and pushes his head out farther. A dark shadow flashes in front of a window. A mere glimpse and then it's gone, but whatever it is, it's too big to be a dog.

A scream pierces the air, and he flinches. That part is real. He remembers that scream from the first time he was here. So much of it, and the sharp scent of iron in the air as blood spills on the pavement.

Shaking his head, he retreats from view and slumps against the tank, wondering what the hell he's doing back here. He knows he's not actually here, but it feels too real, too physical, to be just a dream.

Something clicks, like high heels against concrete. But no one is wearing fancy shoes in Mogadishu.

A knocking sound booms from all sides of the foggy road, its source hidden behind swirling clouds.

Even though the knocking is loud, Simba feels in his core that the real danger lies on the other side of the tank, where something has exited the building. It scurries toward him, clicking and breathing heavily.

But the knocking is persistent. A voice floats from all around him. "Simba."

His name reminds him this isn't real.

This is only a dream.

THERE WAS one last pounding of a fist on metal, and Simba jerked awake. His skin slick with sweat, he stared up at the ceiling of his small room in the staff quarters.

Disorientated, he lay there for a moment, trying to identify the source of the banging, and more importantly, if it was a threat.

*Someone at the gate.*

The cheap, wooden door to his room wasn't remotely sound-proof. Simba could hear every noise.

Someone rattled at the small entrance cut into the compound's gate. When that failed to attract attention, the person pounded a fist against it.

In another context, in another world, this realization would have sent him rolling onto the floor and reaching under his bed for a gun, maybe two.

*But we're not there anymore.*

He had to remind himself, because his heart didn't believe him. It made its disbelief known by pounding an erratic beat against his ribs. His lungs also betrayed him, heaving in oxygen as if he was about to scale a wall and fire down at the enemy on the other side, even if they weren't the enemy. Even if they were merely civilians trying to escape one terror, only to stumble into another.

*The last thing they saw was me.*

Keeping his eyes closed, he tried unsuccessfully to squeeze out the memories. Like the residue of toothpaste in a flattened tube, they didn't budge.

The banging resumed.

For a moment, he stayed still as his mind gradually released the vestiges of the dream and returned to reality. A reality that hurt. Groaning, he gingerly touched his left shoulder and winced.

Grocery shopping right before an alien invasion wasn't exactly a straightforward mission. He'd been lucky the looters arrived *after* he'd already loaded the Land Cruiser and was about to leave.

*And lucky means I'm alive.*

The same couldn't be said for the man who'd attacked him.

Rolling out of bed, he slid a hand under his mattress, fingertips buzzing as they brushed the cold metal. Hesitating, he again reminded himself in a hoarse whisper, "We aren't there. It's done, dusted and finished."

Except it wasn't ever really finished. The past clung to his skin like dust, coating all the surfaces of his heart.

Exhaling slowly, he withdrew his hand. This wasn't Mogadishu, and it was probably the vegetable lady knocking on the gate to find out if they wanted to buy her products. Simba had seen her around the corner, down the narrow side road leading to the village. Desperate, but harmless.

Even still, a part of him wanted to retrieve one of his guns, find the bullets he'd stashed in the locked cupboard in his room, and make sure it was only a harmless vegetable lady.

What would Mrs. Walker think if she saw him with a gun?

The thought stopped him. He didn't know his employer that well, but he'd bet a week's worth of maize meal that she would *not* approve. She was probably one of those anti-gun people.

Not that he blamed her. He wasn't exactly pro-gun himself. But life, necessity, training all dictated otherwise for him.

Forcing himself off his knees, Simba blindly reached for the door, yanked it open and stared in the pre-dawn's murky light at the gate which was a few meters from his room.

He glanced in the other direction, toward Mama Noah's room. It was at the far end of the staff quarters. No way would she hear. And if she did, she wouldn't venture out at this ungodly hour in the morning to open the gate to a stranger.

His eyes roved up to the second floor of the main house. The master bedroom faced the gate and the dirt road, but the thick curtains suggested someone who did not want to be disturbed.

Only he would respond to the noise.

Rubbing a hand down his face, Simba forced himself to move. He shivered when his bare feet touched the cold, dew-dampened grass.

Then, he was on the concrete driveway. He pressed his back to the wall on one side of the imposing gate out of habit, as if expecting insurgents to blow open its inner door and pour into the compound.

Instead, a familiar voice, one from his past that he wished would stay there, echoed from the other side. "Open up. Simba, I know you're in there."

Gritting his teeth, he reached over and pulled the bolt to one side. The metal door swung open and clanged against the inside of the gate. A young, slim man staggered in, almost falling into Simba's arms. Wide, nervous eyes stared up at him.

Not waiting for an invitation, the unwanted visitor pushed past Simba and collapsed on the grass, limbs splayed out.

"What …"

The man held up a hand, eyes closed. "Simba, I'm about to die, and I need your help."

## Chapter Twelve

"IT'S ONLY FOR A FEW DAYS."

Simba stalked away to a chest of drawers in the corner, his broad back hunched over with the tension bulging from his muscles. "Nope. And I would be grateful if you would remove your skinny butt and go back to whatever hole you crawled out of."

Rolling his eyes, Caleb stayed slouched on the bed, eyes twitching as he tracked his half-brother's movements. "No can do, bro. There be dragons in that hole. Or at least rats. Big rats. Real ugly ones, too."

Simba glared over his shoulder, his lips almost disappearing as his mouth formed a neat line. "Let's get something straight. As far as I'm concerned, after your last incident, we are no longer brothers."

Caleb thumped a hand over his heart. "That cuts deep, Simba. Real deep. Okay, so technically we aren't brothers. We're half-brothers. But blood is blood. Am I right? What would good old Dad want?"

Simba slammed shut the drawer he had been rifling through and spun around. The staff quarters were luxurious by slum standards, but the room was still small enough for Caleb to see the dangerous glint in Simba's eyes. His anger seemed to fill the space as much as his tall frame did.

"Good old Dad?" Simba's lips curled back. "There was nothing *good* about him, and I'm amazed to hear you say it."

Caleb pushed himself upright and leaned back on his arms. "Yeah, you're right. Only good thing about him is he's dead. Still, you really gonna kick me out onto the cruel Nairobi streets, defenseless, alone—"

Simba raised a hand. "Don't bother, Caleb. You may be a scrawny little creature, but you can handle yourself just fine. You proved that the last time you crawled to me for help, then screwed me over."

Caleb didn't respond. He wasn't actually scrawny in the least bit, but compared to Simba …?

*Yeah, sure. Standing next to that musclebound oaf, who doesn't appear slim?*

"So things didn't go according to plan the last time."

Simba took a few long strides until he reached the side of the bed and loomed over Caleb. "Oh, I think things went according to plan. *Your plan.* And I still have the scar." He raised his right arm and pushed away the long sleeve of his tee, exposing the jagged line bisecting the inside of his forearm. "Remember?"

Caleb tried not to flinch, but the heat of Simba's rage pounded against him. He counted himself lucky that Simba's large fists weren't also pounding against his face. "Come on, bro. I was young and stupid and—"

"It was only a few months ago, Caleb. But yes, you were stupid. That much hasn't changed." He marched to the door and opened it. "You can spend one night here. Only one. I want you gone tomorrow morning. Understand?"

"Two days. Come on. I have to make plans, call people, and—"

"Fine. Two days."

Caleb bounced off the bed, the metal frame squeaking as he did. "You're all heart, Simba. I knew you wouldn't abandon your only brother."

"Half-brother. And I mean it, Caleb." Turning, he leaned against the doorframe and stared out into the compound. "I just got this job, and I don't want to screw it up like the last time." He swiveled his head to face Caleb. "And by screw it up, I don't mean *I* screwed it up. Your presence seems to do that without effort."

"We all have our superpowers."

Simba snorted and pointed a finger at him. "Forty-eight hours."

Caleb shrugged. "You won't even notice I'm here."

Exhaling heavily, Simba began to walk out. Caleb hurried to follow him, opening his mouth to ask about the fresh cuts on Simba's left arm. His brother was left-handed. Had he been in another knife fight?

Simba spun around and slammed a hand against Caleb's chest. "No way. You stay in here. No one is to see you, hear you, smell you … Speaking of which …" He flipped his hand over so his palm was up. "Hand it over."

Caleb's hands rose compulsively to cover the necklace. He felt the object's bulk under his shirt. How had Simba known?

His eyebrows furled together. "The weed, Caleb. I know you have some. There's no smoking allowed on this compound."

Caleb's shoulders dropped as his tension leaked away. "Oh. That. Nope, no worries. I was running for my life and neglected to pack all my junk."

Simba narrowed his eyes and leaned into Caleb's space with a heavy sniff. "I smell it on you. And if I so much as catch a whiff of smoke, I will personally drag you back to whatever dank, filthy hole you currently inhabit and stuff you back inside with the other street rats. Understand?"

Caleb raised his hands in surrender and fell a step back. "Not a sight. Not a sound. Not a whiff."

Simba held his gaze for a moment longer before shaking his head with a disgusted expression. "Let's see how long this lasts."

## Chapter Thirteen

"SPEAK FAST OR I'LL SMACK THAT WOOLY HEAD OFF YOUR shoulders."

Mama Noah waved her frying pan toward the young man standing in the kitchen entrance. She didn't have to inhale deeply to know he was a druggie. The dreadlocks, the bloodshot eyes, the gangster fashion show hanging off his tall frame. Everything screamed *drug user.*

"Well, speak, young man. I don't have time for this foolishness. And there's no money here. Or drugs." She paused and went through a mental inventory of anything he might possibly want. "And no guns. You hear me?"

The man grinned, and the wide smile transformed his face into something approaching handsome. Holding up his hands, he bowed his head. "Eh! Me, I'm not looking for trouble. But I *am* hungry. I guess you have food in here. Am I right?"

Still not lowering her frying pan, Mama Noah clucked her tongue. "Do I have food here? It's a kitchen. Of course I have food here."

The young man rubbed his hands and wagged his eyebrows.

"Then me, I'm in the right place. Name's Caleb. I'm Simba's brother. He didn't mention I'm staying a few days with him?"

Mama Noah narrowed her eyes. "You don't look alike. Simba is big, strong, handsome. And you, you're—"

"Even more handsome," Caleb finished for her, his mischievous twinkle undimmed by her attempt at an unflattering comparison. "Yeah, yeah, I know. I get that a lot. We're half-brothers, so he's only half as good-looking as me. So, food?"

Mama Noah harrumphed and settled the pan on the stovetop. Using her chin, she indicated the island counter. "Sit and stay out of my way."

"Yes, madam." Affecting a mock bow, Caleb strutted to the island and straddled a stool. "And do you have a name, lovely lady? How about the kid?"

Mama Noah ladled rice and added a scoop of beans before thumping the plate onto the counter. "Mama Noah, and that's Celine. She doesn't talk much."

Caleb leaned his torso to the side until it was almost horizontal with the floor and waved at the girl who was crouching in one corner over a drawing. "Hey, Celine. Nice drawing. Are those the alien ships?"

While Mama Noah didn't expect any response from Celine, her eyebrows quirked upward when Celine lifted her head and met Caleb's inquisitive gaze. The child scratched a hand through her blonde curtain of hair and nodded a couple of times before resuming her artwork.

"Cool." Caleb rapped his knuckles against the marble countertop. "What do the aliens look like?"

Celine didn't look up. Instead, she pulled out a black crayon from her box, followed by a white one, and placed them side by side on the tile in front of her.

"I told you not to leave my room."

Mama Noah turned to face Simba, whose bulk filled the entrance between the kitchen and the rest of the house. She chuckled softly when Caleb rolled his eyes and slouched over the plate.

"Eh, me, I was hungry," the younger man grumbled as he ate. "What, you want me to starve? Your little brother, abandoned and hungry and—"

Simba closed his eyes, gritted his teeth and held up a hand. "Please. Just … stop talking. Finish eating and get out."

"Simba, who is this?"

Mama Noah pretended to be busy drying a silver platter when Mrs. Walker pushed past Simba, her dark blue eyes narrowed and suspicious.

No one spoke at first, and Mama Noah wondered if Simba had asked permission before inviting his clearly troubled relative into the compound. Not wanting to attract attention to herself, she continued to dry the platter and hoped Mrs. Walker wouldn't notice the old cast-iron frying pan. The funny mzungu woman had an issue with it for some reason and insisted Mama Noah use one of her shiny, fancy, silver-colored pans instead.

Mama Noah thought they were useless, and of course overpriced.

Mrs. Walker stared at each of them in turn. "I asked a question. Who is he, and why is he in my home?"

"Sorry, Mrs. Walker. He's not supposed to be here." Simba's voice softened even as his angry gaze fixed on Caleb.

Mrs. Walker huffed and pulled out her phone, already losing interest. "Clearly. But who is he?"

"Caleb Aladdin Makoti, at your service." He stuck out his hand.

Mama Noah frowned at the bits of rice and grease coating his palm.

Perhaps realizing the same thing, he dropped his hand to his pants, wiped it a few times, and lifted it again toward Mrs. Walker. "Simba's long-lost half-brother."

"Aladdin? Really?" Mrs. Walker stared at his hand, the corners of her mouth twitching into a smile while one eyebrow rose as if she was considering the likelihood of catching some communicable disease by touching him. "Delightful." She glanced between them. "You don't look anything alike. It's hard to believe you're brothers."

"Half-brothers," Simba corrected.

Caleb nodded and shrugged. "I can't believe it, either."

Simba muttered in Swahili, "On that, we agree."

Mama Noah swallowed her laugh.

Oblivious, Mrs. Walker dropped her gaze and continued to study her phone. "Are you staying long, Caleb?"

He stopped chewing, cheeks bulging. "Maybe."

Simba lowered his chin, as if preparing to charge. "No."

"A few nights," Caleb said.

"One night."

Mrs. Walker glanced between them, eyes widening, mouth slightly agape. "Okay. Which is it?"

Her phone buzzed. Puffing out a sound of irritation, she tapped on the screen while gesturing vaguely at the kitchen's back door. "Sort it out. I guess you can stay in the staff quarters. There's an extra room."

"He's only staying for one night," Simba said before Caleb could give his thanks.

Mama Noah smirked at the silver platter. She'd rubbed it enough that she could almost see her reflection on its surface.

Caleb leaned an elbow on the counter and smiled broadly at Mrs. Walker. "Yeah, but I can stay longer if you want, Mrs. Walker. I'm real handy around the house."

"I'll think about it. And call me Trisha."

Caleb's grin widened. Simba's expression hardened as he glared across the kitchen. Mrs. Walker didn't notice. Her full attention was fixed on the phone's screen. Mama Noah softly clucked her tongue, marveling at how her mzungu employer could be so oblivious.

"Why, thank you, Trisha. And you can call me Caleb. How can I help?" He scooped in another mouthful of food.

Simba ground his teeth forcibly enough that Mama Noah could hear him.

Mrs. Walker jerked a thumb over her shoulder. "Help Simba bring in the groceries. We need to get everything set up. We have no idea how long we'll have to be …"

She cut herself off as her gaze fell on Celine still huddled in the corner, working on her drawing. "Well, I just want to get everything organized. You understand?"

Not waiting for a response, Mrs. Walker left the room, and Mama Noah waited for the inevitable explosion.

## Chapter Fourteen

SIMBA'S BEEFY HAND SMACKED CALEB AGAINST THE SIDE OF HIS head, catching him by surprise.

And he'd been innocently minding his own business while enjoying the vision of Trisha's backside as she exited the kitchen. His attention was so focused, he didn't notice Simba's approach until too late.

Scowling, Caleb rubbed his head. "Ouch. What was that for?"

He pushed his face close to Caleb's. "You know exactly what that's for. One night, then you're leaving. And stop checking her out."

Mama Noah snorted a laugh while Caleb spluttered an attempt at proving his innocence.

Surrendering the pretense, Caleb slumped on the stool. "Two. You said forty-eight hours. Now, me, I didn't finish school or nothin', but forty-eight hours means two nights."

"Maybe I changed my mind. Are you done yet?"

Ignoring Simba and the maid — she seemed like the nosy type — Caleb scooped up the plate in one hand and held it close to his mouth while using the spoon to shovel as much food into his mouth as possible.

Simba snapped his fingers. "I'll be outside. Soon as you're

finished, come out to the front and make yourself useful. And get a haircut. You look like an unwashed beggar." Then Simba marched out of the kitchen.

A door slammed.

Caleb made a rude hand gesture. "And you're a mkundu."

Mama Noah laughed as she retrieved his empty dish. "You know he can't hear you? He's out of the house now."

Caleb shrugged. "Yeah, that's kinda the idea. I shout at him when he can't hear me. Otherwise, he'd punch my lights out. I take drugs, but I'm not stupid."

"Ah. Not stupid at all, I see. I know someone who can give you a haircut."

Caleb ran a hand over his dreadlocks. "And lose these beauties? Nah. He's just jealous of my gorgeous locks. He wants to change me, make me like him. Uptight, law-abiding, boring."

Knocking his knuckles on the counter, Caleb waited for the maid to turn away before slipping his spoon and a knife into his baggy jean pocket. You never knew when cutlery could come in handy, especially silver-plated.

Twirling, he gave a mock salute to Mama Noah and swaggered after his half-brother, out of the house and to the driveway. He patted the Land Cruiser's front tire. "Nice set of wheels. And an antique. Not too many of the old clunkers still around. How much you think it's worth?"

Simba's shoulders tensed. Caleb wondered if he was going to spin around and punch him in the face.

He stepped back and held up his hands just in case. Not that he'd be able to block a punch from Simba. His older brother had always been big for his age and even as kids he was more than willing to use size to his advantage.

But Simba didn't turn around or respond. He clicked a button to unlock the doors. Stuffed the key into his pocket and opened the rear door. Boxes and bags filled the entire back half of the vehicle.

Caleb whistled and tried to recall if he'd ever seen this much food outside of a grocery store. He was pretty sure he hadn't. "Now that's what I'm talking about. We'll be able to hole up here and outlast the alien invasion. Am I right?"

Simba turned and leaned against the rear bumper. Crossed his muscular arms over his chest and stared into Caleb, his gaze as hard as a drill bit. "The Walker family, yes. You, no. You're leaving tomorrow morning, remember?"

Huffing a laugh, Caleb tugged up his sagging jeans around his slim waist. "You mean, the day after tomorrow."

"Exactly."

"Yeah, sure. Forty-eight hours."

Simba grunted and turned, his thick arms wrapped around a box. "Glad we understand each other."

Caleb rolled his eyes. He doubted they had *ever* understood each other.

Simba stacked a couple boxes on the ground while Caleb reached into the closest box, retrieved a tuna can and tucked it into another pocket. "So what's with the horse trailer?"

"Space."

After a few seconds, Caleb huffed a laugh. *Typical Simba.* "Eh! Don't get too chatty on me. Wouldn't want you to wear out your vocal cords." Under his breath, he muttered, "Mkundu."

Simba ignored him as usual. Caleb waited for the muscle-bound brute to move his big butt out of the way, staring at the tall walls surrounding the compound. They were topped with several lines of electric fencing and barbed wire wrapped around the lines.

Caleb snorted. Paranoid, much? Then again, this was Nairobi. Tall walls and electric fence were the minimum security requirement. The only way in was at the end of the driveway through the black metal gates or the pedestrian door.

His gaze drifted back to the barbed wire wrapped electric fence.

*The only way, unless you want to be cut up and electrocuted.*

He smirked, because security was an illusion and there was

always a way. The stronger the illusion, the safer you were, until someone came along who could see right through it.

Caleb wondered what Madam Zahir was doing at that moment. Had she discovered his treachery?

His hand rose to the shoestring around his neck and the weight at its end. His smile faded when his fingers brushed the pendant pushing up from under his T-shirt, their tips buzzing at the contact.

Why had he given in to his impulse? He might be a thief, but was he really so stupid as to steal from the matron of crime herself?

*Yup, I am truly* that *stupid.*

Shuffling toward the growing mountain of boxes and bags, Caleb cracked his knuckles and ignored Simba's scowl.

The question wasn't *if* Madam Zahir would figure out who stole her pendant. That was a given.

Rather, his gut was twisted imagining what she would do if she ever found him.

*No, not if,* he thought, pocketing a packet of crackers. *When. When Madam Zahir finds me.*

## Chapter Fifteen

*CALEB NEEDS TO GO.*

Trisha frowned at the snarky suggestion. Her inner voice resembled Jake on a bad day. Like most days with him.

But how could she tell Simba to get rid of his brother?

"Because this is your home, and you shouldn't have to host people you don't know or trust."

The words, murmured with an exhale, tightened around Trisha, deepening her unease. The guy seemed all right. And yet, she couldn't help rub her goosebump-covered arms.

She watched as her driver strode toward the Land Cruiser, his brother — half-brother — shuffling behind him, shoulders slouched, dreadlocks bobbing about his head and across his shoulders.

Pacing in front of the living room window, she reminded herself how badly she'd misjudged Simba.

*But Simba doesn't smell like the inside of a junkie's ashtray.*

The men stood at the back of the Land Cruiser. Simba was waving a hand in front of Caleb's face, eyebrows furrowed and jaw tense. Caleb rolled his eyes and looked up at the sky. It didn't seem like a particularly happy reunion.

*One night.* That's what Simba had said. And that's what it would be, despite whatever Caleb might think.

One night.

"I can handle that." She chewed on her cheek, noting her own lack of confidence. She cleared her throat and tried again. "I can handle that."

This was her home, not a hotel. She had two employees living on the compound. And now this one, a stranger, not even employed by her — surely, he had other family or friends to rely on.

Decision made, Trisha continued to watch the men unload the back of the Land Cruiser. Simba had done well with the shopping. Box after box of nonperishables piled high in a mountain around them. They wouldn't have to go out for the next several days. The hoax would be over by then, and the same for all this confusion.

Or maybe it was a glitch in the software. She stopped pacing. *Of course it was.* The photo was probably nothing more than space rock or rocket debris. A small distortion in the telescope's lens or a problem in the imaginative software, and *voila!* Aliens on the other side of the moon. A few unethical bloggers had taken advantage of the possibilities, whispering the notion that these were actually alien spacecraft heading to Earth.

She gave it one week, tops. Probably less.

There were always clever people willing and eager to disprove hoaxes and lies. They would be on this like flies on jam, or whatever the expression was. Soon enough, the world would know the truth. There were no alien ships, and everyone still needed to show up at work the next day.

Either way, Caleb had to go.

She'd seen the bloodshot eyes and had inhaled the sweet scent of pot on his clothes. Not that she needed to be close enough to sniff, either. He hadn't bathed in a couple of days at least.

Crossing her arms, she turned and stared at the shelves. She'd made a feeble attempt at unpacking her books and had stacked a few of her favorites at eye level. Somehow, it made the rest of the room look even emptier.

The men stomped inside. Caleb carried one box while Simba had three balanced in his arms. She heard them exchange words with Mama Noah in Swahili, the conversation fast and fluid, interjected with hearty laughs and climbing voices.

Frowning, Trisha picked up the book at the top of the pile and stared at the cover without really seeing it. Why were they so easy with their words with each other, and yet could hardly meet her gaze or say more than a few words when she was in the room?

The all spoke English. She had been pleasantly surprised by both of her staff members. Simba was educated, even though he only worked as a driver. Mama Noah looked like she had just stepped out of a village, but her English was decent enough. She could even read, much to Trisha's delight, although she refused to offer her real name and insisted everyone call her Mama Noah.

It was an oddity Trisha could live with.

She stepped forward as the men left her kitchen. "Simba. A word, please."

His eyes flicked toward her, then back to Caleb. He murmured something to his brother, who shrugged, nodded and continued outside. Trisha watched as Simba fixed his gaze on Caleb.

*So he doesn't trust his own brother, either. Interesting.*

Her confidence swelled with the confirmation of her suspicions. Dropping the book on the shelf, she rubbed her hands together and hoped her words wouldn't sound as nasty out loud as they did in her head.

"Simba, I would prefer if Caleb left sooner than later. I know I said there was a spare room in the staff quarters, but I think all things considered …"

She left the sentence hanging, unsure how to finish. All things considered, his brother was a drug user? Or how about his brother was untrustworthy, most likely a crook, a lowlife? She knew it was the right thing, but regretted saying anything at all.

Simba nodded twice, his movements precise and sharp. "Yes, Mrs. Walker. I already told him. Is that all?"

Tension flowed out of her shoulders, and her arms fell loosely by her side. Smiling, she shook her head. "Yes, that's it. Thank you."

Still not looking at her, Simba stepped toward the door, watching his brother unload another box as if he suspected Caleb might place it on his shoulder and run off. And for all she knew, maybe that was exactly what Caleb would do.

"He's not going to cause us trouble, is he?"

Simba turned and met her gaze before staring at the small stack of books behind her. He shook his head and murmured, "No. I'll make sure he doesn't."

Trisha watched his dark eyes flick down and up, as if he were trying to read the titles on the spines. His mouth curved into a hint of a smile.

She leaned against the shelving unit and studied the cover of the top book. A zombie glared back at her, clawed hands reaching for her neck.

On an impulse, she picked up the first two books and held them out. The second cover showed a dark and grainy image. The camera was focused on the distant sunset rather than the dehumanized people looming in the foreground.

"You can borrow one, if you want. I have a lot of zombie books. I guess you can say I'm a bit of a fanatic."

Simba stepped back as if the books were about to either self-combust or pounce and devour his brains.

Trisha nodded toward her collection and nudged the box with her foot. "Really. Anytime."

Simba kept staring, his expression inscrutable.

Her cheeks flushed. "Feel free. Just let me know which one you're borrowing."

Simba tilted his head toward her and wordlessly marched outside to the vehicle.

Trisha cleared her throat and watched him effortlessly lift a box. "Okay, then. That wasn't awkward, much."

"Mrs. Walker."

Tensing at the volume and tone of Mama Noah's voice, Trisha spun to face the entrance into the kitchen.

"Oh, God save us. Mrs. Walker, come quick!"

## Chapter Sixteen

TRISHA TRIED TO TAMP THE PANIC which seemed to be pounding in her throat.

Had something happened to Celine?

How could anything happen when only a few minutes had passed since she was in the kitchen with her daughter?

What was wrong with the maid that she couldn't handle a few minutes alone with a child without endangering anyone?

Veering into the kitchen, Trisha stared toward the corner where Celine preferred to sit. Her daughter was still there, contentedly coloring a background of dark blue around three silver discs. She wasn't choking, bleeding, having a fit, or in any way displaying signs of impending death.

Her hands shaking, Trisha spun to face Mama Noah. "What? What is it?"

Shrinking away from her, Mama Noah jabbed a finger at the juke hanging above the counter. She then retreated into the corner next to the kitchen sink, her hands reaching for a dishcloth and a bowl.

Trisha glared at the juke and its shiny screen displaying a view of the world she didn't want to see. A news presenter stared back at her with a somber expression and rattled off the latest Astral update in sharp, clipped words.

Behind her, Simba and Caleb entered the kitchen. Huffing, Caleb dropped the box he was carrying onto the floor. "Wah! That is too heavy. What's wrong?"

Trisha could've answered Caleb in so many ways.

*If my daughter loves me, she never shows it.*

*My husband's a bastard, and I'm glad he's not here.*

*The world is going to hell.*

*And I have no idea what I'm doing.*

Instead, she bit her cheek and tapped on the screen to increase the volume. The presenter — that Greta San Lucas woman with the bulging breasts — declared in a detached tone that she possessed breaking news and begged the audience not to panic. Underneath the serious façade was a delight at being the face of shocking news.

Trisha snorted in disbelief. The media absolutely *loved* to tell people, "the following video contains disturbing scenes," or "some people might find the below description frightening." Those trigger words were candy to reporters. The more disturbing and frightful, the better.

Before she could roll her eyes or scowl at Mama Noah for alarming her unnecessarily, an image stopped her cold. Her hands fluttered in front of her face, pressing against each other in a prayer pose, even though she usually felt that prayers meant nothing.

The entire screen was filled with an image of a vast flotilla of spaceships. But they weren't a distant set of blurs floating in empty space, dots that could, if one stretched one's imagination, be mistaken for shiny asteroids. The ships were clear enough to see the faces of the drivers, if the spaceships had windscreens.

"Oh my God."

Trisha was shocked to recognize the whisper as her own. She pressed her hands against her mouth to stop anything else from leaking out.

This was not a hoax or a software malfunction.

This was real.

"This is Greta San Lucas of Global News, and we have the latest and greatest in breaking news. Today, we received confirmation from NASA scientists that the Astral sighting is not a hoax."

While Greta wasn't one to babble, her expression was a blend of professional seriousness and fearful excitement. Because this time, the breaking news wasn't about some distant disaster or battle that would never touch the presenter or her audience.

This time, the news story of the century was about to land on their planet and change everything forever.

"Like we needed them to tell us what we all see just fine." Caleb smirked a second before his brother smacked the back of his head. "Eh! I resemble that."

Simba huffed. "You mean, you *resent* that, and I don't care."

Pausing in her overview of what was known — very little — Greta San Lucas gave her red-lipped, wide smile for the viewers, as if to reassure them that nothing would stop her quest for an excellent story, and that included a fleet of alien spaceships.

She continued to describe the comments of the NASA scientists before the scene changed. Facing the camera was a woman wearing thick glasses, an anxious expression and a lab coat with the NASA insignia on the right breast pocket.

Adjusting her glasses, the NASA employee cleared her throat a few times. Like Greta, the scientist was doing her best to maintain a dignified pose and a serious expression but wasn't nearly as successful at her guise.

Finally surrendering her pretense, the scientist rubbed her nose, coughed and adjusted the tiny mic attached to her lapel. "Based on the current speed and trajectory, the world has five days before the spacecraft arrive."

The screen split with Greta on the left and the scientist on the right. Greta placed her hands together on her desk and stared into the camera, eyes peering into the heart and soul of the audience, her entire expression a vision of concentration. "And is there any suggestion on the nature of their visit?"

Trisha rolled her eyes. "How the hell would they know?"

Mama Noah clucked her tongue.

The scientist nodded her head a few times as she considered the question. "Um. Well. At this stage, we have no information as to the intent of these spacecraft."

"You mean, aliens." Greta leaned forward, dark eyes glittering. She licked her bright-red lips. "That's what these are, right? This is the first confirmed sighting of aliens."

"Well, at least of their spacecraft." The scientist laughed as if this was all a big joke. "They could be space probes, for all we know. Maybe there's no one in there but computer systems and testing equipment. Like the vessels we've sent to Saturn and Jupiter. Unmanned exploration missions."

"But what are the chances they're unmanned?" Greta tapped the desk with her manicured nails to emphasize her point. "And why so many probes if it's just for collecting rock samples? There could very well be aliens inside. Don't you agree?"

The scientist squirmed as Greta did what Greta did best: pin her down with definitive, polarizing statements. "Yes, it's possible. I mean, I suppose there could be—"

The camera cut to their lead anchor and star reporter. Smiling in triumph, Greta San Lucas straightened up and stared at her unseen audience.

"And there you have it, presented to you by Global News. For the first time in recorded history, we have absolute proof that aliens will be visiting our planet, and they will arrive in five days' time. Stay tuned for our alien expert's five tips for surviving an invasion, coming up next."

## Chapter Seventeen

*THEY WILL ARRIVE IN FIVE DAYS' TIME.*

Numbly, Trisha reached up and muted the volume. She had no interest in hearing the presenters and their experts dig into the vague comments squeezed out of the NASA scientist. The media would analyze, digest and dissect every nuance and word. Then, once that was exhausted, they'd return to the images and regurgitate more nonsense.

As far as she was concerned, they were trying to generate new stories out of nothing. Yet they really only knew that there were mysterious vessels moving toward Earth with unknown intentions. The facts hadn't changed.

But the level of fear certainly had.

They had five days before …

If silence had a sound, the kitchen drowned in it. Trisha looked up to see all three Kenyans staring at her, waiting for her decision.

Why was it up to her?

*You're used to this,* she reminded herself even as her fingers squeezed the edge of the marble counter behind her. *Once upon a time, you directed a whole department. And everyone listened to you. So why shouldn't this group?*

Before the nasty voice in her head could answer — *that was seven years ago when you were younger, confident and well-rested* — she cleared her throat as if about to commence a speech.

"Nothing has changed. Let's finish unpacking the food. Simba, start filling containers and buckets with water, and also the spare tank. Fill everything. You bought chlorine tablets, right?"

He nodded and Trisha allowed herself a moment of smugness. Jake might dismiss her as ignorant, but who had made the decision to stock up before inevitable chaos hit the streets?

She smiled for the first time since yesterday morning. "That's good. We don't know what will happen next."

Simba rubbed a hand over his head, the soft scratching of skin against stubble filling the conversational void. He looked ready to speak.

But Caleb said, "Don't ya think we should leave?"

"Leave?" Trisha stared at him, puzzled. "You mean, leave Nairobi? And go where?"

As far as she was concerned, the only things outside of Nairobi were national game parks and hostile land. Probably wasn't accurate, but she wasn't about to risk the relative safety of her house to find out.

Simba stared down and scuffed his boot against a floor tile. "Things could get …" He hesitated, as if searching for an appropriate word. "Difficult."

Caleb snorted. "You mean total chaos, confusion, riots in the street and looting." Grinning, he winked at Trisha. "At least, that's what happens every few elections."

Except this wasn't an election. This was the arrival of an alien force, even if the ships were unmanned. If people reacted poorly to the uncertainty of an election result, what would they do in this situation?

That was the million-dollar question.

Trisha threaded fingers through her hair and shrugged. "That's the typical response to a zombie apocalypse."

Mama Noah's jaw dropped while Caleb laughed. Simba stared at her, an eyebrow raised.

Not sure if she should laugh, blush or change the subject, Trisha looked at her bare feet. She had read every book and watched every movie and TV series related to zombies. She'd always had a fascination with them, ever since she could remember. Jake, on the other hand, found the whole notion disgusting and disturbing. He hated the zombie movies particularly, which of course made them more fun to watch.

Meeting Simba's gaze, she straightened up. "Listen, this is just like a zombie apocalypse or a nuclear war scenario. Panic and perish."

Caleb's laugh died as he joined the other two in mutual confusion.

*In for a penny, in for a pound.*

"The safest thing to do when the world goes sideways is to stay put. Everyone else is rushing around like headless chickens, trying to escape population centers and find a safe haven out in the countryside. In the process, they clog the roads, fight each other, lose their gear. They end up either getting shot or shooting others. The same thing will happen now, in this possible but not yet confirmed alien invasion. For all we know, the aliens are just passing by."

She thought about *The Hitchhiker's Guide to the Galaxy* and laughed. "Maybe they recently built a galactic highway through our solar system, but without blowing up the planet. And they're trying to call us right now and say, 'Sorry, earthlings. We didn't send you the memo about the interstate running through your backyard.' After all the panic dies down, those who stayed calm will be fine."

She looked around the kitchen. Mama Noah had covered her cheeks with both hands, perhaps trying to keep her jaw firmly closed and her eyes stowed in their sockets. Caleb made no such effort, and his mouth hung open as he gawked at her.

Only Simba maintained a cool façade, providing no indication of how he thought or felt about her word dump.

Turning her head to the side, she studied the clean plates drying in the rack. "Anyway, that's my zombie theory. I just don't see the point in joining all the mobs that will form out there. Jammed roads, chaos and confusion." She shrugged. "We have enough food here for the next week, at least. And by that time, we'll know if the aliens are passing by or …"

She shrugged.

Because if the ships didn't keep flying, if this wasn't merely traffic zooming past them on an intergalactic highway constructed close to Earth, if the aliens actually *stayed* for a visit, the real question wasn't if the Walker household should leave Nairobi.

Instead, they should ask if anyone would survive the encounter.

"But if you really want to go, I'm not stopping you."

The gentle hum of her fridge sounded like a roar.

Clearing his throat, Caleb scratched between his dreadlocks. "Where would we go?"

Her phone buzzed in her pocket.

*Saved by the bell.*

Her relief at the interruption was short-lived.

Holding up a hand as if to interrupt the nonexistent conversation, she pressed the phone to her ear and hurried out of the kitchen. "Jake."

"Are you guys okay?"

He meant Celine. For all the difficulties they had between them, at least she couldn't fault him on that. The man was utterly dedicated to his daughter.

"We're fine. I stocked up on food and other supplies yesterday, so we should be good for a while." She waited for him to praise her quick thinking. When he said nothing, she huffed a laugh. She should've known better. "Where are you now?"

His hesitation was enough. "I'm still in Geneva. Just waiting."

Trisha didn't bother to ask what he was waiting for.

"I think you should get out of Nairobi."

Trisha stopped in front of the bookshelf and looked at the stack of zombie books. Her fingers skimmed the titles. "That's exactly what everyone is going to do, Jake. It'll be madness out there. Why are you still in Geneva?"

"They grounded all the planes the moment the Astral sightings were made. I think they're going to resume normal flights in the next few hours. It doesn't matter. Have you seen the news?"

Her finger paused on the spine of a favorite. Stroking it like a cat, she decided not to ask where in Geneva Jake had been staying. Like he said, it didn't matter, even if he had shacked up with his lover. If the aliens landed, the world would change, and nothing from their past or their failed marriage would be relevant.

"I'll think about it."

Jake swore. "Do more than think about it, Trisha. It isn't safe in the cities. If those things come any closer to Earth, people will panic, if they aren't already."

"I said I'll think about it."

"Damn it. Stop being so obstinate." He launched into a monologue of all the reasons she had to take *his* daughter to a safer place.

She disconnected the call.

Glancing through the kitchen entrance, she watched as Celine stood and stretched. Bending at the waist, she picked up two crayons — a black one and a white one. Celine straightened and held out the crayons to Caleb.

And despite the oddity of the moment, Trisha's thoughts returned to Geneva, and she wondered when she'd stopped caring about Jake and his lover.

## Chapter Eighteen

"FORTY-EIGHT HOURS."

The dull thud of a knife hitting the wooden chopping board accompanied Simba's words. Mama Noah stood facing the back window, her blade mincing vegetables, her head bowed in concentration.

Not looking up, Simba continued placing a few items of food into a small backpack. "That was the deal. Two days, and then you go. Well, by my watch—"

"Yeah, yeah." Caleb held up his hands in surrender, then pushed his fingers through his dreadlocks.

Leaning against the island counter, he watched his half-brother place a can of beans precisely on top of a box of crackers. With that food, plus what he'd stolen, he had enough for five days. A week, if he was careful.

"I get it. You're a man of your word and all that. But hey, I'm used to it. I'm used to being tossed out into a cold, cruel world."

Simba snorted and stared into the backpack. "Whose fault is that? Wait." He waved a hand at Caleb. "I don't want to know."

Dodging around Mama Noah, Simba opened the fridge. "And it's hardly cold out there. I'm sure you can make your way back to your pack."

"Gang, not pack. We're not dogs."

Mama Noah chuckled behind Simba, the thumping knife punctuating her chuckles.

Straightening up, Simba placed some leftovers from the previous night onto a piece of tinfoil. "I'm giving you a couple days' worth of food."

*Thud. Thud.*

The bag was almost fully packed when Simba finally met his brother's gaze. "Listen, it's not just me. Trisha … I mean, Mrs. Walker also wants you gone. I guess you have that vibe."

For once, Caleb said nothing. His big bro and the white lady had been talking about him. So what? He didn't need them.

Looking down at the marble counter, he traced a golden vein with one finger. "Yeah. Don't worry about it. I'll be fine." His eyes cut sideways, and he saw Simba's scar, a ragged reminder of a ruined life carved into his skin. "I'm sorry."

Simba paused, a tin of beans held aloft.

Caleb lowered his gaze and tapped the counter. "About … you know. What happened that night. I didn't know they'd be waiting there. I swear it wasn't part of the plan. Someone must've told them. And …"

He shrugged, wondering why something as simple as picking up a couple packages from the post office could turn into a scramble for life and limb. Madam Zahir had nearly killed him for losing one of the parcels in the scuffle; instead, she'd added the loss to his ever-mounting debt.

Simba cleared his throat and dropped the tin in the pack. "Okay."

Yawning, Celine shuffled into the kitchen, box of crayons in one hand and a drawing in the other. Looking up, she tilted her head toward Caleb and climbed onto a stool beside him.

*Finally, someone who doesn't talk bad about me. Probably because she doesn't know better.*

Caleb winked. "Hey, kid. Whatcha got there?"

Celine slid a drawing toward him. A jagged mountain covered in snow with forests along the bottom.

"Cool drawing. Looks like Mt. Kenya. Right, Simba?"

His brother ignored him, his attention on Trisha, who had followed her daughter in.

She smiled, then frowned as she looked across the island. "Caleb. You're still here."

Huffing a laugh, he pushed back from the counter. "Not for long. Just on my way out."

*Thud.*

The box of crayons thumped onto the floor, bits of waxy color scattering underfoot. Eyes wide, Celine stared at her mother, mouth open.

Trisha smiled. "Are you hungry, Celine?"

Snapping her mouth shut, Celine slid off her stool and latched onto Caleb's arm with both hands. Her knuckles whitened as she tightened her grip.

"It's okay, kid. I'll be fine." Awkwardly, Caleb patted Celine's head with his other hand, half-smiling at the child's concern. *Kinda cute. Guess this is why people have kids.* "Thanks for caring. 'Preciate it."

Simba stared at him, his jaw working. "Did you bribe her to do this?"

Caleb rolled his eyes. "Me, I'm saving everything I have. Because, you know, I'm going out there alone, armed only with a bag of groceries and my wit."

Simba pressed his lips together.

*Probably wants to call me a halfwit and tell me to get a haircut.*

Trisha drifted around the counter toward her daughter. "Celine, let Caleb go. He has his own home. Let's make some hot chocolate. I have those little marshmallows you love so much."

A small tick fluttered along Celine's jaw, and she tightened her grip. Eyes fixed on her mother, she shook her head and tugged at Caleb's arm. Bemused, he allowed her to move him to the other side of the counter, opposite Trisha.

Mama Noah's shoulders quivered, surely from suppressed laughter.

"I'm not going to ask you again, Celine." Trisha circled the counter, her pace slow and measured, gaze never leaving her child's face.

Celine wrapped her arms around Caleb's waist.

He raised his arms, eyes wide and darting from side to side. "I swear I'm innocent this time. And to be clear, I don't get to say that often."

Simba stepped backward and stood next to Mama Noah, hard gaze fixed on his brother.

Shrugging, Caleb leaned against the counter by the sink. Dampness sank into the back of his T-shirt, a reminder that he needed to do some laundry. If Trisha allowed him to stay, maybe Mama Noah would wash his clothes.

As if hearing his thoughts, Mama Noah placed her knife flat against the chopping board and glanced over her shoulder at him. Lips quivering, she pressed her hands onto the counter and shook her head slightly with narrowed eyes.

Then elbowing Simba, she murmured in Swahili, "That little girl, she's keeping Caleb. You watch."

Trisha thumped a fist on the counter. "Celine, this is ridiculous."

Caleb circled his arms around the girl's shoulders, earning a nasty look from Trisha. "Hey, don't call her ridiculous. Besides, I can be useful. I'm good around the house and … I have farming experience. That greenhouse in the backyard? I can look after it. You'll never go hungry with me around."

Mama Noah muttered something under her breath, not especially flattering.

Maybe she wouldn't wash his clothes, but at least he'd be fed.

Keeping his gaze fixed on Trisha, Caleb watched her inner battle play out on her expression. Anger, frustration, concern, and finally surrender.

"Fine. You can stay. Now make yourself useful and …" She waved her hands toward the window as if to indicate the entire back-yard. "I don't know. Find something to do."

Scowling, Trisha twirled around and paced the length of the island counter until she reached the other end. Squatting, she reached into a lower shelf and retrieved a tall biscuit tin with a fancy design. It looked imported and therefore expensive. She twisted the top and pulled out a long, tubular biscuit. The thing was shaped like a bread stick, but Caleb could smell the sugar coating.

Her expression distracted and eyes distant, Trisha crunched on one end of the biscuit. Then, as if sensing all their eyes, she shook herself out of her daze and gestured to the large jar. "Anyone else want one?"

Simba shook his head while Mama Noah continued with her meal preparations.

*She's just being polite, but hey, why not?*

Smirking, Caleb ignored his brother's warning glare and stretched out an arm over Celine's head. "Sure. Thanks for offering."

If Simba had been a real lion, he'd be growling.

*We all live here now. If they wanna play the humble servants, screw 'em.*

Celine tipped her head back and eyed the treat. Caleb snapped his biscuit in half, and ignoring Trisha's sharp inhale, handed it to Celine.

Trisha huffed. "She shouldn't be eating those until after lunch."

"*We* didn't have to wait," Caleb said, figuring he sounded like a reasonable and mature adult. "You know, for a retarded kid, Celine ain't that bad."

Trisha's hand tensed around her biscuit. "Don't call her that."

Caleb scratched his head, his eyebrows scrunched together. "I shouldn't call her Celine?"

Trisha's knuckles went bright white as her fingers tightened. "Don't call her re … the R word. She is *not* that."

Caleb cocked his head to one side. "So if she ain't retarded, what is she?"

"A little girl." The biscuit crumbled with a soft pop in her hand. Crumbs scattered beneath her shaking fist.

Caleb crowed. "Holy crap. Did you see how that just exploded?"

Simba stepped forward, his fists pressing onto the island counter and his forearms bulging.

Snickering, Caleb wondered if the vein on Simba's neck might explode as well. "You don't need to loom over me. Me, I get it. The mzungu doesn't like her kid being retarded. Just like you don't wanna hear the truth about your mama—"

Mama Noah hissed and half-turned to wag a finger. "That's enough, young man. No one is talking about anyone's mama."

Shrugging, Caleb slouched, his T-shirt picking up more water. His teeth crunched noisily against the biscuit.

Trisha brushed her hands together over the counter, spilling crumbs everywhere. Not bothering to clean up, she spun around and hurried out of the kitchen.

Simba pushed himself away from the counter and smacked Caleb on the back of his head. "You better behave. Or one night I'll drag you out myself, when your little protector isn't around."

Caleb grinned. "Love you too, bro."

Celine wiggled out of his grasp and began gathering her crayons.

Enough was enough, so Caleb exited the kitchen through the washing area and strolled into the backyard. He needed a smoke. And if he was going to survive these people, he needed more than one. The aliens had nothing over this mad house.

And why couldn't the kid eat a biscuit before lunch? Weren't they there to be eaten?

Shaking his head at the weirdness, Caleb jogged through the garden until he reached the tool shed. It was as big as some of the huts he'd lived in, but only for rakes and wheelbarrows.

"Now that's wealth," he said and slipped around the small

building to the back where he was out of sight of even the eagle-eyed Mama Noah.

Sliding to the ground, he pulled a joint out of his pocket, lit up and inhaled. A groan rose with the smoke.

"There is a god, after all." Glancing up at the sky, he grinned. "Wonder what the aliens smoke?"

Movement flickered at the corner of his vision.

He rolled his head to the side and met Celine's stern gaze.

"Serious? Shouldn't you be inside eating your disgusting veggies?"

Celine drifted to his side and sat.

Caleb fingered his joint and watched the small trail of smoke curl around his hand.

"You're not gonna tell anyone, are you?" He cackled. "Nah. Of course you're not. I kinda see why people keep retarded kids around. I can say whatever I want, and you won't tell a soul."

He leaned closer to Celine, lowering his head until his eyes were level with hers. "Especially my half-brother. Man, that guy's got a stick up his ass. Oops." He giggled. "Guess I shouldn't swear in front of you, either."

A few moments later, he said, "You know, for a mute, you sure are chatty. Your eyes talk a lot, I mean."

Celine shifted closer until her thin shoulder pressed against Caleb's arm.

He looked into her pale blue eyes. He'd never seen eyes that color before, not in person, not even in the movies. She really did seem to have a lot on her mind.

"I see why they keep you around."

Humming softly, he closed his eyes and inhaled some more happiness. As his mind floated up with the smoke, Caleb heard a voice, soft and sweet, murmuring through him.

*It's going to be okay, Caleb. Everything will be fine.*

And for just a second, before reason left him entirely, he could've sworn the voice belonged to Celine.

## Chapter Nineteen

THE SKY TURNED BLACK ON THE FIFTH DAY.

Simba was in the kitchen with Celine, watching her drink marshmallow-infused hot chocolate when it happened.

He didn't notice at first. The juke was on, and a nervous reporter — not Greta San Lucas but some bug-eyed white guy — was delivering an update on the day's breaking news. A few hours earlier, the media had informed the world, unnecessarily in Simba's view, that the ships were now clearly visible using home telescopes.

Shortly after that, scenes of chaos, panic and mass looting appeared on newsfeeds around the world. The media was having a field day. The rest of the population, not so much.

Celine held up a finger to her chocolate-lined lips.

"What is it?" Simba asked and reached up to mute the juke, as if expecting the girl to say something.

That was when he *felt* the silence, the kind that preceded a storm. An ugly sensation crawled across his skin and constricted his chest.

Leaning on the island counter, he looked through the large window at the backyard in time to see a formless shadow creep into view.

Celine didn't blink or move her head at the strange shift in the day.

His bare feet padded against the cool tiles as he stepped up to the sink and stared toward the back of the compound. At the far end he could see that the tool shed and small greenhouse were lost in unnatural twilight.

"Stay here, kid. I'll be right back."

Pushing away from the sink, Simba strode toward the side door and tugged on his boots. He reached for the doorknob and a scream shattered the silence. Swinging open the door, he almost bumped into Mama Noah.

"Oh, it's the end of days," she shrieked and grabbed onto the front of Simba's shirt. "The Four Horsemen, the day of judgment. My preacher, he told us about this time. He gave us a lengthy sermon only a month ago, God bless him. Told us about The Rapture, too, when the faithful servants of Jesus will be whisked into Heaven right before the end of days. This is it. This is the end!"

A stool scraped the kitchen tiles, and small feet pattered toward him. A tiny hand slipped into one of his big ones.

He gave the flustered maid a hard look and switched to Swahili. "You'll scare the child. Keep quiet."

Mama Noah drew herself up to her full height, the top of her head barely reaching his chest. "She has a right to know as well. The Rapture is coming, mark my words. Go outside and see for yourself, young man. You think you're so big and strong and … Well, the big part, I'll give you. But not big enough for what's out there."

Pushing past them, Mama Noah marched into the house and collapsed on a stool.

Not bothering to tell Celine to stay — she would come or go as she pleased — Simba stepped out into the courtyard where the laundry still hung dripping. Fat drops *plunked* against the irregularly-shaped paving stones.

A soft thumping filled the air, and he thought of a large fan twirling overhead. Except this sounded and felt like a giant fan or perhaps countless smaller ones, hanging from the sky.

Glancing up, he gasped at the darkness. His hand involuntarily tightened around Celine's.

A thick blanket of moving feathers obscured the sun. Countless birds flocked in the sky, wing tip to wing tip, the beat of their wings becoming a deafening *flap, flap, flap* as more avians added layers of feather until not even a glimpse of blue could be seen above the house.

And it wasn't just one type of bird. All colors, shapes and sizes flew in a monstrous flock. Flashes of pink indicated flamingos from Lake Nakuru. They mingled with yellow weavers, kites, ravens, giant marabou storks, ibises and hornbills.

Mesmerized, Simba stepped off the stone and onto the grass, his eyes fixed on the multitude of birds.

"What the hell are they doing together?"

Behind him, the plunking of water from their drying clothes highlighted the absence of other life in the garden. Where had all the resident birds gone?

A tapping on glass invited a glance over his shoulder. Mama Noah stared at him through the small window in the door and gestured with one hand, reminding him there was safety in the house. Out here, he was exposed.

*Plunk. Flap. Flap. Plunk.*

"They're just birds." His voice was a hoarse whisper, and the words failed to reassure him.

Kenya was a major hub for migrating birds. Surely, he was witnessing an unusually large migration.

Despite his churning stomach warning him how wrong he was, curiosity won out. He stepped farther away from the house, the child following him.

As the blanket of birds expanded to cover more and more of the sky in every direction, other sounds filled the spaces between flapping feathers against the air. Caws and whistles. Screeches and hoots. Clacking of bills. Flapping of wings.

It drowned out the soft *plunk, plunk* of drying clothes behind him.

Wave upon wave of birds joined the expanding flock, and the noise crescendoed.

Celine tugged at his hand, but he stared entranced at a world transitioning into a deranged version of itself. The mad beating of wings caused dust and small leaves to swirl in eddies around the garden. His nose wrinkled at the sharp bite of fresh bird droppings.

Some of the birds peeled away from the main flock. They created a living arrow and swooped down and around as one.

"We shouldn't be out here."

The words came from his mouth, and yet they didn't seem to be his. Glancing down at Celine, Simba was startled to see her eyes fixed on him.

*We shouldn't be out here.*

Her tiny, pale hand squeezed against his. Black and white mingling into one. His hand felt warmer than usual, and he suppressed the urge to pull away from her, and sever their connection.

*She's just a little girl,* he reminded himself while turning to face the line of wet clothes.

*Plunk. Plunk.*

A storm of caws drowned the flapping of thousands of wings, mocking his attempt at logic and sanity.

*We shouldn't be out here.*

Not his words or his voice.

Grasping his hand with both of hers, Celine tugged at Simba as she staggered backward toward the house. Her eyes were bright, almost glowing as she stared at his face.

The shrieking and hooting of birds sounded closer now, and a feather-scented wind pounded against him as if some avian creature was fanning his body.

Except it wasn't a creature at all.

It was a wave of birds who shouldn't be here. Not like this. Not in these numbers.

And definitely *not* sweeping toward him.

Gasping for air, Simba dared to look behind him and stared into a myriad of eyes glaring out of a storm cloud of birds. The multicolored swarm careened toward the house.

No, not toward the house. Toward *them*.

The strange lethargy caused by the sight of the mega-flock dissipated. Dropping to one knee, he grabbed Celine into his arms and bolted towards the kitchen door with a surge of energy.

The flapping grew louder while the smell intensified. It reminded him of his father's hen house at the back of the farm. The stench of feather and bird droppings were concentrated in a small, enclosed space.

But these weren't chickens peacefully pecking at the ground.

Wings brushed air overhead. He felt the birds hovering behind him. Their diverse noises melded into a loud, angry chatter that bombarded him from all sides.

His breath scratched at his throat as he sucked in the tainted air. He surveyed the distance. Five more long steps, and he would be inside, momentarily safe from whatever was happening to the planet.

Talons snatched at the back of his shirt as he stumbled onto the paving stones. Sharp tips dug into his shirt and clawed at his back.

Three more steps.

Something pointed and hard pecked viciously at his left shoulder, right over the place he'd been stabbed while grocery shopping. He grunted as the bird's beak tore at the recently formed scab.

Two more steps.

Mama Noah's face appeared in the door's small window, her eyes and mouth wide in horror and desperation. Pushing the door open, she screamed at him, but her words were lost in the cacophony of beating wings and hungry shrieks.

One more step.

His shirt tore, and the talons raked against his skin before losing their grip.

He fell into the kitchen, and Mama Noah slammed the door behind him. Collapsing at the base of the island counter, he clutched Celine to his chest and stared at the birds crashing against the back door.

"Lock it," he wheezed as he met the gaze of a larger-than-average raven with a blood-speckled beak. "Lock it. Lock it, damn it!"

Gasping, Mama Noah dragged the bolt into place. Turning her back to the crush of birds and feathers visible in the small window, she slid to the floor opposite Simba and cradled her bent legs.

For a few minutes, the three of them were still and silent, crumpled on the floor.

Gradually, the angry noises of birds diminished as they flew off to rejoin the flock. Only a marabou stork remained, its large, ugly head filling the door's window. It tapped at the glass a few times, giant wings fluttering behind it. The bird was at least five feet tall.

Clutching at her chest with both hands, Mama Noah rolled her eyes to the ceiling. "Are they gone?"

Simba's gaze hadn't left the window. "All but one." He looked down at Celine and almost smiled in disbelief. She had fallen asleep in his arms.

Mama Noah stretched her legs, straightening her skirt and kikoi before slapping her hands on her thighs and staring at him.

"It's the end of days, I tell you. It's the end of days."

## Chapter Twenty

"WHAT THE HELL IS GOING ON IN HERE?" TRISHA YELLED as she ran into the kitchen.

Simba craned his head back. Celine was still in his arms, her slow breath tickling his neck. He met Trisha's astounded expression and wondered what she thought might be happening.

Wordlessly, he lifted an arm and waved at the back door. Unable to summon more energy, he dropped his arm to his side and watched her.

He knew the moment she saw the marabou stork, because a gasp slipped from her mouth. She staggered forward, one arm lifted out to the side, hand pressed against the wall, as if she were afraid she might collapse without something to support her.

*Maybe that's exactly what would happen*, Simba thought when seeing her pale skin and strained expression. Deep lines bracketing her thin mouth.

With one last vicious peck at the glass, the stork retreated. Taking a few bouncing steps on its long, gangly legs, it leaped. Wings stretched wide as it rose to rejoin the swarm that had obliterated the sky.

Mama Noah stretched her arms to block Trisha. "Don't open the door."

Simba softly huffed a laugh. *As if anyone is crazy enough to do so.*

Then again, maybe they were descending into insanity gradually enough that they wouldn't notice until they hit the bottom.

"Yeah, no kidding." Trisha peered through the back window, which was now clear of all but a few feathers. "What the hell are they doing?"

No one had an answer.

"Hey guys, have you seen this?" Caleb trudged into the room, his bleary eyes blinking at Simba.

"Yes, Caleb," Trisha scoffed. "We're seeing it right now."

Caleb shook his head, red-eyed gaze still fixed on Simba. "No. Not the Hitchcock birds. The others."

Slowly, one step at a time, Trisha turned to face Caleb. Her face was paler than usual, with dark rings floating below her eyes. Even still, she looked beautiful. "What others?"

Shrugging, Caleb slouched around the other side of the island and flicked on the juke. Its screen buzzed, and the theme song for Global News summoned them to the latest alien-related story.

Laying Celine on the floor, Simba pulled himself up and stared at the juke, wondering what new horror awaited them.

Familiar footage of cities tearing themselves apart streamed across the juke's wide screen. Global News anchor Greta San Lucas eagerly narrated each incident with the genuine fervor only a reporter could summon in the face of mayhem and disaster.

Even still, Simba could see a twitch that occasionally flickered at the corner of one of her eyes. This might be the biggest news in media history, but everyone was feeling the strain.

Simba rubbed his face. "We've already seen it, Caleb. Chaos across the world's urban centers."

Hissing, Caleb shook his head and manually searched for another station. "You're not gonna see this on Global News, not yet. Because this … Well, *this* news is only Nairobi. No one else has picked it up yet, 'cause it's happening right now."

He paused at a local station. The juke flashed onto different scenes across the city. First downtown, where looting was well under way. Grocery stores in the city center had been cleared of anything edible, so people were stealing jukes and devices that may or may not work once their visitors were here.

The video flashed to Mombasa Highway as it spilled out of Nairobi onto the Athi Plains. Bumper-to-bumper traffic stretching to the horizon, and no one moving. Throngs hurried along the roadside carrying or dragging whatever they could manage of their worldly possessions.

Another camera came online, showing the road leading to Limuru and down the escarpment into the Rift Valley. Choked with traffic, though at least it was moving, even if only at a snail's pace.

Trisha sighed. "Just like I said."

Caleb winked at her. "Yeah, boss lady. Your zombie theory is holding out."

Simba planted his hands on the countertop, the sound of skin smacking stone loud in the exhausted silence. "Okay. So there's a lot of traffic leaving Nairobi. That's why we're staying here."

He glanced at Trisha, expecting to see an expression of vindication and self-righteousness. Instead, she creased her forehead and chewed her thumbnail.

Caleb switched channels a few more times. "Those video clips? They're a few hours old. History, not news. And that's not what I wanna show you." He stopped changing channels when he reached the site of a well-known Kenyan blogger.

Simba squinted at the juke. "What …?"

Trisha leaned against the counter next to Simba, her arm brushing against his. "Is that …?"

Caleb turned to face them, clearly having seen the video already. With a self-satisfied smirk, he nodded. "Yep. Downtown Nairobi *right now*."

"But what are they doing? Why are they there?" Trisha asked, as if any of them might possibly have the answer.

Mama Noah huffed as she shuffled toward the sink. "It's obvious. They're escaping."

"Escaping what?"

No one answered Trisha because no one had to.

The juke was still muted, but there was no need for narration. A camera hovered over Uhuru Highway; the edge of Nairobi's city center was visible along one side. Traffic was bumper-to-bumper. That wasn't unusual.

Of course, traffic usually didn't have pickups carting away household furniture and suitcases hastily stuffed with clothing and food.

Normally, cars didn't have entire families packed inside and their worldly possessions strapped to the roof.

Typically, Nairobi traffic didn't include a herd of zebras cantering along the sidewalk.

Or a pride of lions prowling between lanes.

Or a giraffe and her tall baby sauntering along the roadside, ears flicking back and forth when a motorcycle veered too close.

In the silence, Simba could hear the clock squatted atop the wooden mantlepiece in the living room ticking off the seconds. Each tick marked another heartbeat gone.

*Tick. Tock. Tick. Tock. Tick …*

Trisha exhaled loudly. "Where are they going?"

Without having to consider it, Simba knew. The words spilled out of his mouth before he realized it. "The Limuru Highlands. About twenty kilometers north of us."

Staring at the video, Trisha tapped her nails against the countertop, a nervous *click, click, click* that matched the *tick, tock*. "But why the Highlands? None of those animals are from there."

Mama Noah clucked as she began putting dishes away. Porcelain clattering against porcelain punctuated her words. "There's only one reason animals head for high ground that isn't their natural place."

Everyone except Celine swiveled their heads to look at her.

Lifting her chin, she straightened her shoulders and puffed out her chest. "The animals, they know. They're going to escape the flood."

## Chapter Twenty-One

"ME, I DON'T KNOW ABOUT ANY FLOOD OR WHATCHA BEEN smoking, but you definitely don't wanna go outside the compound."

Wearily, Trisha looked at Caleb and wished everyone would just go away.

Maybe she should have followed Jake's suggestion. Instead of playing host to three strangers, she should've packed Celine and herself into the fully stocked vehicle and driven off. How difficult could it possibly be to drive an antique with a manual transmission? Mama Noah, Simba and Caleb knew people in Nairobi who could help them. They could have stayed in the house. The landlord had better things to worry about.

But now, with the roads blocked, there was no leaving Nairobi.

Even as she mulled over the idea, Trisha was glad she'd stayed. There was only trouble and growing lawlessness out there.

*Besides, how many people get a chance to test out their theories on surviving a possible apocalypse?*

Grinning, Caleb stared at her, waiting for her to question him.

*He is entertaining.*

Trisha surrendered to his silent demand. "And why don't we want to go outside the compound, Caleb?"

He shrugged, his grin slipping at the corners. "Because the great migration has already migrated to Kinanda Road."

Simba huffed a laugh beside her. "What great migration?"

Trisha rubbed a hand down her face. "Isn't that what happens in the Masai Mara every year? All those wildebeests jumping over crocodile-infested rivers?"

Caleb switched the juke back to Global News. Greta was eagerly interrogating some unfortunate expert. "Yep, and the Masai Mara just strolled into our neighborhood. You can see the show from your bedroom."

Trisha tapped her nails on the counter, a metronome for her breathing.

*Inhale one, two, three.*

"What were you doing in my bedroom?"

*Exhale one, two, three, four —*

Caleb cackled with a shake of his head. "Checking out your underwear collection, and boss lady, you need to work on your lingerie. Serious. Come on. You have to see for yourselves." Pausing, he winked. "The migration, not the underwear."

Her mouth strained under the forced smile. "Thank you for clarifying."

With a jaunty swagger, Caleb led them upstairs, and Trisha didn't bother arguing when he, Simba and Mama Noah entered her bedroom. Celine paused at the threshold and watched.

Standing at the large window overlooking the front of the house, Caleb waved them over and tapped a finger against the frame. "See?"

Trisha's hands fluttered over her mouth, but that didn't stop the gasp from leaving.

Caleb chuckled. "The safari has come to us."

Pacing down the main dirt road, a large male lion sniffed the air. Several lionesses and their cubs trailed behind him.

Trisha carefully eased the window shut and tightened the latch. Dropping her voice to a whisper, she asked, "Do you think they're staying?"

Caleb pushed the window open. "What? You think they're gonna scale the wall, climb over an electric fence, chew through the security grills and creep into your bedroom while you're sleeping?" He chuckled, seemingly unconcerned about his volume.

Trying to shush him, Trisha slapped his arm. "Lower your voice. I'd rather not draw attention to ourselves."

Caleb shrugged. "Too late. They've been sniffing around our wall for the last half hour."

Standing to one side, Simba crossed his arms over his chest. "They've been here that long, and you only thought to tell us now?" His voice was soft and calm, yet his anger sliced through the air, more lethal than a shout.

Trisha's eyes opened wider, and she gawked at Caleb. "One of us could've been going out to get supplies from the village. You should've told us immediately."

Caleb shrugged, his gaze still fixed on the lions. "If one of you'd approached the gate, I woulda made a noise and warned you. Probably. Maybe. Depends who it was." Grinning, he winked at her. "For you, absolutely. Besides, you wouldn't be much of a meal for a pride."

"You're incorrigible." Trisha stepped back from the window, her gaze staying on the lions. She bumped into Simba, then sidled around him and strode toward Celine with a shiver. "What else is out there?"

Caleb snickered. "A troop of baboons. Now *those* are nasty. And some zebra. Eh! If we finish off our groceries, I nominate Simba to hunt us a zebra."

Spinning around, Trisha glared at her staff. "Okay, show's over. You can all leave my bedroom."

"Probably the best show this room has seen in a while," Caleb muttered.

## Chapter Twenty-Two

"IF SOMEONE DOESN'T START TALKING RIGHT NOW, I START USING this." Madam Zahir lifted a machete, its blade sharpened into a gleaming edge. "Do we understand each other?"

Truth be told, even if one of these numbskulls answered, she might still use the thing. She was in that sort of mood, and justifiably so.

*Maybe they think I'm going soft because I let Caleb go.*

Her hands quivered at the outrageous notion. Soft? Her? Bile scorched her throat.

The men cowered before her rage. Of all her crew, only Samuel remained unfazed by her threat, even though he knew well enough she would carry it out.

As if sensing her observation, he lowered his gaze. Maintaining a respectful tone, he asked, "What exactly are you missing, Madam Zahir?"

Hadn't she already told them?

She felt her entire face contort into a snarl as her rage found a deeper groove. Before anyone noticed what lurked under her normal veneer of calm and confidence, she suppressed the emotion and forced her features into a mask of mere anger. To expose the extent of her fury …

Well, that was one beast she needed to keep locked away. Fear was critical to maintaining order, but outright terror made people lose their minds and do stupid things.

And she couldn't afford stupidity right now, not among her crew.

"A pendant. It's an heirloom with sentimental value. A trifle, really. But it's the thought that someone stole from me that's more important." She waved a hand as if to brush away a fly. "It was in the van's glove compartment."

Despite her attempt at downplaying its value, she mentally kicked herself in the proverbial backside. Why had she left it there? Normally, she was so careful to keep that item in her possession or locked safely away.

The one time she slipped up …

Truth was, she had utterly forgotten she'd left it in the van until *after* the Astral announcement. Such lapses in judgment weren't common for her, but she was only human, after all.

She might have laughed if not trapped in the grip of a creeping rage.

"I want it and the thief found. Who used the van last?" Tilting her head, she did the calculation. "In the past one week or so. Who has been in or near it?"

The men shuffled from side to side, heads down, low murmurs drifting between them as they tried to decide who was to blame or, more importantly, who they could throw under the wheels of her fury.

They knew how terribly the thief would suffer. Madam Zahir was infamous for her creativity.

Timothy scratched his head, his expression glazed and thick. He wouldn't have the brains or imagination to steal from her.

Not surprising, Samuel spoke again. "Didn't Caleb use the van for that last job?"

There was a communal exhale and several eager expressions of agreement.

As soon as Samuel uttered the words, everything clicked into place in her mind: Caleb and the embassy job they did the day before the Astral App alerted the world to a new reality.

Caleb drove the getaway van. *Her* van.

*Of course.*

Caleb with his incessant curiosity, impulsiveness, foolhardy behavior, and lack of insight into the resulting consequences.

And there would be so many now.

"Caleb," she repeated out loud, her mouth twisting as she tasted the bitter word. "Find him."

## Chapter Twenty-Three

*IT'S JUST LIKE AN ECLIPSE.*

Even as he thought it, Caleb giggled softly under his breath. This was *nothing* like an eclipse. An eclipse was a natural event, the passing of one big hunk of space rock in front of another. And while once upon a time it may have inspired terror and the sacrifice of virgins, nowadays it barely warranted mention on the news.

Caleb glanced at Celine, who was crouched on his left. Perhaps sensing his gaze, she peered up and huddled closer until her shoulder pressed against his arm.

Trisha didn't notice her daughter pulling away. Like all of them, she was awed by the spectacle unfolding above the city. She stared through the large living room window, her forehead creased, lips pinched together. Lines he hadn't noticed before were prominent across her features as she gawked at the descending disc.

Just as NASA had predicted, the alien flotilla entered Earth's orbit six days after the Astral App's initial sighting. And now one of those craft was hovering above Nairobi.

With every minute, the disc …

No, not a disc.

*A spaceship.*

As in an *alien* spaceship. From another planet across the galaxy or universe or … Well, it could be from another dimension, for all they knew.

Caleb wondered how many breasts the alien women had. Three would be perfect.

When he dragged himself out of *that* little fantasy, the spaceship appeared bigger.

*We'll be safe here. We have food and water and …*

Caleb shook his head to clear the infiltrating thoughts. The voice was Trisha's. Desperate to make sense of everything, he opened his mouth to say something, anything. Safety? That was an illusion. Caleb knew how easily walls could be scaled, electric fences cut, security bars sawed away, locks picked.

Celine elbowed him. He looked at her and she stared up, transfixed him with her pale blue eyes, unblinking, her lips pursed into a line.

On his other side, Simba stroked his chin, eyes also fixed upward. *Chaos.*

Accompanying that word whispered in his half-brother's voice came images of people running. Mouths opened in silent screams. Trembling hands grabbed whatever they could, lawfully or otherwise.

Frowning, Caleb wiggled away from his brother. He had to stop smoking so much. Those images didn't feel like his, same for the whispered thoughts drifting through his mind like tendrils of inky smoke.

*She can't leave the house without me.*

Another voice swirled around, except it wasn't in exactly those words. It was more a sensation of fear, determination and protectiveness. And despite the oddity of the experience, Caleb knew it was Trisha discussing Celine.

"Stop being so overly protective," he blurted, his throat constricting around each word.

Simba hissed at him to keep quiet. Celine looked up, her mouth quirking into a suggestion of a smile. He'd never seen her smile before.

A shadow crossed over them, swallowing light and leaving behind a sudden chill in its wake.

Only Mama Noah didn't crouch by the window. She stood behind them, softly humming a vaguely familiar church song. It provided a background theme along with the *tick, tock, tick, tock* of the clock above the artificial fireplace.

The shadow darkened and the song faded away, but her lips continued to move in a constant stream of unintelligible whispers.

Caleb knew without actually knowing that she'd moved from song to prayer, fervently begging God for mercy at the end of days. All her nonstop babbling about The Rapture and Judgement Day and all that other religious crap.

*Then again, we can use all the help.*

Caleb smacked the palm of his hand against his forehead a couple of times. Since when was he a believer? Since when did he know about other people's prayers, fears, and memories? Not just know about them. He was experiencing them.

*It's official. Dude, you're finally flipping.*

Outside, the world fell silent. The birds who usually squabbled in the tree by the front door retreated to wherever birds go when a predator prowls nearby. Except this predator loomed above all living creatures, blocking out the day's sun.

*Oh my God.*

Caleb couldn't tell if Trisha had gasped those words out loud or in her head. What drugs had Samuel mixed into that last batch of pot? If he ever saw Madam Zahir's right hand again, he'd have words with the man.

Then again, if he ever saw Samuel and Madam Zahir again, he'd probably be hanging over a fire, getting roasted alive while they sliced off his privates.

Just thinking about the crime queen caused him to instinctively cover his chest. Through his T-shirt, he could feel the stolen item pulsing in time with his heartbeat.

*Man, I've got to stop the drugs.*

*Don't do that*, whispered another voice in his mind.

Trisha whimpered and wrapped an arm around Celine's shoulder, pulling the girl tighter against her. Caleb almost sighed with relief. It still didn't stop the swarm of other people's thoughts and emotions, like the buzzing of bees after their nest is disturbed.

*Maybe we should have left.*

The texture of that thought belonged to Trisha. Yet her mouth hadn't moved.

Simba cleared his throat. "Is everything locked up?"

Caleb scoffed, though the words were directed at Trisha. "You think locked doors will stop a spaceship from landing on our house?"

"Shh," Trisha hushed even as she thought, *I shouldn't let Celine see this. She's too young and …*

Caleb gaped at her, trying to ignore the large, slowly approaching silver disk. "Serious? You think she's *not* gonna notice a giant spaceship descending from the sky? How is that helpful, hiding her away?"

Trisha shrank away while Simba reached over and smacked the back of his head. One of these days Caleb would turn around and slap Simba back.

*Yeah, maybe in a dream where you grow an extra three feet and a hundred pounds of muscle.*

Details of the large silver spaceship were now visible with the unaided eye. A pulsing, glowing blue line encircled the widest portion.

Every minute that passed, Caleb had to reassess how big he imagined it was. At this rate, the ship might cover the entire Kinanda Village and squash it upon landing.

But surely, something that big wouldn't touch the surface? They had to have smaller vehicles, scout ships, they would send out.

And what would those scout ships do?

*It's okay.*

The flavor of that thought was different from all the others. Caleb didn't have to turn to the side to know Celine was watching him, assessing his reactions.

Meanwhile, Trisha stood and stepped away from the large bay window. "Come on, Celine. It's time to … go have a snack."

She tugged at her hand, but despite Celine's small size, she didn't budge. Instead, Celine squeezed against Caleb and grasped his forearm with a tiny hand.

*It's going to be okay.*

And while he desperately hoped the imaginary voice in his head was correct, the eclipse cast a shadow on more than just the land.

## Chapter Twenty-Four

ALTHOUGH TRISHA HAS NEVER BEEN TO MOSCOW, SHE RECOGNIZES THE iconic Saint Basil's Cathedral in Red Square. Its rounded, multicolored domes remind her of Christmas candy.

Celine tugs at her arm, and Trisha looks down, happy her child is able to view this heritage site before it's gone.

Nodding, Celine purses her lips. "I know, Mommy. The aliens haven't destroyed it yet, but they will."

As in the ways of dreams, Trisha doesn't think it strange that her mute child can speak. Instead, her amazement at seeing the cathedral shrivels up in a surge of terror. Glancing into the sky, she sees the spaceship hovering so close, too close. Yet none of the other tourists seem to notice. They stream past her, taking photos of the cathedral and each other, laughing, chatting and acting oblivious to the danger looming above.

"We should go. Celine?"

The warm presence by her side is gone. Spinning around, Trisha searches the crowd for a pale blonde head. Ever-growing numbers of people crowd the square, blocking her passage.

Waving her arms, she swivels back and forth, searching for an opening, searching for her daughter.

*She's gone. They've taken her.*

The thought is like a punch to her gut. Air rushes out of her in a long scream. Struggling against gravity and the suffocating terror only a mother can feel, she claws her way through the swirling masses of disinterested humanity.

But someone stands in her way, blocking her efforts.

As she twirls in place, searching for a way out of the crowd, a shadow lurks into view. Everywhere she looks, there's another one, each a piece of living night exhaling death and crackling blue light.

And then, from above, a blinding illumination swallows them all.

## Chapter Twenty-Five

THE SCREAMING WOKE HER.

For a moment, Trisha thought she was still in a nightmare. She rubbed her eyes, sorting through the thin strands of dream memory. She had been traveling somewhere with Celine and had lost her daughter in a crowd.

*Moscow.*

Coldness blossomed in her chest. That part had been real. What happened to Moscow …

"God, no," she whispered, the vestiges of the dream fading into the horror of reality.

Two days ago, the alien flotilla had arrived. Each spaceship had flown to a different city and silently hovered above it. Yesterday, along with the rest of the world, she had watched in morbid fascination as Moscow launched a missile against one of the ships. The attack failed to leave even a scratch on the silver surface.

Moments later, a burst of blazing light obliterated the city and everything — *everyone* — in it.

Shrinking away from the images of an obliterated city, Trisha instead tugged at the threads of her dream, grappling to understand them. What were the shadow beasts? Where had those come from?

Gasping for breath, Trisha gazed around the room, her brain scrambling to make sense of what she was hearing and seeing. Unnatural light pulsed through the windows — just like the light in her nightmare, the one that had demolished Moscow. It cast distorted shadows and created shapes from nightmares.

Except the terrors were real.

Clutching the blanket, she stared up at the ceiling and listened as another scream shattered the stillness.

"Celine."

She rolled out of bed, her legs entangled in the sheets. Her breath punched out of her as she collapsed to the wooden floor. "Celine!"

No response to her shout. Simba was in the staff quarters along with Caleb and Mama Noah. None of them would hear her cry.

More screaming and shouting. As Trisha kicked at the sheets, her senses finally caught up to the stimulation. The noise wasn't coming from inside the house, and neither was the light.

Blood swooshed through her head and pounded a battle song against her eardrums. Rolling onto her back, Trisha closed her eyes and focused on her breathing.

*Inhale one, two, three.*

She imagined she was in a pool, fully submerged in a protective bubble of water.

*Exhale one, two, three, four, five.*

The screaming came from the village.

She scrambled up and leaned against the bed frame, staring at one of the windows facing Kinanda Village. She forced herself to stumble around the bed, still gripping it for balance. She reached the window and pressed herself against the wall, lifting the curtain to peer through the crack.

Something crashed against the window.

Screaming, she jerked back before realizing it was a bat.

As her eyes adjusted, she saw another bat career out of control and crash into a tree.

"But bats don't bump into things," she protested.

Then again, the night shouldn't pulse with this much light.

Alien ships shouldn't destroy entire cities in a blink.

Ignoring the bats' erratic behavior, Trisha focused on the bigger picture. The garden landscape, the house in a neighboring compound and the tops of the village huts glowing under a white light.

She tried angling her head back to see the source, but it was too high. But there was only one possible source for the strange light from above. The alien ship was finally doing something beyond hovering above them.

Saying *hello* with a light show.

Another scream caused her head to jerk painfully around, her neck twanging with the motion. A whimpered shriek dribbled out of her open mouth as she watched a shape rise up in a column of neon light.

The shape moved, limbs flailing.

The light was sucking a man into the sky.

Her hands clawed at the curtains as she moaned. Another shaft of brilliant light slashed through the darkness, followed by more screaming.

People floated up, up, up toward the unseen spaceship.

"Oh. My—"

"Trisha?"

She yanked at the curtain hard enough to tear a portion of it off the rails. She spun around and slapped a hand across her mouth to block the terror about to explode out of her. A large man stood in the doorway.

"It's okay. It's me." Simba stepped forward into the glow of the light, his eyes wide, his face creased with concern, but his gaze steady. Confident, unflappable. Reassuring.

Dropping her hand, she gasped. "Simba."

"You've seen?"

She pushed herself away from the wall with a nod, away from the window, away from the nightmarish vision of people — her neighbors, humans, fellow earthlings — getting inhaled into an unknown fate by faceless aliens.

"I'm sorry. I came in here without your permission, but—"

"Thank you." Trisha continued to babble her gratitude until she reached him. Her knees wobbled as if she'd run a full marathon. Gripping his arms with both hands, she willed her legs to behave. "Thank you."

Nodding, he stepped aside to let her pass, as if knowing where she needed to go.

Grateful for his presence, Trisha dashed across the hallway and into Celine's room. The bed was empty.

"No," she shrieked.

"Trisha?" Heavy steps pounded the hallway behind her.

She ignored Simba, clutching at the doorframe and gawking at the bed before motion by the window alerted her.

Celine stood there, small hands pressed against the glass, face peering upward, her entire form bathed in light.

"Celine!" The name poured out of her in a high-pitched scream as Trisha stumbled and tried to run.

But as if in a nightmare, gravity clawed at her, slowing her every movement.

She gritted her teeth and forced herself past the fear. She reached Celine, yanked her away from the window, and pushed her deeper into the room. "Stay away from the windows. Understand?"

Momentum from Trisha's shove carried Celine toward her bed, where she fell onto her back.

Trisha hurried to Celine, not daring to look up at Simba for fear of seeing judgment there. "I'm so sorry. Are you okay? I didn't mean to … Did I hurt you? You have to stay away from the windows."

Did it matter? These aliens were powerful enough to create spaceships that traversed the universe and beams of light that sucked people into the air. Surely, they didn't require open windows to access their prey?

She wasn't taking any risks. Scooping up Celine and ignoring her silent protests, Trisha scurried out of the room.

"It may be safest in the kitchen," Simba suggested, his face once again a mask of neutrality. "There's only one window, and it's covered in security bars."

Trisha hurried downstairs after giving her driver a relieved smile, her bare feet slapping against the stairs in time with her heartbeat. She paused in the living room and grabbed an elaborately carved, wooden walking stick she'd bought at an artisan's market. It wouldn't stop an alien ship from levitating her, but at least it made her feel better.

Stick in hand and Celine clinging to her, Trisha entered the kitchen where Mama Noah and Caleb waited. At least here, the window faced away from the village, and away from that pulsing, unearthly light.

Without asking, Mama Noah reached for Celine and pulled her into an embrace. Immediately, the child stopped her wiggling and collapsed against the maid.

Mama Noah brushed a hand through the tangled mop of pale hair and made reassuring sounds as she stared up at the ceiling. "It begins."

Caleb tugged at a dreadlock and yawned. He opened the fridge door and began to sort through the leftovers. "Yeah, but when does it end? And can we eat?"

Mama Noah clucked.

Trisha leaned against her stick. "How can you think about food right now?"

Caleb stared over his shoulder at her, half his face bathed in light from the fridge. "Boss lady, it's one of the ways I know I'm still alive. 'Cause dead men, they don't eat."

"Unless they're zombies."

Caleb saluted her with a drumstick. "You craving brains?"

"No."

"Then we're good."

A ridiculous conversation, but Trisha smiled anyway.

## Chapter Twenty-Six

*NEVER.*

That, Mama Noah decided several hours later, was the answer to Caleb's question. It never ended. If the stories shared by the Elders were correct ...

*But why wouldn't they be?*

She considered that as she staggered up the stairs. So far, they'd always been faithful to the underlying truths, even if a few details changed in the retelling. That meant the events of last night were part of a larger continuously-repeated cycle.

"Kind of like these stairs. God is great, but who needs three floors in a home?"

Mama Noah huffed from the exertion as she hiked up to the attic. She reached the top landing and leaned against the wall to catch her breath. The door leading into the third floor was closed, and again she wondered what anyone would want with so many floors.

"One is enough. Two is luxury." She clucked her tongue. "But three? This is more work. More dust. More space to collect junk."

Not to mention a devious way to exhaust a poor maid, as if she didn't have enough to do. Her legs weren't accustomed to so many stairs. Walking long distances to get from place to place? Absolutely.

Bending over to yank potatoes out of the ground or drop seeds into small holes? She'd been doing that her whole life.

But hiking up three floors to enter yet another unnecessary room was a different matter altogether.

And of course, they had to store the camping equipment in the attic.

Mama Noah harrumphed, waiting for her lungs and heart to resume a pace approaching normal. She'd worked hard to afford electricity and piped water. It was a sign of success. Yet here these foreigners abandoned a perfectly good house to live in the bush for days at a time. And they did so *of their own free will.*

"Bah. Who does that?"

Shaking her head at some people's crazy ways, she squared off with the closed door. Simba had asked her to find the camping equipment, "just in case." He didn't elaborate as to what that case would be; nor did he need to. After all the recent activities, she suspected they were close to reaching the "just in case."

Mrs. Walker still insisted they stay, despite the night's abductions and the morning's exodus from the village. In stoic silence, she had stood in front of the upstairs hallway window watching the steady procession of villagers with their worldly possessions piled on their backs or in hand-pulled carts. At breakfast, when Simba had again suggested they leave, she'd shaken her head in response.

But how much longer would she cling to her zombie theory? How long could they huddle in the kitchen, praying the aliens left them alone? They were comfortable for now, thanks to a solar-powered inverter and a water pump, but eventually even those modern conveniences would break down.

And that assumed the aliens didn't snatch the remaining humans before things fell apart.

Mama Noah rubbed her hands down the red kikoi wrapped around her waist and stared at the ceiling, wondering what had happened to the taken. When she'd heard the screaming in the middle of the night, she'd thought, *Well, I've lived a good life, for the most part. Good enough, anyways. I'm ready to go, Lord. Amen.*

But then Simba and Caleb had banged on her door and insisted she follow them. Seeing the villagers floating up in tunnels of light, she immediately realized what was happening.

The Rapture, of course.

The preacher had warned his congregation that The Rapture would sneak up on them like a thief, or something like that. Mama Noah didn't believe this was what he had in mind. At least, she hoped not.

But to repeat an oft-repeated truth, God moved in mysterious ways.

"Oh, God, my God," she'd called out, arms aloft, just in case this was the real deal. "Don't forget me. I've been faithful, Lord Jesus. Well, except that one time. But I'm ready to be taken. I'm ready for Heaven and the New Jerusalem. Amen."

Scoffing, Caleb had grabbed her arm and dragged her into the house. "Lady, this ain't no Second Coming."

She should've known that. The tunnels of light strobed overhead, and she'd woken up completely.

The lights reminded her of that *other* time.

Rubbing her hands together, she pushed past the memories and opened the door to stare at the space looming before her. The attic was smaller than the other floors, a single room with only one window facing the road. Dingy curtains covered the glass, adding to the gloom. An empty light fixture dangled from the ceiling.

Shaking her head, Mama Noah stared at the boxes squatting in the far corner like a misshapen creature preparing to pounce. The attic seemed to expand before her, filled with more shadows than should be there.

Hesitating, she wondered if she should go downstairs and call Simba or his drug-using half-brother to search for the camping gear.

She clucked her tongue at her own foolishness and wiped her hands. "It's a pile of junk, and guess who has to sort through it? Well,

I'm not hauling it up and down stairs. There are two strong, young men who can make themselves useful. God knows that's what men are good for, carrying heavy loads and not much else."

She knew that from hard experience. Mama Noah had raised and fed her children, paid for their school fees and made sure they wouldn't spend their days cleaning other people's toilets, all by herself. And now, they were off being big and important and forgetting about home and her.

Shivering in the artificial twilight, she pattered across the dusty floor to the large window and tugged the curtain to one side. A shaft of late morning sun peeled back the murkiness. She exhaled and was about to march to the stack of boxes when a motion flickered at the edge of the cornfield.

Squinting through the dusty glass, she studied the road and clucked. "Must be those lions. Imagine. Lions in the city. Aliens in the sky. If these aren't the end days …"

Her words fell apart around her when a shadow shimmied out from between cornstalks.

Except shadows didn't cause physical objects to bend and sway around them.

Shadows didn't lift a toothy snout and snuffle at the air.

And although there was no way she should be able to hear the shadow from three floors up, she'd swear on her well-used Bible that the thing *purred*.

Or maybe that was a memory — someone else's, but still vivid and real — superimposing itself on her frantic brain.

As she gawked at the living shadow, the air in her lungs solidified into a cold, hungry beast that crawled out of the primordial ooze of blind terror.

Then, as quickly as it appeared, the shadow retreated into more shadows.

Mama Noah stumbled back with a gasp, her limbs and brain momentarily disconnected.

The Elders had warned them: *Keep the faith. Obey the law.*

And not the religious laws or the rules brought by invading barbarians. The tribal Elders had been referring to something far more ancient, pure and not adulterated by human greed.

The truth.

A low whimper echoed around her, and it took several ragged breaths before Mama Noah recognized the sound as her own.

Words gargled in the back of her throat, trapped by the thought of all those lurking shadows.

Caleb was wrong. The Second Coming *had* arrived. But there was no heaven at the end of those tunnels.

## Chapter Twenty-Seven

CALEB KNEW THEY WERE ALL SUPPOSED TO STAY IN THE kitchen, but when had knowing something ever stopped him from doing the opposite?

Besides, Mama Noah had left to search for camping gear while Trisha and Simba went upstairs.

He left Celine in the kitchen with her drawings, then crept up the stairs with a smirk, wondering why Simba and Trisha had broken their own rule. Was he about to catch them in bed? More likely the uptight Mrs. Walker was raiding a secret stash of antidepressants. If so, he hoped she'd be generous. Sharing was caring, after all.

"It's a third wave."

The whispered words caused Caleb to pause near the top landing and crane his head. Simba and Trisha were standing shoulder to shoulder in front of a window at the end of the hallway, facing Kinanda Road and the corn which had overtaken the empty plot across the road. The built-in desk held them back. Otherwise they'd have their faces smushed against the glass for sure.

"What do you mean?" Simba sounded hesitant, as if he still wasn't sure of his identity as a lowly driver or something else.

*What a mkundu*, Caleb thought as he eased a foot onto the next stair.

Trisha cleared her throat. "The first was the animals coming into Nairobi. The second was the abductions. Now this. A swarm of whatever the hell those things are."

Curiosity won over caution, as usual. Bouncing up the final few steps, Caleb strutted toward them. "What things?"

Simba glanced over his shoulder. "I thought I told you to stay in the kitchen."

"And I thought I told you to get a personality. But eh! I don't see you doing that, either."

Trisha flicked a hand at him. "Keep it down."

A stair creaked behind them. Mama Noah plodded down huffing. She hesitated, then muttered, "Stay inside," before she continued downstairs.

*As if.* Ignoring the maid, Caleb squeezed in between Trisha and Simba. "What are you calling a third wave? What are those things? They're almost as ugly as Simba."

"*Shh.*" Trisha smacked him on the shoulder.

Even though it didn't hurt — he didn't think she could hit hard enough, unlike Madam Zahir — Caleb rubbed his shoulder and pouted. "Eh, it's a valid question."

Simba pushed a beefy hand against his chest. "We don't know how keen their hearing is." His voice was low but clear. "They could be looking for survivors."

Caleb rolled his eyes. "Serious? No way. Anyone from the village who wasn't sucked up like the bottom of a milkshake into a straw? There's no one there."

"We're still here," Trisha whispered.

And just like that, the conversation ended.

But those words, *We're still here*, closed in on them, squeezed them into a deeper sense of claustrophobia. Or maybe that was just him and his drug-induced imagination.

*Yeah, I may have to slow down on the smoking.* Caleb scratched at his dreadlocks with a grin. *Or maybe not.*

He couldn't imagine going through whatever *this* was without assistance. Bad enough that aliens were invading. Now he was stuck in the same house with his half-brother. And after spending most of last night sleeping on the cold kitchen floor, he was about ready to call it quits.

*Serious. If you're gonna live through the apocalypse*, he thought with a sideways glance at Trisha, *at least it should be alone with a beautiful woman and no cockblockers.*

He giggled softly. *Yup, that's Simba, all right. Such a joy kill.*

Motion outside sobered him enough to heed the reason they were crowded by the window. A creature, whatever it was, paused in the middle of the dirt road directly in front of their gate. Unconcerned about the pride of lions lurking in the cornfield, the four-legged alien tilted its head, as if studying the best way to breach the compound walls.

The windows were all closed, but Caleb swore he could hear a purr, like a giant cat. Except this wasn't any feline. At a glance, it could pass for a black panther, but even from this height, he could see something was wrong about it.

Panthers didn't have scales or a blue glow shimmering from the skin underneath. The creature had a reptilian feel even as it stalked forward like a lion about to pounce. Everything about it screamed apex predator. And when it decided to move …

Caleb blinked as the creature scuttled forward with the rapidity of a mutant insect, limbs buckling and shifting as if they weren't limited by bone or the normal laws of evolution.

Another pair of the lizard-panther creatures appeared. Yellow, serpent-like eyes fixed on a point to one side of the hallway window. The original abomination joined them, and their heads bobbed in unison.

Scratching his dreadlocks, Caleb wondered if his weed would

last. At this rate, he was in danger of running dry before the food did, and now he needed to up his dose. "What are they looking at?"

Trisha was already moving, her breath vented in a frantic pant. She ducked into the closest room with a shriek.

Caleb followed Simba into Celine's room, curious more than alarmed. There he found Trisha whisper-arguing with her child.

"Celine, come away from the window."

The girl's back was to them. Her small hands were pressed to the glass as she ignored her mother's command.

Caleb stood on tiptoe to get a better view of the child's line of sight. It looked like the kid and the aliens were having a staring contest. "Eh, they really like Celine."

"Shut it," Simba growled.

"Celine!" Trisha crept up and wrapped her arms around her daughter, then carried Celine to the door. "What did I tell you last night? Stay away from the windows. It isn't safe. Why aren't you downstairs?"

Caleb smirked. Despite being south of normal, Celine was still a child. *Of course*, she had to sneak upstairs to see what all the excitement was. What healthy kid wouldn't?

He waited for Trisha to push past him, then straightened and craned his head to see the alien lizards' reaction.

But the aliens were already gone.

## Chapter Twenty-Eight

*THEY'RE CALLING THEM REPTARS.*

That had been Caleb's big reveal during lunch as he sat across from Trisha at the island counter and shoveled food down as words came out. "Those reptile-looking, alien panther things? They're calling them Reptars. Kinda like reptiles except not quite. Cool, eh?"

Trisha tried not to watch his grotesque table manners, although she found it morbidly fascinating. When had she decided it was okay for the staff to eat with the family? She couldn't pinpoint the moment. Somehow, over the past week of self-imposed isolation, social norms and unspoken rules that normally governed relations between employer and house staff had broken down.

*Not just broken down,* she thought as she crunched on the salad grown in their greenhouse. *Disintegrated into dust, never to be fixed again.*

Not that she minded. Their presence, especially Simba's, reassured her that she wasn't completely alone. The village had emptied after the abductions, adding to the sense that they were the last humans on Kinanda Road.

What if they were the last humans on Earth?

Trisha gulped her food past a constriction in her throat. Of course, that was ridiculous. The kitchen juke was proof. It was on, although reception had become fuzzy at times. Ever since the destruction of Moscow, the video occasionally disappeared into a haze of static before resolving itself.

Greta San Lucas of Global News — *Does that woman ever sleep?* — was providing the latest breaking news.

Despite Trisha's negative view regarding jukes at mealtime, she didn't have the energy to turn the thing off. Besides, it was muted. Never mind that her gaze kept drifting toward the unending carousel of spaceships, chaos, and human fear.

Celine was the only one disinterested in the news, focusing only on her food and her drawings.

"Reptars," Caleb continued to chatter. "Cool name. There've been sightings all over. Crazy, eh?"

Trisha gave up on the pretense of eating, pushed her plate away, slipped off the stool, and wandered off, ignoring Simba's raised eyebrows. The rules may no longer exist, but she didn't owe an explanation to anyone.

She plodded upstairs, then drifted to the end of the hallway and stared out the second-floor window facing the street. Her hands brushed the built-in desk under the window. When she'd first seen the bright, open space and desk, she had imagined using it as an office.

"Maybe I can start consulting once Celine goes to school," she'd told Jake, eyeing the table and farmland.

He'd turned to his email with a shrug. "We won't be in Kenya long enough."

He *should* have said an alien invasion might put an end to her plans.

"I guess we're all unemployed now." She laughed. Her voice sounded off, and she quickly pursed her lips closed.

Trisha's gaze drifted to the cornfield across the road. Over the past week, greenery had surged upward. Tall stalks swayed and swirled as something passed between them.

Trisha rubbed her hands up and down her arms with a shiver.

What was in there? The lions? Or those aliens that looked like distorted panthers and ran like demented insects?

*They're calling them Reptars.*

Trisha called them alien nightmares.

Another movement caught her eye, a flash of red. A small child in a red dress scurried down the middle of the dirt road. Black hair stuck out from messy braids, as if no one had bothered to care for her in the aliens' wake. She glanced around her, probably sensing the predators lurking nearby.

Trisha leaned forward, her stomach pressing against the built-in desk. "What are you doing out there?"

Not that it was any of her business. If someone thought it was a good idea to allow their young child to wander alone out there, that was their problem, not hers.

The child looked about Celine's age.

"Dammit." Trisha knew she shouldn't go out there. It wasn't her problem, or her child. It *definitely* wasn't a good idea.

That's what she kept telling herself as she skipped down the stairs. The house had an empty feel, and without understanding how, she knew Simba, Celine and Caleb were in the backyard. Mama Noah was probably hanging laundry.

*I should really ask Simba for help.*

*Better yet, I shouldn't do anything at all.*

And just as Trisha hesitated at the front door, she recalled the little girl's startled eyes, too big for her small face. Minor details pressed against her as if they were important: her red dress was muddy and tattered; the thick rows of black braids were unravelling from neglect; her expression seemed vacant if not entirely haunted.

She had seen the child before, lingering at the entrance to the village. Why was she still here? Between alien abductions and the resulting mass exodus, Trisha had assumed the village was now empty of human life, abandoned to the wildlife and the alien monsters.

Was the child alone?

Wiping a hand across her mouth, Trisha tried once more to reason with herself.

It wasn't her problem. The child had survived this long. Someone must be caring for her, right?

*She's just a little girl.*

What if it had been Celine out there? Maybe the child's mother was hurt or, worse yet, maybe the girl was on her own, abandoned or forgotten in the rush to escape all the predators in, around, and over the village.

Trisha's stride lengthened as she strode down the short driveway past the Land Cruiser and horse trailer. She reached the door cut within the big gate and paused. Her hand trailed over the bolt keeping the door firmly closed and secured.

She didn't dare look up to the sky, but felt the alien ship pressing down on her. Her breath hitched. That little girl was out there all alone.

"I'll just take a peak," she whispered to herself.

She glanced around, half-hoping someone would appear from the house and tell her to stop being such an idiot. Then she slid the bolt open, wincing as it squeaked in protest. When had anyone last oiled it?

She held her breath, wondering why as she eased the metal door open, creating an opening in the solid gate. The compound was now accessible, a fact that weighed on Trisha. What if a lion jumped out of the cornfield and attacked her, then slipped through the opening and tracked down Celine?

Clinging to the door's edge, she stared across the dirt road at the thick forest of corn. She found no amber eyes surrounded by tawny fur staring back at her. There was no alien monster (*They're calling them Reptars*). Apart from a slight breeze rustling the tips of the corn-stalks, there was no movement ahead of her at all.

Of course, with predators, that didn't mean much.

"Way to be confident," Trisha muttered, peering down the road in the direction the girl had gone.

The girl looked over her shoulder as if sensing an observer, large eyes dark and liquid like a deer's and just as startled. For a heartbeat, they stared at each other. A frozen moment trapping them in paralysis.

A bird screeched overhead.

The girl turned and ran.

Without thinking, Trisha followed. "Wait, don't go. Are you alone?"

*What if it was Celine out here, lost and alone — what would I want someone to do?*

The thought spurred her forward, arms and legs pumping faster. Trisha rounded the corner of her compound and lurched to a halt at the narrow side road leading into the village. The girl wasn't much farther ahead, her red dress bright and bold against the dusty road and the green vegetation lining either side.

They ran, the girl forever just ahead of Trisha. And as Trisha reached out to snatch at the dress, the girl twisted to the side and dashed down the narrow alley created by the walls of several small houses.

Fueled by a compulsion to save this child, Trisha followed. Several steps later, the girl disappeared into a small shack of concrete blocks, covered in metal sheeting.

The door was no more than a piece of flimsy plywood. Trisha pushed it open. From behind her, light illumined a wedge of the interior, enough for her to see the child cowering next to an elderly woman.

The old woman's eyes were milky, and she clutched a walking cane in her gnarled, wrinkled hands.

Squatting with care to avoid the filthy floor, Trisha whispered, "Are you okay?"

The old woman's head craned upward. She looked from side to side as if trying to see with broken eyes. The little girl whimpered and hid her face behind the old woman's withered arm.

Trisha stared around the small room. A large plastic bottle was filled with water, bits of sediment floating in the liquid. A small pile of charcoal stained the concrete floor in one corner. Trisha's nose wrinkled at the sharp scent of kerosene and an undertone of burning wood. Three ears of corn were scattered on the floor, the leaves still fresh and green.

Trisha picked up an ear. "So that's what you were doing out there. Do you want to come with me? I can give you more. You must be very hungry."

Even as she offered, a part of Trisha resisted. Didn't she already have enough mouths to feed? Simba had done well with the groceries, but they would only last so long, and all the shops had surely been looted to empty by now. Yet she didn't retract her offer. How much could a little girl and a frail, old woman possibly eat?

She shuffled forward, still squatting. The old woman flinched and held up her shaking hands before her face.

"I'm not going to hurt you."

The woman began to wail, the sound growing louder until it pitched into a shaky scream. The child added her voice behind her.

Dropping the corn, Trisha backed away, hands up. "Okay. I'm leaving. I'll come back with some food for you. If that's alright?"

Not sure if either one of them even understood English, Trisha hastily retreated and began to march up the narrow alley toward the side road leading her home.

The wailing and screeching continued behind her. She hoped it didn't attract the wrong kind of attention. The other villagers seemed to be gone, but the place obviously wasn't as empty as she'd first assumed. And there were always those who took advantage of fear and chaos.

She took one step into the narrow side road, then scurried back before she could fully comprehend the scene. She pressed against the brick wall of a better-built hut, squeezing her eyes shut and focusing on her breath while her brain processed what she saw. Two young men. Strangers who didn't look like they were from the village.

Only then did she hear a long, raspy inhale behind her. Followed by a long and loud and terrifying purr.

## Chapter Twenty-Nine

THE CHILD SHOULDN'T HAVE STARTLED HER, BUT SHE DID.

*Then again, what child hides inside a washing machine?*

Mama Noah clutched a hand over her chest, her erratic heartbeat fluttering like a trapped bird in a cage.

But it wasn't Celine who'd scared her. It was the memory of that living shadow.

The shadow and the tunnels of light had stirred up too many memories — not hers, yet so vivid. When the Elders shared their stories, the audience felt they were there, transported into an age of legend and myth.

Instead of dwelling, Mama Noah had decided to do laundry. What else was there to do?

*The aliens might be invading again, but we still need clean clothes and dinner on the table.*

All thoughts of clothes and dinner disintegrated at the sight of a living creature in the machine. "Oh, good God, protect me!"

Celine remained curled inside. Her large, pale eyes stared up unblinking, surrounded by sheets of blonde hair.

Mama Noah's shoulders slumped. She exhaled loudly as her

brain caught up with her eyes. "Oh. It's just you. What are you doing in there, mtoto? This is no place for playing. I know your mama told you to stay downstairs, but there are better places to …"

Her next word came out gargled and strangled.

"The Lord loves me, truly He does, but really, mtoto. What are you doing playing with *that*?"

Celine held up her cupped hands to reveal the field mouse sitting inside.

Mama Noah shambled forward to get a better look. "At least it's not a rat."

Celine brought her cupped hands closer to her mouth and breathed over the mouse. The tiny creature stood on its hind legs, nose and whiskers twitching as it sniffed at the air. The odd child then peered up, eyebrows scrunched, teeth nibbling at her lower lip.

Mama Noah huffed, then patted Celine's head. "Don't you worry, mtoto. If it was a rat, we'd be having a conversation. But field mice? They're as innocent as you. Now come out of there so I can do some laundry. As long as we're still here, living and breathing and not being abducted, the work will need to be done. That, child, is the way of the world."

Something approaching a smile ghosted across the girl's lips before she finally crawled out. She sat back on her heels, stroking the creature's miniature head.

Mama Noah softly laughed and began to remove clothes from the basket. "You're a smart one to keep quiet. Most people talk too much and say very little."

Celine's eyes flicked up, then down.

"When I was your age, me and my brothers, we played with all sorts of things." Mama Noah dropped a white shirt onto the growing pile. "If our mama had known, oh! She would not have been happy. But that's what children do."

She upended the basket and sat on it. "Rats, they are another problem altogether. Most of them are too smart to be caught, but once, I caught a stupid one sitting on the counter, eating a banana, bold as anything. So I took my pan — you know the one, the old, heavy one your mama hates — and I banged it down once. Bam!" Mama Noah smacked her hands together.

Celine looked up while cupping a hand protectively over the mouse.

"You can't do that with those fancy, state-of-the-art, nonstick frying pans your mama wants me to use. They're just like her. Pale, skinny and no weight." Leaning over, she began sorting the clothes by color. "But that old pan of mine? It's made with real metal. Solid and heavy. Why, I can break a hyena's skull with it. Those fancy ones? The bottom would crack in two if I tried."

Mama Noah sat back and gazed at the garden, already spent by the day. At the far end, Simba entered the greenhouse. She'd sent him out to get a few tomatoes. No sign of his brother.

"Do you want to hear a story?"

She hadn't meant to ask. But recent events had awoken old memories …

*No, not memories. Stories. Vividly told stories.*

*That's all they are.*

Mama Noah huffed at the lie. Oh, sure, the Elders had called them stories, but only the ignorant or well-educated actually believed they were no more than fables. Anyone still connected to the land of their ancestors could feel the truth, that the myths had once been someone's memories, passed from Elder to Elder in a digestible form. Even after all these generations, the stories still held the essential truths of their tribe's history.

Because how else could the Elders have known about the shadow monsters and the strange lights from the sky?

Celine's mouth formed a small circle, and she nodded. Mama Noah dragged a bucket to her side, turned it upside down and patted it. Celine slid onto the top, keeping a distance between them. Still cupping the mouse in her hands, the child stared at her and waited.

Mama Noah smiled and closed her eyes, recalling the many

nights her family gathered around the fire and listen to her grand-mother, an Elder, recite the stories of her people.

"In the days of giants and monsters, my ancestors, the Kikuyu, lived at the foothills of Mount Kenya. We were a prosperous people as long as we obeyed the laws left by our creator.

"Our Elders taught us that God — or Ngai — lived at the top of the mountain whenever he came to visit. Legends say that when Ngai descended from the sky, his feet first touched the ground atop Mount Kenya.

"During those visits, the mountain would be bright with radiant, unnatural light, even during the blackest nights. That's why we call the mountain Kare-Nyaga, Kikuyu for mountain of brightness. We believe our mountain is Ngai's throne on Earth, God's resting place."

Mama Noah's hands rested on her knees. It had been many years since she had shared the story with anyone. Young people were no longer interested in history. They watched fake stories on their screens and forgot about their past.

She cleared her throat and stared at the empty washing machine. "Gĩkũyũ, the father of our tribe, was the first person on Earth to ascend our mountain, and for many lifetimes, the only person who ever succeeded in doing so. He was favored by Ngai, who allowed him to pass into the clouds and reach the ice-covered summit. There, Gĩkũyũ would converse with Ngai and receive guidance, wisdom and our laws.

"But anyone else who attempted such a feat would be tossed into one of the deep crevices that cut through the glacier, never to be seen again. Or one of the giants guarding the summit would rip the tres-passer into pieces. Over time, we learned that anyone who tried to climb beyond the bottom edge of the clouds was doomed to never return. We feared and respected the place as a holy site, not to be tampered with by mere mortals. That fear protected us."

Mama Noah paused to check her audience. The last thing she wanted was to give the child nightmares. But Celine looked placid as usual, pale eyes unblinking as she waited for Mama Noah to continue.

Mama Noah leaned a little closer and lowered her voice. "There was one young warrior, Gichinga the Firebrand, who did not believe the legends of a god who lived on the top of the mountain. Nor did he cower and tremble at the stories of the giants who guarded God's resting place.

"He scoffed at the limits our myths placed upon us, boasting that one day he would travel to the top of the mountain and bring back proof that Ngai and his guardian giants did not exist. Or that they were no more than a tribe of mountain men if they did.

"The Elders begged him to leave the mountain in peace. They would tell him, 'Where Ngai lives is no place for mere mortals.'

"But the bold young warrior was not dissuaded. In preparation for his journey, he changed his name, instructing everyone to call him Gashoki, meaning *The One Who Returns*."

Mama Noah clasped her hands, recalling her childhood and the stories which once bound her people together.

Her mind drifted to thoughts of her adopted brother, also named Gashoki. Unlike the legend, her brother was a timid and fearful creature who lived in the barn on her family's farm and looked after the livestock. Her face pinched with worry as she wondered if anything had happened to him since her last call. He was so frail and easily alarmed.

A small, pale hand brushed over hers, its smooth softness contrasting with her dark, wrinkled skin. Mama Noah's eyes cut sideways, and she smiled at Celine and pushed away her concerns. Her brother was in a safer place than she was.

"Gashoki was no ordinary man. In fact, he was second to none in his power of utterance, his skill as a hunter, and his ferocity as a warrior. The young women adored him, and the young men admired him. And perhaps the constant praise he received by everyone made him believe that he, alone of all mortals, could venture uninvited to God's resting place.

"And so, the day arrived when Gashoki packed a few supplies and ventured along the path that wound through the mountain's forested slopes. The young women wailed and pulled at their hair while the young warriors pounded their chests and chanted funeral songs.

"But Gashoki was not discouraged by these signs of grief. Laughing, he turned his back to all of them and marched up the mountain and into the clouds.

"Years passed, and the family of Gashoki accepted that, like others before him, he was lost to the mountain, sacrificed by an enraged god into the crevices of the glacier.

"Ngai and his giants passed into the mists of myth, and people neglected our ancient gods and their sacred places. The modern world finally reached even us in our villages on the slopes of the mountain of brightness, clearing our ancestors' wisdom from collective memory."

Clapping her hands softly, Mama Noah sighed, and in that moment lost the nerve to continue, to share the rest of the story. Tribal myths normally provided a reassuring narrative that life had divinely guided purpose and meaning. Sometimes, the Elders resorted to fear and awe of unknown forces to protect, usher and instruct. But on occasion, they told the literal truth.

To the initiated, those were the most terrifying tales of all.

So she stopped before the end because, unlike Gashoki, Mama Noah had no desire to climb that mountain.

Silence followed. A peace settled around the house, and she imagined the home sighing in relief.

Mama Noah patted Celine's hand and pushed herself off the basket. She wasn't one to lie, but decided to do so for the child's sake.

"And now, the age of legends is finished."

## Chapter Thirty

*THEY'RE CALLING THEM REPTARS,* CALEB HAD SAID.

Trisha's exhale came in painful chunks, as if the air had solidified somewhere between her lungs and her lips.

Something was behind her.

The harsh raspy inhale of the reptilian alien drowned out every other sound. Or perhaps all other creatures had retreated into silence, deeply aware that an apex predator hunted in their midst.

*They're calling them Reptars.*

"Oh, God." The words whistled out of her, a faint breath of air squeezed past her constricted throat, unbidden and desperate. She wasn't particularly religious, but maybe it was time to make an exception.

Her legs wobbled, and she collapsed to the ground, her eyes still facing forward. She dug her fingers into the grime beneath her, the rough grit a welcome reminder that the world still existed, even if it no longer made any sense.

She'd initially retreated into the alley because of the two men. She couldn't quite put her finger on why she thought they were strangers. Maybe their clothes, the hard lines around their eyes, the way they skulked along the outside of her compound wall. Maybe she was relying too much on stereotypes, but they looked like hired thugs. Mean, tough, on a mission.

Yet now, they were no longer the primary source of danger. They were only men, after all.

Metal clinked behind her, and Trisha shrank closer to the ground until she inhaled the mineral smell of clay.

A shadow passed overhead as something large clattered over rooftops. With a raspy purr, it leaped into view, landing in the middle of the side road. It paused and crouched close enough for her to see its nostrils flare.

Before she could fully grasp any other details, it scurried down the village road in the opposite direction.

She'd left the gate door open.

Desperation squeaked past her trembling lips. If the creature turned around and decided to explore the main road … What had she been thinking?

Trisha crawled forward, willing herself to move, breath rattling loudly in her ears. Pebbles scratched against her palms. Sweat tickled her armpits and stung at her eyes.

She had to close the door.

Trisha peered around the corner of the brick hut and stared down the side road. Four more of the beasts slunk into view a dozen meters away. Joining the first one, they stood in a semicircle, surrounding the thugs. The two men had their backs to the wall of the Walker compound as they stared into the jaws of death.

*What if one of them is Caleb? Or Simba?*

They weren't. Of that, she was certain. Still, the idea caused her stomach to convulse. Whoever they were, whatever their reasons for lurking around the abandoned village, she could do nothing to help them.

But she could protect her family.

"Close the door," Trisha whispered.

She leaned her shoulder against the hut and forced herself to stand. Only a hundred meters separated her from that open door and the relative safety of her home. This knowledge did nothing. Her feet remained rooted in the ground, her legs so stiff they ached. When the time came, would she even be able to run in the open, down to the main road, then around the corner to her gate?

She exposed only the tip of her nose and one eye while holding her breath, watching the men as they faced off against five alien lizards. They didn't look so tough now. She could see even from this distance a wet stain down the front of the taller man's pants. Whatever they'd been planning on doing, Trisha felt a pang of sympathy. Even thugs were human. She didn't want to see how this ended.

Her rational brain screamed at her to run while the beasts were distracted.

*Let the Reptars devour the men,* it said.

Meanwhile, her lizard brain scuttled and scurried in a circle, wanting to crawl inside a hole to hide forever.

She continued to watch, her heart conflicted and her breath a shallow wheeze.

The bigger thug clutched a crowbar in his hands, and the other held a gun. The muzzle was pointed down, his hands shaking too hard to raise it.

Hissing, the alien lizards stalked toward them in a coordinated formation, unhurried, unfazed by their weapons. Then, as if they shared one mind, the beasts stopped and crouched down. Black, scaly skin rolled as if covered by a layer of snakes or shiny beetles. The vision repelled her and yet lured Trisha in with a horrifying seduction.

The smaller man finally raised his gun and pointed it at the closest lizard. He yelled something in Swahili, and in the silence, his words echoed through the quiet village.

The Reptar opened its jaws, wider than should be possible, and exposed many rows of needle-sharp teeth.

The man pulled the trigger.

The gunshot boomed in the silence. Trisha involuntarily clasped a hand over her heart at the sudden volume.

The lizard didn't flinch.

The shot faded and the five creatures simultaneously burst into movement. They were so fast, Trisha could hardly track their movements. They didn't exactly run or leap. They *flowed*. In and out of spaces so fast she grew dizzy watching.

Only after they reached the two men did they finally slow down enough for her to see each distinct limb. And then, Trisha wished she hadn't stayed to watch.

The men's screams, guttural and animalistic in their agony, couldn't drown out the sounds of claws ripping off skin or jaws crushing bone.

One of the Reptars ripped off an arm as if it were a twig, while another crunched on the other man's head. Within seconds, the five beasts had swarmed over the two men and shredded them into bloody nuggets.

Those seconds ranked as some of the longest in her life.

"Run. Run. Run."

It took a few panting breaths for the words to penetrate her shocked state, and even longer for her to recognize the voice as her own.

Wasted seconds.

At any moment, one of those beasts would turn around and realize she was there, standing visibly at the corner of the hut, gawking in horror.

Jerking her head in the other direction, Trisha pushed a hand against the wall to give herself momentum. Stumbling, she forced herself not to fall, hesitate, or give them any opportunity to catch her.

She ran down the narrow road, toward the main road, arms pumping in time with her heart. Gulping at air, she hoped — no, *prayed* — the others were already inside. Because she was under no delusion how long the outer wall would keep these beasts out. The wall she once thought impenetrable and prison-like now seemed a flimsy barrier, designed only to slow them down with a minor inconvenience.

Her family's only hope was to lock themselves inside, seal themselves in a windowless room and pray that the beasts would grow tired and seek easier prey elsewhere.

She rounded the corner and saw her gate. Motion distracted her. Trisha's eyes rolled to the side.

One of the beasts was staring at her, its jaws smeared in blood, eyes pulsing with azure light.

Gasping through her tears, she willed herself to run even as the beast surged toward her.

## Chapter Thirty-One

IF ANY OF THEM HAD SURVIVED MOGADISHU, HIS TEAMMATES WOULD'VE laughed him to scorn, seeing how he'd swapped his guns for a basket of tomatoes.

*Let them laugh,* Simba decided as he followed Celine through the expansive garden. *Veggies over guns any day.*

Not that he'd abandoned his gun collection completely, but at least he no longer lived by them.

They were in the far corner near the greenhouse and tool shed, the main house hidden by the thick cluster of shrubs boasting trumpet-shaped white flowers, each as large as his hands. He had a clear line of sight on the black metal gates which provided the only opening into or out of the compound. They were firmly shut and locked. While he couldn't see the inner door cut into one side, he had checked it last night. No reason anyone would've opened it since.

The compound was as secure as it could be, all things considered, leaving aside the alien spaceship.

Celine's meandering path led them to the tool shed. She paused in front of the door. Tilting her head to one side, she rubbed her bare feet against the thin concrete platform where the metal structure had been built.

Simba stopped behind her. "Let's get back to the house. We don't want to keep Mama Noah waiting, now do we?"

Celine craned her head back and to the side until her pale blue eyes stared at Simba's mouth, then into his eyes. She pursed her lips, then faced forward and reached for the lever handle.

Simba sighed, then lifted an arm to stop her. He hesitated, not wanting to startle her with his touch. "Celine, we can come back later. Let's …"

He stopped as his nostrils flared at the overly sweet smell. "What the …?"

He reached past Celine, slammed down the lever and yanked the metal door open. He stepped forward and stared into the shed's gloomy depth. A growl formed in his chest at seeing his half-brother slouched near the back wall.

Caleb waved a long, thick joint their way and coughed out a lungful of smoke. "Eh, bro."

Simba bit back a series of curses and held out a hand, twitching his fingers in a come-hither gesture. "Hand it over."

Caleb's bloodshot eyes widened and he clutched the joint to his chest. "Wah! This may very well be the last weed in the apocalypse. Just let me enjoy it in peace before we all die, okay? The aliens may blow up the planet any day. You wanna deal with that sober?" He shuddered. "Me, not so much."

Conscious of the child standing beside him, Simba gritted his teeth and swallowed the colorful epitaphs bubbling within him. Celine wiggled past his legs and skipped into the shed. She leaned against a canvas bag of fertilizer that was almost as big as she was. She peered over the top and waved at Caleb.

He grinned and waved back.

Simba opened his mouth to say something. At the very least, the girl shouldn't be in that stuffy, confined space, inhaling whatever garbage his halfwit of a half-brother was inhaling.

But metal clanged against metal before he could say anything.

Simba spun around and found himself staring at Trisha stumbling into view with the gate at her back.

She ran toward him screaming, "Get inside the house. Get. Inside. Now!"

Even as his legs tensed to run — but in which direction? — motion froze him.

A large, black-scaled limb reached over the gate, its talons hooking onto the top of the electric fence. Unfazed by the surge of electricity, the creature yanked down on the wire.

A second limb appeared.

"Simba!"

Trisha's scream tore through his frozen state.

He sprinted toward her on instinct, wrapped his arms around her waist and yanked her toward the tool shed.

In a pant she said, "The house."

"No time." Grunting, he swerved into the tool shed and snapped the door closed behind him.

From outside, the screech of metal sheering off of metal perforated the air, followed by nails scratching against a smooth surface.

Grimacing, Simba dropped Trisha in the far corner behind the bag of fertilizer and gestured to Celine to sit beside her mother. He waited for his eyes to adjust to the gloom. A machete hung from its hook. He removed it with care before sliding down to position himself between the door and the others.

Celine hugged her knees, back to the wall and watching him, expression unflustered by the commotion. Did she even understand what was happening, what horror lurked outside?

Caleb waved the fat joint in front of Simba with a grin behind tendrils of sweet-scented billowing smoke. "Wanna puff?"

"Quiet," Simba hissed and snatched the joint close to the burning end. He gasped at the stinging pain and tossed it toward the door.

The joint rolled and bounced until it landed close to the noticeable gap between the door and the concrete floor. Tiny embers glowed from its end. Noodles of pungent smoke weaved through the air.

"What a waste," Caleb whispered with a giggle.

Simba slammed a hand across his mouth and gripped tightly, his eyes narrowed. With his other hand, he raised the machete and held it against his brother's cheek. Only after Caleb closed his mouth did Simba finally lower his arms.

The click of large, hard nails against concrete rang out louder than it should have, or maybe even had a right to.

Her breath hitching, Trisha met his stare, eyes so wide Simba felt he could drown in them.

*Click, click* preceded a raspy, inhaling huff of breath.

Simba pushed his fear into that dark box he kept for all such occasions, and focused on mentally summarizing what he knew about the enemy. That's what he did, or rather what he used to do. He studied, analyzed, and assessed, searching for weaknesses even if there appeared to be none.

But everything had a soft spot, including this beast. No creature was independent of the food chain or circle of life. Even humans fell prey to disease-causing bacteria or venomous bites.

This alien was no different.

*Click. Click.* Inhale.

The creature stalked around the tool shed, pacing its length. Simba couldn't see it and hoped he never met it face to face, but he could hear it. Only a thin sheet of metal separated his head from the creature's toothy jaws.

He looked around the shed, searching for anything else he could use as a weapon, and again met Trisha's gaze.

Her horror and desperation were tinged with expectation. She thought he might be able to rescue them, but how? Nothing in his training or experience had prepared him for this.

Terrorists? Check.

Armed insurgents? Check.

A human army? Double check.

But aliens with clearly superior technology who could destroy an entire city in a burst of light?

The clicking of skin-shredding talons against concrete moved around the corner as the beast padded in between the shed and the compound's wall.

Simba eyed the machete, gently running his thumb along the sharpened edge. Would it even make a dent on those black scales?

The creature now paced the other length, passing behind Celine and Trisha, their beating hearts millimeters from death.

*Keep walking.*

*There's nothing here. Just leave.*

The Reptar paused when it neared the front of the shed. The momentary silence was deafening.

Simba leaned forward, watching as a shadow fell under the gap between the metal door and the concrete flooring. A black limb slid into view. The surface of hard, scaly skin undulated, followed by a second leg with a pale gray splotch near the base.

*Click. Click.* Inhale.

Was this creature ever going to exhale?

Or was its exhale the scream of its victims?

Simba glanced over his shoulder at Trisha. The bag of fertilizer blocked her view so she couldn't see the limbs. But the sound was enough, maybe worse. Her face was drawn and sickly in pallor. Her eyes beckoned to him like twin pools of ocean water.

*It's okay,* he mouthed.

They both knew it was a lie, but she blinked once in acknowledgment.

Caleb slumped against him, his legs pulled up and fists shaking atop his knees. Taking pity on his half-brother — they were about to die, so he could afford to be forgiving — Simba pressed his shoulder against him.

Caleb's head jerked up. Bloodshot eyes glittered through a drug-induced haze with the certainty of impending death.

Maybe he shouldn't have taken Caleb's drugs.

Maybe it would be easier to die if they were all …

"*Celine*," Trisha sharply whispered, her words a bare whisper on a sharp exhale.

Simba's neck twanged as he looked over at her, wondering what was wrong with everyone. Couldn't they just keep quiet for two bloody minutes?

Then he too wanted to shout.

He pressed his lips together instead, shaking his head several times, trying to catch Celine's attention.

Ignoring him, Celine wiggled away from her mother, eyes fixed on the gap under the door. The child started to crawl across their legs and toward the Reptar, her expression set in a determined frown.

Trisha whimpered and bent at the waist, stretching her arms over her legs and trying to grab her daughter.

Metal creaked behind her.

The tapping of the alien's claws against the concrete finally ceased.

In the resulting silence, Simba blinked away a dribble of sweat stinging his eyes.

Celine lifted her hand as if to continue her crawl toward the door. But then what? What was she thinking? Why did she choose this moment to take an active interest in her environment?

Not daring to move, Trisha clasped her hands in a prayer pose, tearful eyes fixed on Celine. Her lips moved soundlessly, forming words at her wayward child.

Before Celine moved closer to the door, Caleb shifted forward and grabbed her. As she writhed, he hugged the girl close, trapping her in his arms and legs, and pressing his hand against her mouth, forming a dark band of skin against her creamy pale cheeks.

The two stared into each other's eyes, watery blue fighting against chocolate brown.

Some understanding seemed to pass between them. Celine stopped struggling and slumped against his chest. But Simba didn't dare to exhale as the alien lifted one of its legs, skin contorting with the movement.

*Click. Click.* Raspy inhale.

Trisha covered her mouth with both hands, tears streaming down in silent horror as she stared at her daughter.

The tip of a snout appeared in Simba's line of sight. How big were these things? From a distance, from the safety of the house, he'd guessed they were approximately the size of a large lion.

Yet now, the length of the beast seemed to stretch on and on.

Or maybe that was the terror.

He used to think he understood fear. Despite his experience fighting terrorists in Somalia, this enemy redefined terror.

Scratch that.

It redefined *everything*, taking all the carefully constructed social norms and beliefs and then dumping them on their head and down into a deep, dark abyss from which there was no return.

The snout pushed against the gap under the door and snuffled, nostrils still flaring.

Simba mentally prepared himself for the worst. Surely, it could smell them and the acrid bite of fear-induced sweat which drenched the air.

*Any minute*, he thought, glancing over at Trisha, then at Celine and Caleb. He'd failed them, and now they would all be torn to shreds. The machete in his hands felt brittle and flimsy.

The reptile snuffled and snorted, then inhaled deeply with a long, raspy intake of violent breath.

The joint fluttered and slipped under the door toward the alien's flaring nostrils, a tendril of smoke drifting in its wake. There was another husky inhale, and the entire joint disappeared inside one of the nostrils.

Wrinkling its snout, the Reptar snorted and hissed. The muzzle jerked back, and the alien made a sound that sounded like a sneeze before stalking out of sight.

Minutes passed.

"Where'd it go?" Caleb whispered, flinching when Trisha and Simba both shushed him.

Simba pressed an ear against the metal wall, then held his breath and waited for the telltale raspy inhale, the *click, click* of talons, the approach of death.

"Simba."

His name, whispered on an exhale, made him turn to Trisha. She was staring past the bag of fertilizer at the door, her breath coming in wheezes and gasps.

He turned his head to the side and caught sight of something that stole all his breath.

The lever handle on the door was swiveling down.

Simba tightened his grip on the machete and rose into a crouch, preparing to lunge at the beast. Maybe he could distract it enough for the others to run to the house.

As the handle slid into a vertical position, the door clicked open.

Caleb whimpered.

Hinges creaked. A pool of light widened until it filled half the shed.

Looming in the entrance, her heavy cast-iron pan in hand, Mama Noah stared down at them. Her tongue clucked in disapproval, and she glared at Simba. "Young man, where are my tomatoes?"

# Chapter Thirty-Two

"GOD IS GREAT AND HE LOVES ME. HE TRULY DOES. That's why he sends me these tests." Mama Noah sniffed, her nose wrinkling. Maybe she'd caught a whiff of the lingering smell of pot. "And by these tests, I mean you men. Why he thought to create you in the first place is beyond me."

Simba blinked in the bright light, wondering if the Reptar had already eviscerated him, and he was experiencing a pain-numbing hallucination while dying. It took a few breaths longer to realize the maid was talking in Swahili, her words flying out faster than buckshot and almost as lethal.

Mama Noah shook a fist at him. "I send you on a simple mission. Bring me some vegetables. Simple! And then what? I might as well do everything myself. It's faster that way, and at least the job gets done."

Her scowl shifted into a confused frown as her gaze wandered the tool shed. "What are you all doing in here? Is this a party? And what's that smell? Mrs. Walker?"

Trisha hiccupped and sobbed. That was all Simba needed to break from the stunned spell Mama Noah's arrival had cast upon him. He leapt up, pushed past the astonished maid, and studied the compound.

Walls: clear.

Roofs of buildings: clear.

Greenhouse: clear.

No sign of the Reptar. How long would that last?

He spun around, grabbed Mama Noah by the shoulders, then directed her to the path leading to the main house and away from the tool shed.

"Young man, you may be big and scary, but nothing is as frightening as Mama Noah armed with this." She raised her frying pan and tilted it toward him.

Simba leaned into the tool shed, ignoring the sincere and obvious threat. "Get up. Now. Into the house."

Even focused on moving everyone to a more secure location, his voice still surprised him. Pitched with the exact depth, force and intonation he once used when commanding his team in the heat of the moment.

*I'm not their leader. I just need to get them into the house. Then they can figure out what to do.*

But as he watched each one of them stumble out, Simba felt the insincerity of his own thoughts. An untrained woman, a young child, and a man who acted like a child: this wasn't a recipe for survival in a post-invasion world. Of the four civilians, the maid was the best equipped mentally and physically. All she had was a frying pan.

Simba lingered behind them, keeping an eye out for any motion, hint of black, scaly skin or glowing eyes. Only a yellow weaver bird dared to disturb the unearthly stillness of the moment. Warbling raucously, the little avian fluttered from tree to tree, searching for nesting material.

Huffing a laugh, he saluted. "Good luck to you, sir."

He reached the Walker household just as they filed into the house through the kitchen's outer door. He pushed his brother ahead of him, then closed the metal door and made sure it was locked.

"Mama Noah, go around the house and lock up every door, grill and window."

Scowling, she opened her mouth and paused when Trisha slumped onto a kitchen stool. She rested her face against the island counter and covered her head with her arms, shoulders shaking.

"Madam? Mrs. Walker?" Mama Noah hesitated over every syllable.

Trisha's body shuddered, but she didn't lift her head. "Just do it."

Simba and Mama Noah traded a worried glance, then she lumbered away, pan in hand. Simba closed his eyes as he heard her slam windows shut. Hinges creaked. Locks snapped into position.

But would it be enough?

Silent as a shadow, Celine skipped to the corner of the kitchen, a box of crayons in one hand and a sheaf of papers in the other. Squatting, she began to color. Instead of the silver and blue crayons, she held a black one only.

Exhaustion rushed over Simba, and he rested his back against the wall, staring down at Celine as she scribbled black lines across the white paper. He wondered if she'd run out of her regular colors. It was the first time he'd seen her use black. The crayon looked untouched.

Coughing, Caleb opened the fridge door and leaned in. "Well, this is fun, but we can't stay locked up in here forever."

"We leave."

Simba and Caleb both swiveled to face Trisha. She still hadn't raised her head. Words muted but clear enough.

Caleb yawned, wedging himself between the refrigerator's door and main compartment. "What do you mean, leave? What happened to your zombie apocalypse theory? You know, stay put, don't follow the ignorant masses. They're all sheep plodding into a massacre."

Trisha's arms slid onto the island's countertop, and she drummed her nails against the cold marble, her nails clicking softly. She lifted her head until her chin rested on one arm and her eyes faced forward, staring past Caleb as if she could see the fridge's interior through his ribs.

"That was before the apocalypse landed in my backyard. Before I saw a pack of those monsters tear two of our neighbors apart. Or thugs. Whoever they were."

Trisha pressed her hands onto the countertop and pushed her body upright, dark blue eyes sparkling with fury. "That was *before* they threatened us. They know we're here. They abducted half the village in one night. The other half have fled. We're pretty much the only ones left and they know it."

Her body shook, in sharp contrast to the cold hardness of her words and the rage contorting her face. "This house, the doors and grills, those walls and the electric fence, none of it will stop them. None of it! This place isn't a sanctuary. It's a prison, one they can enter whenever they damned well want to. They're targeting major urban centers. Well, guess what? Nairobi fits the bill. How much longer before our luck runs out?"

Simba stepped toward her, raising a hand to placate the fury, but she knocked it aside.

"Are you going to argue with me, Simba?" She spun off her stool, almost knocking it over. "You think we were clever? We barely survived that encounter. Have you seen what they can do?" No one answered and she screamed, "Have you seen?"

Her chest heaved with the effort of holding herself together.

A small whimper distracted her. She stared past Simba toward the corner of the kitchen where Celine crouched over her drawing. The girl's eyes were large, wide and fixed on Trisha.

The vision of her daughter huddled in a corner calmed Trisha's inner storm. Simba saw the exact moment everything deflated, and Trisha covered her mouth with both hands. "I'm so sorry, Celine. It's okay. Mommy isn't angry with you. I'm just … angry. Tired."

"I know where we can go."

Simba swiveled partially around and turned to face the doorway where Mama Noah stood. Her cast-iron pan hung at her side while her other hand rested on her hips. "I know a safe place. God's resting place. Mount Kenya."

Caleb scoffed, turned his back to them and pushed his head into the fridge. "Eh. There is no God. Look around."

Mama Noah raised the frying pan like a sword. "Watch your mouth, young man, or I'll wash out that filth. Maybe there is no God you can see, but He's been in my life plenty."

Caleb glanced over his shoulder and rolled his eyes. "Yeah? I hope he gave you more than a frying pan on his way out. 'Cause we're gonna need a lot more than that to survive."

Mama Noah stomped into the kitchen and slid the pan onto the counter near the sink. Stooping down, she picked up Celine and hugged her close. Glaring over the child's shoulder, she ignored Caleb to fix her gaze on Simba. "I don't know anything about zombies, but I know a little something about survival. And us, we're not going to survive here much longer. No food. No shops. Only chaos, confusion and mutated reptiles."

"They're aliens, not mutated reptiles," Caleb muttered as he pulled out a loaf of bread.

"Same thing." Mama Noah whispered something in Celine's ear and lowered her to the ground.

Without looking at anyone, Celine scooped up her box of crayons and scuttled out of the kitchen. The pitter-patter of her bare feet slapping against the wooden stairs was the only sound for a moment.

Simba stared at the abandoned drawing, something about it bothering him. He bent to pick it up.

"Mount Kenya. There aren't too many people, no cities, only a few towns. And I have a farm in the area." Mama Noah nodded at each of them, a self-satisfied expression settling on her face, as if the decision were already made. "If we can farm, we can survive. No reptiles are going to hang around empty farmland."

An uneasy stillness settled around them. Only the hum of the fridge and the *tick, tock* of the living room clock to disturb their silence. Ignoring the maid's words, Simba placed the drawing on the island. Unlike all the others, this one wasn't of silver discs against a blue sky, or a scattering of dots and circles.

"Mount Kenya." Trisha spoke the words as if tasting them, testing their flavor and texture, trying to determine if they met her expectations.

Simba rubbed a hand over his shaved head, invisible bristles scratching against the skin of his palm. "Mrs. Walker."

"Trisha." She sighed and plopped onto her stool. "I told you to call me Trisha."

He slid the paper over, watching her reaction shift from defeated to alarmed.

She peered up at him, the paper shaking in her hands. "Just now?"

He nodded.

Caleb shrugged and dropped the loaf of bread on the island counter. "What's the big deal? It's just a stupid lizard."

Trisha licked at a corner of her mouth, diverting Simba's attention. "Until last week, Celine's drawings were the same. Mostly colored dots and circles. She never drew anything different until then. First, the silver discs." She covered her mouth with a trembling hand and closed her eyes. "And now … of all things, she draws a Reptar."

"Whatever, dudes." Caleb ripped open the bag covering the bread. "She drew a Reptar. Big, fuzzy deal. Are we going or not? If we do, pack a lot of food. 'Cause me, I don't do road trips on an empty stomach."

Something clattered in the background, but Simba was still focused on Trisha. Would she agree to go? And since when had her approval of a plan been so important?

*Since the moment she became your employer.*

Yet it had been a few days since Simba had thought of Trisha Walker as his employer. Something about an alien invasion destroyed all previous social constructs, only to recreate them in a new image. They were part of a team now. Mama Noah's confident swagger as she stomped toward the island counter only reinforced the point. The maid met Trisha's gaze with chin up, expression determined.

The clatter repeated itself.

Simba took a distracted step toward the kitchen door but stopped when Trisha cleared her throat.

"You have a home around Mount Kenya?" Her nails tapped against the marble counter. *Click. Click.*

Mama Noah's shoulders relaxed, and she exhaled. "Yes, madam. I have a home and a farm and no giant reptiles. There's nothing for them."

"So we just have to get there." *Click, click.* "How difficult can that be?" Trisha laughed, the sound warbling until she snapped her mouth closed.

Simba's mind turned over the clattering until it stumbled upon the cause. The back screen door. He could hear it flutter against its frame, like a wheezing cough as the house drew breath and blew it back out.

He turned to face Mama Noah, wondering what else she had forgotten. "Why didn't you lock the screen door out back?"

Mama Noah crossed her arms over her bosom and met his glare with one of her own. "I locked up everything."

In the moment between words, the screen door rattled in its frame.

Mama Noah's eyes widened, and her confidence leached away in the light of a creeping fear. "I know I locked it. Why is it open?"

Simba shook his head as he turned to investigate. "More importantly, who unlocked it? Trisha, wait."

But she wasn't waiting. Squeezing past him, Trisha dashed up the stairs, taking them two at a time. "Celine. Darling, where are you?"

Simba left her to search upstairs and strode toward the rear. Even from the other end of the hall, he could see the back door was slightly ajar. Through the gap, he caught sight of the screen door fluttering in and out, inhale and exhale.

A bellow echoed from upstairs, a single name reverberating through his soul.

Simba bolted for the back door and crashed through the opening to stare around the yard. Even before Trisha shouted for him, Simba felt the truth.

*Celine was gone.*

## Chapter Thirty-Three

CALEB WATCHED TRISHA FALL APART. IT WAS AS IF SOMEONE had cut her strings from the marionette frame. She collapsed, limbs askew as she crumpled in a heap on the living room floor.

Mama Noah trotted in, full of useless reassurances. They'd seen what was out there. Predators of all sizes, earthling and alien alike. If the lions didn't sniff her out, surely the Reptars would.

"Well, there's no point standing around here."

Only when Simba looked up at him with raised eyebrows did Caleb realize he had spoken those words himself. He blinked in surprise at his impulsive offer to …

To what? Go out there and brave the lions and killer aliens to find some kid he barely knew and wasn't his? To get himself killed in the process?

*Whoa, boy. You're not the hero in the story.*

*You're never the hero.*

His legs disagreed and were marching him toward the front door.

"Give me a couple minutes. I'm coming with you," Simba said from behind him.

Caleb tried to ignore the worry squirming through his stomach.

He gave a jaunty wave. "Sure thing. Meet you at the gate. I hope you bring more than that frying pan." He gestured to Mama Noah.

She raised the pan with a scowl even as she hugged Trisha. "Young man, you'd be surprised what I can do with a frying pan."

Caleb grinned. Better than collapsing next to Trisha in a puddle of terror. Ignoring the rational part of his brain screaming *What the hell?* he opened the front door and continued striding toward the gate.

A set of long scratches trailed down one side of the gate. The automatic swinging arm on that side was snapped off and dangling uselessly. The Reptar must've done that when it climbed into the compound. If they wanted to open the gates, they'd have to do so manually.

His gaze swept down, and he could see the inner door wasn't bolted shut. Someone had snuck out.

*What's that kid thinking?*

An image flashed before him in response. Celine, the lions, and the Reptar that had inhaled his joint. They swirled around each other like colorful playing cards caught in a whirlpool.

He shook his head, yanked the gate's inner door open, stooped down and stepped through. Only once outside the compound and its safety did he realize how stupid he'd been.

No weapon. Not even a frying pan.

And he hadn't bothered to check if anything was lurking on either side of the gate. Convulsively, his head turned quickly in both directions.

Nothing but landscape and the cornfield across the road.

The cornfield.

Something rustled through it, away from him.

He rolled his eyes because snark beat the fear-soaked alternative. "Great. Just like the movies. Of course the little girl heads into the cornfield. 'Cause why not? Let's go into the one place that's most likely full of carnivores."

"Do you always talk to yourself?"

He looked back and watched Simba scoot through the doorway

before closing it behind him. His eyes brightened as a vestige of hope settled in. "Nice."

Simba shouldered the rifle while patting his belt. A gun hung from either hip. "Never leave home without them."

Caleb grinned. Maybe this wasn't a suicide mission after all. He held out his hand. "And mine?"

Simba snorted. He pushed past Caleb with a shake of his head and began loading the guns with clips from his pocket. "Get your own. These are for the adults."

The door in the gate rattled behind them, and Caleb turned in time to see Mama Noah push her way out, frying pan in hand, followed by Trisha.

He snorted a laugh. "Serious?"

Mama Noah clucked. "Don't you *serious* me, young man. I have just as much right to …" Her words drifted off as she stared across at the cornfield. "She went in there, didn't she?"

"Yup."

Simba nodded. "Afraid so." Staring over Mama Noah, he frowned at Trisha.

She stared at the rifle. "You have guns? I didn't know that."

Caleb guffawed. "You don't know nothing, boss lady, so chill."

Mama Noah reached over and slapped Caleb on the head.

"Hey." Caleb rubbed his skull, deciding that if the carnivores came at them, he merely had to outrun the slowest person. He narrowed his eyes at the maid. *Yeah, and that will be you, ol' lady, not me.*

Simba placed a hand on Trisha's shoulder. Her head jerked back, and Caleb watched his brother's face darken in a flush. Still, he held his arm steady. "They're usually locked away, and they only go off when I pull the trigger."

Caleb cackled and shook his head. "Yeah, soldier boy. That's kinda how guns work. Speaking of which." He again pushed out a hand. "You're not gonna leave me defenseless, are you?"

Simba straightened his shoulders. "Of course not. I'll defend you. And look. There's a stick over there." Not waiting to see what

Caleb would do, Simba turned around and marched toward the cornfield.

Caleb traded glances with Mama Noah, who clutched her pan closely. "Don't look at me, young man. I'm armed." She strutted after Simba, a swagger to her hips, red kikoi horrifically bright against the green foliage ahead, like a walking blob of fresh blood.

Her eyes red-rimmed, Trisha stared at Caleb. She held up a fancy walking stick, the overpriced kind they sell to tourists in markets around the city. "Don't try to stop me. That's my daughter in there."

Caleb held up his hands. "Lady, I ain't stopping nobody."

Together, they followed Simba into the cornfield.

## Chapter Thirty-Four

"IS THIS WHAT CARNIVORES SMELL LIKE?"

"Shh," Simba hissed at his brother, lowering his rifle and using it to separate the stalks ahead of him.

Caleb gestured to Trisha to move forward while muttering to himself. She couldn't understand the language, but knew the tone. He was definitely saying something unsavory about Simba, but not loud enough for the big man to hear.

Despite their efforts, there really was no point in trying to be quiet. Long leaves snagged on their clothing, causing the cornstalks to shiver. Every motion created a whisper of rustling and crackling around them. If there were lions or aliens anywhere nearby, they'd have to be stone deaf not to hear the trumpeting of their arrival.

Trisha inhaled, her nose wrinkling at the stench of rotting meat. What had died here? Or more to the point, what had been killed here, and by what?

*They're called Reptars.*

A shudder started from her core, and Trisha almost dropped her walking stick. She'd been so close to being caught by a pack of those beasts. Only dumb luck had helped her to survive the encounter.

That kind of luck didn't last long, and neither did people who relied on it.

"Celine, where are you?" Trisha whispered under her breath. "What were you thinking?"

More to the point, how had she not heard her daughter leave the house? What kind of failed mother was she?

Rather than answer that question, she focused on Simba's broad back immediately in front of her. Out here, surrounded by thick foliage, oppressive heat, and a tinge of humidity, Simba looked the part of a soldier. Guns hung from his muscular frame like extra limbs. She wondered if Jake had known that about their driver before he hired him.

Or maybe that was why he'd hired the ex-soldier.

She wasn't a fan of guns in the house, having read too many stories of little children accidentally shooting themselves or a family member. Yet the sight of those guns strapped to Simba's body improved her mood. Not a lot, but in his competent hands, those guns might be the difference between surviving the day and being eaten.

Trisha clutched her own weapon tightly, wanting to laugh at herself. It was a fancy walking stick from a touristy crafts market. At the first contact with the scaly skull of one of those aliens, it would snap in two. And several paces behind her, struggling to keep up, her maid was brandishing a frying pan.

So yes, Simba's guns were several levels of better compared to what she had. If they were really lucky, they'd find Celine before anything else found her or them. Apart from her close call with the Reptar pack, her and luck hadn't been close acquaintances. But maybe today …

She flinched as she stepped on a brittle stick. The resulting *snap* ricocheted around them.

Simba held up a fist and squatted.

Caleb scoffed behind her. "Yeah, like that's gonna help. We ain't in a war zone, Simba."

She too stayed standing, wondering what squatting would do for them. Lions had an astonishing sense of smell and didn't have to see them in order to know they were there. And as for the Reptars? Her guess was as good as anyone's, but they looked lethal enough to have all five senses working better than any human's.

Trying to be silent, or stay out of sight, was as pointless as pretending the aliens didn't know they were hiding out in the only house with lights on in the area.

Simba pointed to his right. Trisha could almost feel Caleb's eyes roll behind her. She slapped a hand over her mouth to cover her giggle. Not that it was funny. Or maybe it was, or would be in hindsight. Lots and lots of hindsight.

Simba led them through the maze of corn, shifting direction often. She heard only her own harsh breathing and the rustle of leaves from their passage. The world beyond their green bubble lay silent.

Sweat dribbled into uncomfortable places. Trisha wiped a hand across her eyes, blinking away the sting. The stalks shielded them from the direct sun, but their close presence trapped them in a warm, moist, living oven.

She stumbled into Simba when he abruptly stopped at the edge of a clearing somewhere in the middle of the field. And as she stared into the wide space, her mouth opened to scream.

## Chapter Thirty-Five

SIMBA KNEW TRISHA WAS GOING TO SCREAM. HE DIDN'T KNOW how it was possible, but it was. Not so much a *knowing* as a *feeling*. He *felt* the scream bubble up through Trisha, her mouth opening to release it, almost as if they momentarily shared the same body.

Before her emotions could erupt in audio, he spun around and slapped a hand across her mouth. He stared into her wide, ocean-blue eyes, her tension brushing through him. He shuddered with its force but stayed his hand. At some gut level, he knew if he moved it, she would fall apart and take them all with her.

"Don't. Make. A sound," he whispered.

He waited until she nodded before dropping his hand and returning his attention to the clearing.

Celine stood there, her expression vaguely interested in the creature sitting by her side. Her arm was draped around its neck, and she gazed down, stroking it. The positioning was the same as when he'd seen her with the village dog near the Walker compound.

Simba remembered Trisha screaming at her to get away from the dirty animal. She'd lectured Mama Noah about allowing her precious daughter to play with stray animals, talking over the woman's soft protest that it was only a friendly dog owned by one of the local families.

This time, it wasn't a village dog.

It was a vicious killing machine from another planet, and Celine clung to its neck as if it were nothing more than the neighbor's pet.

"Celine." He croaked her name from his parched mouth.

Trisha made a whimpering noise beside him. The Reptar snarled, but something was off.

Simba studied the rest of the clearing, searching for the source of the stench of rancid meat and death. There was a lump of black-and-white fur in one corner, its insides spilled on the ground around it, most of the flesh already eaten.

Closer to the center, a lioness lay stretched out, its muzzle pulled back in a snarl, its eyes glazed, its limbs not yet stiff. A fresh kill. Trampled stalks, blood and bits of fur suggested a battle. Some of the blood had a blue glow.

*So aliens bleed blue.*

Caleb squeezed between him and Trisha. "Wah! That thing, it's big. Where're the lions?"

Simba's eyes narrowed as he studied the surrounding forest of corn. No eyes glared back at him. For now, they were alone with the alien.

"Do you think that thing wants to eat us?" Caleb sidled closer to Simba, as if suspecting the answer.

Simba snorted and stepped away. "Definitely. I bet it would love a drug-flavored meal."

"Eh! Aren't you the comedian. So why isn't it, you know, attacking or whatever?"

Trisha flinched as if Caleb had struck her.

Simba jutted his jaw to one side, then another. "Something's wrong with it."

The Reptar's eyelids lazily flickered, its gaze unfocused.

Caleb snorted a laugh. "Ain't that the truth? This is the one that sucked in my whole bloody joint. Look at it. The thing is flying high in the sky. Serious."

"You're the expert."

"Simba, my bro, you missed your true calling as a clown."

Simba studied the Reptar more closely, doing his best to ignore Caleb. There was a light gray splotch on one of its front legs. As if sensing his attention, the beast opened its snout to reveal several rows of sharp teeth.

But Simba could see that just the effort of lifting its head took all the energy the creature had. After a few seconds, the eyes dimmed slightly, and the head fell forward as the creature collapsed on the ground.

He glanced between the drugged-up alien, the dead lioness and the zebra kill. "Wonders never cease. You're right."

Caleb did a mock bow. "More often than you know."

Trish whimpered, and Simba felt more than heard her low murmur of her daughter's name. Behind him, Mama Noah huffed and puffed as she finally caught up.

"What's going on?" she wheezed.

Simba held up an arm, almost covering her entire face with his hand. "Stay with Mrs. Walker."

He took a step forward, half-expecting the alien to snarl. Nothing happened. "It must've stumbled into the lion's kill, and they attacked it."

Trisha was doing her best not to fall apart next to him. But he could hear the hitch in her breath, the soul-stirring sob she tried to suppress. Her quivering hand gripping his arm reminded him that this was no place for an overly emotional mother. Because predators honed in on that; they sniffed out fear and weakness of any sort.

While he'd never thought of Trisha as particularly weak, in this moment she was utterly vulnerable.

And the Reptar knew it.

Even drugged up, its muzzle twitched in her direction, and its eyes narrowed to fix on her. The jaws opened slightly. Rows of teeth and a blue light glowing from its gullet.

"Mama Noah." Simba focused on keeping his voice calmer than usual, soft without inflection. "Take Trisha back to the house."

He could almost feel the protest erupting from the two women as if it was his own reaction. Glancing at Trisha, he leaned closer until he could see only her dark blue eyes. "You need to go. That thing is picking up on your ..." He hesitated, trying to find the right word and failing. "Upset."

*Upset* didn't come close to describing her state, but she still understood. She wrapped her arms around herself and stared at Celine, mouth quivering and eyes glazed with unshed tears and shock.

"I'm not ... How can I just leave my child?"

The Reptar shifted, large, claw-tipped paws scraping through the crushed cornstalks. The sound of rustling leaves under the heavy body caused them both to look at the creature squatting beside a very tiny child.

Simba didn't take his eyes off the alien. "You need to leave *because* of your child. I promise I'll get Celine and bring her to you. But I can't do that if I have to worry about you. If anything happened ..."

He didn't finish. He'd said enough.

"Come, Mrs. Walker," Mama Noah murmured. "He's right. You'll distract him. Let the soldier deal with this."

"Eh!" Caleb huffed. "What about me? I'm dealing, too."

Simba spared a quick look to judge her response. He thought Trisha would push through her horror and argue. He wouldn't deny her the right to stay and share the danger if she did. Even if it increased the risk to all of them, she was Celine's mother.

He heard their retreat through the cornstalks and some of the tension across his shoulders eased, even as his throat constricted with disappointment.

He didn't have long to dwell on the confusing brew of emotions. The Reptar's glowing eyes settled on him, as if it understood that of all the humans in the area, he was the only genuine threat.

*Alien, you have no idea.*

Then again, would a bullet impact that scaly skin? The creature looked like a living tank.

Simba eased forward, his rifle at the ready, every muscle tense and preparing to leap, run, fight. Anything but die, even though that was always an option.

"Eh. Simba?"

He continued studying the alien, wondering what it would do if one of them walked over to Celine. "What?"

"Simba," Caleb hissed.

He glanced up in time to see several lionesses drift into the clearing.

## Chapter Thirty-Six

TRISHA ALLOWED MAMA NOAH TO LEAD HER AWAY. HER heart kept screaming at her to return, get back to her child and do whatever it took to push through the bone-deep, limb-freezing terror and face the monster sitting next to Celine.

But some logical, rational part of her brain — the sliver that was still functioning and hadn't dissolved into a spineless, chattering monkey — understood that Simba was right. She was only a distraction, and he couldn't afford one right now.

Why was she a distraction?

It didn't matter. If there was any chance to rescue Celine from the monster, he needed to focus, and her presence interfered with his efforts.

Why did he find her distracting?

*It doesn't matter. He's just the hired help.*

But even as those words drifted up from a less appealing corner of her mind, she felt their wrongness resonate through the core of her being. Maybe it was living together in a post-invasion world, surviving the chaos, abductions, Reptar attacks. Over the past nine intense, insane days, Simba and Mama Noah, even Caleb, had ceased being employees or *others*. They were so much more.

"What am I doing?" Trisha stopped, her eyes stinging. "How can I leave Celine? What kind of a mother am I, abandoning my child?"

She started to turn around, blindly whacking at the cornstalks with her stick. "I didn't stay with her at school, and look what happened. And now … I'm a coward. I'm a horrible, terrible—"

Mama Noah clucked. "You're not abandoning her. You're letting Simba do his job."

"And what's mine?" Trisha stopped thrashing around and stared down the uneven path leading to the clearing. "To be a mother, and I've failed."

In the conversational pause that followed, leaves rustled around them, and a bird warbled nearby. Trisha sniffed loudly. The air was heavy with the scent of warm soil and ripe greenery.

Mama Noah looped an arm around her waist and plucked the walking stick out of her limp hand. "Do you know the story of Solomon and the two mothers?"

Trisha wiped a hand across her eyes and shook her head.

"Two women came to the court of King Solomon, both claiming to be the mother of a baby boy." Mama Noah resumed walking away from the clearing, her grip on Trisha unyielding. "As there was no way to prove who had the stronger case, Solomon suggested they cut the baby in half, so that each woman would receive a share. One of the women agreed, while the other begged the king not to do this. 'Give the baby to her,' she cried. 'Just don't kill him!' In this way, Solomon knew who the real mother was: the woman willing to sacrifice her own self-interest for the benefit of the baby."

Sighing, Mama Noah made the sign of the cross. "Staying there just to prove you're a good mother won't help Celine. A good mother does whatever must be done to protect her children, and that's your job. Now watch your step."

Trisha jerked her head up, surprised they reached the gate so fast. If anyone had asked how much time they'd spent searching for Celine, she would've sworn they had marched through the cornfield for an hour instead of minutes. And yet, here they were already.

She glanced over her shoulder. No motion disturbed the dense rows of cornstalks. Who would guess that a deadly alien sat next to a child, maybe a hundred meters away?

Giving into Mama Noah's gentle tug, Trisha ducked through the doorway in the gate and shambled up the driveway.

"Mrs. Walker."

Wearily, Trisha pushed her hair off her face and lifted her head, looking toward the house. The front door was open and the hallway was full of shadows despite the bright sunshine. She pictured herself walking inside and collapsing on the living room sofa. And when she woke, Celine would be there, coloring her dots and circles as if nothing had happened.

"Mrs. Walker, do you see?"

Before Trisha could reply, Mama Noah jabbed a finger at the front door.

A terrible fatigue clawed up her back and clung to Trisha's shoulders. It dragged down her eyelids and urged her to curl up on the grass and sleep. It took all her effort to push out one word. "What?"

"The door. It's open."

Trisha closed her eyes. "Okay."

A hand clasped around hers. "I closed it behind us."

Trisha opened one eye, wishing Mama Noah would leave her alone, and willing herself to provide words of reassurance. Instead, she choked on air as motion stirred the hallway's shadows.

Someone or something was in the house.

## Chapter Thirty-Seven

*THIS MUST BE ANOTHER HALLUCINATION.*

That was Caleb's first reaction to the scene. Even as a more logical part of his brain resisted his attempts to candy-coat the situation, Caleb kept telling himself that.

*It's only a hallucination. It, too, shall pass.*

There was only one problem with this reassuring notion. Lions circling the clearing in the middle of the cornfield didn't vanish in a puff of smoke. Neither did the alien panther/insect thing. They were all solid and going nowhere.

But Celine was what really froze his blood and made him wish the Reptar hadn't swallowed his joint. She stood in the middle of the clearing, surrounded by snarling lions, right next to the head of the scariest thing Caleb had ever hallucinated.

Except it probably wasn't a hallucination, if he was being honest with himself, which he hated to be.

Honesty was so overrated.

Caleb stared at Celine.

She stared right back, her expression calm, with no indication at all that she was aware of the predators prowling around her or the giant, scaly one lying at her feet.

"Why aren't any of them attacking?" Caleb whispered. "Not that I'm complaining, but what the hell?"

Simba slipped the rifle off his shoulder and hefted it into a better position.

"You'll hit the kid."

Simba snorted. "No. I won't."

*It's injured.*

Caleb rubbed his forehead, wondering why he would think anyone was injured. Though if he was sticking to that whole over-rated honesty trend, he had to admit it wasn't his thought at all.

Celine's eyes brightened. Her small arm, seeming so fragile, hung around the reptile's neck.

*It's injured. We have to help.*

Simba half-swiveled toward him. "Who's injured?"

Caleb's head jerked up, and he met Simba's confused gaze. His mouth fell open, then closed as he tried to formulate a response.

*Did I say that out loud?*

But it wasn't even his idea. Of course, they weren't going to help. It was an alien reptile thing, sent down to hunt and destroy.

*No. Not really.*

His gaze drifted past Simba's bewildered face to Celine's. Her stare didn't waiver.

Did she really expect him to help?

*I ain't no hero, kid.*

*But you could be.*

Talking with his mind wasn't the weirdest thing Caleb had ever imagined. Besides, this was all still an elaborate hallucination, so he went with the program.

*Wah! Serious. I'm really not.*

"Celine."

Simba's harsh whisper broke Caleb's focus. God knew he only had so much to begin with.

"Celine ... step away from that thing and get over here now."

Celine lifted her chin, her eyes shockingly cold and calculating, something he had never imagined seeing in the girl before. She shook her head and tightened her grip on the Reptar's neck.

Its giant jaw opened, as if the creature were panting like a dog, except it wasn't panting at all. Rows of pointed teeth lined its gums. Strange blue light pulsed from its throat, matching the illumination glowing between its inky black scales. Dark liquid oozed from its neck between Celine's fingers.

He rubbed the back of his neck. "Eh, Simba? It's injured. Maybe we should help it."

*Good, Caleb.*

Ignoring him, Simba raised his rifle, settling the butt against his shoulder.

"Whatcha gonna do, soldier boy? Shoot us all?"

"The thought crossed my mind."

Caleb lifted an arm. "Simba. Serious, dude. You could hit the kid."

"Not a chance."

Caleb stared beyond Celine to the lions pacing the opposite side of the clearing. Why weren't they attacking? Why weren't they showing any interest in the two big, human-shaped snacks on the other side? Or the kid? They were clearly capable of injuring a drugged-up alien.

The Reptar was starting to wake up. Its head bobbed back and forth, up and down. Toothy jaws snapped open and shut, as if it couldn't quite decide if it should eat them, tear them apart, or lick their faces.

Caleb giggled. "Dang. That thing is stoned."

Caleb's legs started to stumble forward until he put the brakes on them. No way was he going near that thing or the lions. Nothing that might tear off a limb. He was seriously attached to his limbs and hoped to keep them where they were, firmly attached and functioning.

He tried to keep eye contact with Celine, but his gaze inadvertently dropped to the creature by her side. Its eyes glowed reptilian yellow, and it seemed to sneer at him, revealing teeth that were sharper and bigger the closer he approached.

The creature smacked its jaws, as if smelling the fear.

Why the hell was he even here?

"Of all the stupid ideas," he muttered under his breath, "this ranks right up there with stealing from a crime lord."

Well, almost. The Reptar would probably rip him apart much faster than Madam Zahir would if she found him. He took a step backward, away from the monster, and something crunched underfoot.

A leaf? Twig? Bone from the creature's last meal?

"Celine," he said, wishing his voice didn't quiver so much. "Let's go. Let's leave your new friend in its cozy home, and let's go to ours."

*It needs our help.*

Caleb wanted to roll his eyes or scream, but he wasn't prepared to take his eyes off of Celine and her pet. Besides, screaming would certainly remind all the beasts of the food source.

*Run away,* he thought. *Just run away. You're good at that.*

His legs appeared to be in a state of mutiny, refusing to heed his jabbering brain. Still several paces from Celine, they stayed rooted, not going forward but also not retreating. He couldn't stand being so close to the alien.

Just thinking about the creature made him lower his gaze. It didn't have to go far. Even lying down, the beast's presence filled the clearing and radiated lethal skill.

He stared at the claw marks across its back, shoulders, and neck. "Do you think it'll survive?"

"Who cares?" Simba said behind him. "Go grab the girl and get back here."

Caleb's shoulders itched. How did Simba get behind him? And was he pointing the gun at his brother? How good was Simba's aim? Because right now, he and Celine were too close. Maybe he was using this as an excuse to get rid of his pesky, troublesome brother.

*And I wouldn't blame you, Simba.*

Celine frowned.

Caleb shook his head. "I ain't approaching that thing, man."

"Like you said, it's injured."

Unable to look away from the yellow eyes, Caleb cracked his knuckles. "Then you give me the gun and go over there, soldier boy."

"You couldn't hit the broadside of an elephant."

"Mkundu." He was too far away to reach her, but Caleb still stretched out his arm. "Hey, kid. Come here. Let's go play with some crayons while we still have all our fingers and toes. Before the alien snaps them off and eats them for a snack."

The Reptar's front legs straightened, claws digging into the ground as it lifted its tremendous ugly head until its yellow eyes were nearly level with Caleb's.

The snarl deepened, a strange mixture of a really loud purr and a death rattle. Except Caleb was pretty sure it would be *his* death, rather than the Reptar's.

"Nice kitty. Good alien monster thing."

Motion behind Celine caught Caleb's attention. "Serious? Can this get any crazier?"

Of course, the answer was always *yes*, especially for Caleb.

A large lion padded into the clearing, its mane floating around its head like the hair in a shampoo commercial. Its entry hardly stirred the cornstalks. A few more lionesses slunk into view beside it, the pride now in full force.

"Serious." The word hissed out of him.

The Reptar's purr deepened.

Was that a happy sound, the way a house cat purred when rubbing up against the furniture? Or was it the alien version of, *And now, human, I shall eat you?*

Something clicked behind Caleb.

"Did you just flip the safety off?"

"Yup." Simba didn't have the decency to sound guilty that he had armed the weapon which probably pointed in the vicinity of Caleb's head. "Don't move."

"Eh? What—"

Something zipped past his head right as one of the lionesses leaped.

A first gunshot echoed, followed by a second.

The leaping cat collapsed right behind Celine. The male lion roared before retreating. The others scattered, their passage marked by the rustling of leaves as they didn't try to silence their escape.

"Wah!" Caleb looked over his shoulder, shaking. "Serious?"

Simba smiled with the rifle still pressed to his shoulder. "Serious."

## Chapter Thirty-Eight

SIMBA WASN'T SURE IF HE SHOULD BE IMPRESSED OR
SCARED out of his wits.

Probably a bit — or a lot — of both.

Without a trace of fear or concern for life and limb, Trisha's kid
continued to casually lean against the alien, and the thing *let* her do it. No
teeth gnashing, hackles raised or whatever they did to show their displea-
sure. The Reptar lay there, its sides heaving with the labor of breathing.

Another emotion crept over him, one that surprised Simba more
than the sight of a little kid taming a wild alien beast: curiosity. He
might never have another opportunity to study one of the Reptars up
close.

The creature reminded him of a ridiculously large lion, but heavier. It wasn't just muscular; somehow it was more *dense*, as if the beast
wasn't actually made of the same sinew and muscle as Earth creatures. It had a solidity that suggested its composition included some
element not of this world.

Its skin, made of black, undulating scales, looked harder than any
lizard he'd ever seen. Simba squinted against the sun reflecting off
the scales. He could see the skin move.

It reminded him of the time he'd helped his father clear a field for planting. By himself in one corner of the field, he'd rolled aside a log and found a nest of black baby snakes underneath. Exposed to the light of day, the snakes squirmed and swirled in and out of each other's coils, acting as both individuals and a collective, their existence almost indistinguishable between the states.

This creature's skin reminded him of black snakes slithering in their nest. And his halfwit of a half-brother was babbling on about helping it.

Simba wasn't the eye-rolling type, but was prepared to make an exception. He grunted and took a step closer, wondering when — not if — the Reptar would attack.

Despite his middle name meaning lion — his father's drunken idea of a strong, manly name — Simba had little experience in handling wild animals. But he'd listened to the stories of the old men whenever visiting his father's village near the coast. Some of those stories were certainly exaggerated to the point of fantasy, but there were always grains of truth nested inside.

Of course, the animals in those stories had been from this planet, and these yellow glaring eyes were utterly alien. But predators were predators, and one thing was consistent. You never turned your back on them, or ran. Both made you look like prey.

Simba was many things, but *prey* wasn't one of them.

"Caleb, make yourself useful. See if you can get close to the kid. On my mark, grab her."

He expected the coward to protest. Hell, he was amazed Caleb hadn't turned tail already. Self-preservation was built into his half-brother's DNA along with a predilection for intoxicating substances. The fact his father's bastard child was still present … was unexpected.

"Yeah, yeah, don't spare the flattery," Caleb muttered and took a step toward Celine.

With the clearing free of lions, Simba shifted his rifle's sight to the

Reptar. Caleb had dared to shuffle closer and stood to one side of the girl, doing his best to tug her free of the alien.

Despite being a diminutive six-year-old, the girl was surprisingly strong. She resisted Caleb's physical and verbal efforts. Her grip on the Reptar's neck tightened, and she pressed her face into its scales.

Caleb glanced over his shoulder and wrapped both arms around Celine. His face was covered in an unhealthy sheen, and his eyes kept blinking. Still, his expression was determined. "A little help."

Simba tilted his head at Caleb in a silent salute to the unexpected courage. Their previous interactions had always left Simba disgruntled and wondering how they could be related, more often than not. Yet here his little brother stood adjacent to death incarnate, pushing through his fear and self-interest.

*Impressive. And if we survive this, I'll let him know.*

"Caleb, get ready to pick up Celine and run."

He huffed a laugh. "Bro, she's like a leech on this thing's neck. If I pick her up, the alien's coming with us."

Simba narrowed his eyes, stalking closer. "Then break her arm if you have to. Just get her away from that—"

*No.*

A line of sweat dribbled into Simba's eye, and he blinked it away. "What do you mean, no?"

Caleb's Adam's apple bobbed convulsively. "Wah! You can hear her, too. Am I right?"

Before Simba could process the strange statement, the alien's front legs collapsed. Its head flopped to the ground, and its eyelids flickered closed. The strange blue light pulsing from between its scales finally dimmed.

"What's happening?" Caleb asked.

Simba lowered himself to one knee and shouldered his rifle in case this was a ruse.

"Do I look like an alien expert?"

Despite the situation, Caleb dared to chuckle. "Nope. You look like an idiot."

*Help.*

Simba gritted his teeth. Was the stress finally getting to him? Were they all experiencing a group hallucination caused by the past week's insanity?

Maybe he'd inhaled too much of Caleb's joint.

Celine squirmed out of Caleb's arms and tucked herself between the alien's front legs. She stroked its muzzle, cuddled against its chest, her cheek resting against the side of its massive head.

"Celine," Simba whispered.

Her large eyes peered up at him. Her hands floated across that mouth full of rows of teeth. Then, shockingly, Celine smiled.

He'd never seen her smile like that. It made her face radiant.

"Yeah, isn't that amazing?" Caleb squatted and stared at Celine. "I wonder why she doesn't smile more often."

Simba eyed his brother, then Celine, who contentedly sat in danger's arms. What were they doing? And had he spoken out loud? Why else would Caleb respond like that, as if they were having a conversation?

Maybe Caleb had smoked one joint too many, because despite the man-shredding claws in striking distance, he sat cross-legged in front of the killer alien. He placed his elbows on his knees and cupped his chin.

Simba breathed past the burst of fear-induced adrenaline.

*Jesus, he's crazy. It's not a pet dog.*

Caleb laughed, his body convulsing with every fresh guffaw.

Simba flinched. "For Christ's sake, shut up."

Caleb laughed harder, the sound booming in echoes around them. He fell backwards and rolled on the ground, arms crossed as if hugging his ribs.

He ignored Simba's warning hiss, continuing to chuckle.

The alien's eyelids twitched but stayed closed.

Still giggling, Caleb rolled to his side, propped up his head with one hand and stared at Simba.

"'Course it's not a dog. Don't you get it, bro? This whole thing is crazy. That's why we have to help the alien."

## Chapter Thirty-Nine

IF HE EVER MADE IT OUT ALIVE, CALEB WOULD DEFI-
NITELY ask Samuel what was in that last batch of pot. Assuming
Madam Zahir didn't order Samuel to shoot him first.

Caleb pushed himself upright, rocking back and forth, scratching
his head and glancing between Celine, the Reptar and a confused
Simba. "We can't leave it here."

Caleb could almost feel Simba's denial of the truth.

"Sure, we can." The rifle dipped slightly, as if Simba was read-
justing his aim from the alien's head to its chest. "Maybe we should
shoot it. Put the thing out of its misery."

Still sitting on the ground, Caleb looked up to where his brother
still kneeled, the rifle pressed to his shoulder. "Aren't you feeling this?
She's not gonna leave it here. We need to help it."

"No. We don't. And the only thing I'm *feeling* is a need to get out
of here before the lions return. Or maybe some of this monster's
friends."

Caleb half-swiveled so he didn't have to kink his neck back.
"Don't be an ass. I know you can feel it. You can hear her, too, same
like I can. And if you say no, you are in denial."

Simba clenched his jaw. "And you are in a drug-induced delusion."

"Denial it is."

Celine's eyes twitched as she watched their volley. Then, as if she'd had enough of their indecision, she stood so abruptly that Simba jerked his rifle her way.

"Wah!" Caleb swiveled his hand a few times, as if removing an invisible lightbulb. A typical Kenyan gesture used to indicate, *What the hell?*

Simba swallowed hard and shifted his rifle to one side, redirecting it at the alien's big head.

Caleb rolled his eyes. "Dude, if that thing fires, you're as likely to hit Celine as you are the Reptar. And then, she'll be pissed."

Simba didn't so much as look at him or acknowledge the point. He stared at Celine instead. "Time to go, kid."

"She ain't going."

"She's a six-year-old who doesn't know any better. She probably inhaled some of your smoke, which would explain the situation. As usual, you mess everything up. Now, get on your feet, pick her up, and let's go."

*No.*

Caleb started to laugh when he heard Simba's teeth grinding against each other. Loud enough that the Reptar stirred with another effort to shake off the drugs.

"Told you, bro. We ain't leaving that thing here. Like it, hate it, tolerate it. Your choice, but we have to take it."

Again, that eerie, radiant smile graced the girl's petite face. Celine looked angelic.

Caleb tilted his head to one side. Maybe she was an angel. How else had they survived so far? An alien carnivore, a pride of lions, and yet here they were, still breathing, with every limb attached to its torso.

"Do you think she's an angel?"

Simba muttered something unsavory under his breath.

Caleb frowned. "Eh, not in front of the kid."

Simba eased up from his crouch, his every movement controlled. "Aren't you the model of a good father? Okay, genius. If we have to take this creature with us, how do we do it without getting eviscerated?"

Caleb shrugged and leaned back on his arms. "I never said I'm a genius. You're the smart one. You figure it out."

Celine stomped a foot, dragging their attention back to her. She patted the Reptar's head, satisfied. The beast inhaled, one eyelid peeling upward to reptilian yellow. It pushed itself into a sitting position, shaking its head and looking like the giant mutant offspring of a dog and a lizard.

Caleb stretched his legs and brushed bits of corn off of his pants. "Let's go."

"What do we do with it?"

The Reptar clacked its teeth.

Caleb frowned at his brother. "I think *it* is a *her*."

"How do you know it's a female?"

"I don't know. Maybe the sleek body."

Simba lowered his rifle and rolled his shoulders. "That doesn't mean anything. It could be a male. This is stupid."

Bending to the side, Caleb tilted his head. "Nope, no manly stuff underneath."

"Are you looking for its junk?"

Cackling, Caleb straightened and rested his hands behind him. "Yup. And there ain't nothing underneath. Maybe they lay eggs."

Simba shouldered his rifle strap, still eyeing the alien. "Lay eggs. And here I thought you couldn't get any dumber."

Caleb grinned. "Which proves you don't know everything. Reptiles lay eggs, don't they?"

Simba exhaled heavily. "It's not a reptile, Caleb. It's a *Reptar*."

"And we don't know squat about them. For all we know, it's an alien's version of a reptile that lays eggs. And if it lays eggs, that means it's a hen."

"It doesn't look like a hen."

Celine's head bobbed as if observing a tennis match. A confused frown formed between her eyebrows.

"Kid's right. We gotta move. Let's call her Spot."

The Reptar snarled.

"No? How about Grumpy?"

Its front limbs shook as the creature struggled to keep itself upright, lips peeling back to jagged teeth.

Caleb raised his hands. "Spot it is."

Simba scraped a hand down his face and said, "I'm surrounded by idiots."

## Chapter Forty

*OF ALL THE STUPID NAMES.*

That wasn't Simba's only thought, but even he had to censor the rest of it, especially if they were sharing thoughts.

*Which is impossible and isn't happening,* he tried to reassure himself. It didn't work.

This was beyond madness. Were they seriously going to help this creature?

Yet looking at Caleb, who had miraculously grown some courage, and Celine, whose backbone he never doubted, Simba knew the alien must be saved in order to fulfill his promise to Trisha.

"Fine. You want to adopt an alien? Then come help me." He chuckled as Caleb's face twisted into a sour expression. With one eye on the alien, he strolled over to his brother's side and reached down. "Come on. That beast isn't going to move itself."

"Herself." Caleb tilted his head back and grinned. "It's a she, remember?"

He clasped Simba's hand and for a moment — the few seconds between an inhale and an exhale — Simba could imagine how things could have been between them. Two brothers, facing the world together, having each other's back.

Except this was Caleb, and the only back he ever protected was his own. Simba had the scars to prove it.

Yanking Caleb up, he pulled away his hand and studied the alien. Not surprisingly, the creature returned the favor, its yellow eyes unblinking. "You first."

Caleb waggled his eyebrows. "Age before beauty, bro."

*If a little girl can stand next to that thing, it can't be that bad.*

Except Simba knew it could be. He could see the evidence ripped into the skin of the lioness Spot had killed earlier. Those claws weren't for decoration. Still, the creature seemed too wounded and drugged up to do more than blink maliciously at them.

Simba shouldered his rifle and circled the beast until he was approaching from one side. Caleb mirrored him on the other. Celine stepped in front of them and peered at one of them and then the other, as if she too was curious about their intentions.

Simba kept his hand firm, free from any trembling that might reveal his fears. He reached out and stroked the creature's back. The scales felt as he imagined they should, like a python, smooth and cool to the touch. Yet despite their hardness, there was somehow a softness, as if the creature was constantly shifting between friendly puppy and lethal killer.

Simba nodded at Caleb and pressed up close. Wrapped one arm under Spot's neck and reached the other around its back. Despite his size, his arm couldn't reach the bottom of the creature's belly. Caleb mirrored his actions until they were almost cheek to cheek.

Caleb cackled. "Ain't this cozy?"

"Not the word I would've used. Ready?"

Together, they tugged the creature to its feet. Simba was under no delusion; the only way they were moving Spot anywhere was if the alien wanted to move.

Snarling and hissing, it complied. It staggered out of the cornfield with their help, one painful step at a time. Simba's face was covered in a sheen of sweat by the time they reached their gate, T-shirt clinging to his back and under his arms.

Celine continued to stay next to Spot's toothy muzzle, matching their stride and leading them forward. Apparently unconcerned by the oddity of their situation.

"We need to open the gate. Spot can't fit through the door."

Celine skipped ahead and through the open door before Caleb could reply. One side of the gate creaked open a moment later.

"Caleb, help Celine open the back of the horse trailer," Simba ordered, blinking away beads of sweat from his eyes.

The kid tilted her head, staring at Simba as if questioning the decision.

Spot wavered on its legs, about to collapse in the driveway.

Simba grunted with the effort of holding the neck up. "It'll be comfortable there. I promise. But we can't have it wandering the compound, for its own safety."

*Because if I find it wandering around, I'll shoot it.*

*Her. Whatever.*

Shrugging, Celine followed Caleb as he opened the trailer's rear gate and lowered the ramp. After some pushing, shoving, grunting and softly muttered curses, they managed to settle Spot in the trailer. The alien turned until it faced the entrance before collapsing. The yellow in its eyes dimmed, and its eyelids quivered shut.

Caleb and Simba retreated.

Once outside, they stared at the sleeping alien.

Caleb glanced at him. "You really think this will hold her?"

Simba gripped the butt of his rifle. "For its sake, I hope so." He swung the back of the trailer closed.

Celine was tugging on Caleb's arm and pointing to the garden faucet.

Simba nodded at the girl with a smirk. "It's good to see there's at least one woman in the world who can control you."

Caleb snorted a laugh but smiled. "Hilarious."

"Once you're done, bring her inside." His eyes cut sideways to stare at the trailer. "I don't want you guys out here when that thing wakes up."

Caleb gave him a mock salute before following Celine to the faucet. "Yes, sir. Celine, let's get a bucket first. Okay?"

Exhaling heavily, Simba left them to deal with the alien while he wandered inside the house. He stepped into the hallway and a tingling started up his back.

It was silent. Too silent. While Trisha and Mama Noah weren't bosom buddies, he would expect at least some clatter from the kitchen, the whistling kettle or running faucet as the maid washed another batch of dishes. *Something.*

Instead, the house felt empty.

"Trisha?" One hand drifted down to the rifle at his side while the other brushed the wall. He reached the kitchen doorway and saw her standing in the far corner. "Are you okay?"

He took one step inside.

Cold metal pushed against his temple.

Everything slowed down. Simba saw Trisha wipe away tears. Nearby, Mama Noah sported a blossoming bruise under one eye. A large African woman, her arms almost as beefy as his, stared at him with mild interest. Something about her felt off.

He twirled around, lifting his arm up for a block. His forearm connected with the man holding a gun. Knocking the weapon arm to one side freed up space for Simba's other fist to connect with his assailant's nose.

Garbled curses spilled out over the mouth along with blood from his nostrils.

Gripping the gun arm, Simba's hand slid down the arm, grabbed the wrist and twisted it painfully. The other man's grip loosened enough that Simba could wrench the gun from his hand.

As he spun around and lifted it toward the strange woman, something heavy smashed against the back of his head. Stunned, Simba stumbled forward, still lifting the gun.

The woman's lips, painted bright red, rose in a mocking smile.

Another assailant latched onto his arms and tugged them

painfully back. The first one, his nose still bleeding profusely, cursed again and viciously drove a fist into Simba's stomach.

He doubled over, groaning, and dropped the gun.

His two assailants forced Simba to his knees, then one of them tied his wrists behind him with twine. The strange woman paced around the island counter, pausing just in front of him. His vision was filled with her shoes peeking out from beneath her long, black skirt.

A hand slipped in front of him. Long colored nails, the same red as her lips. Like talons, they dug under his chin and lifted his head until he met her dark gaze.

"You must be Simba. Caleb has told me so much about you." She leaned closer. "Is your brother here?"

Simba gawked at her, but why was he surprised? Typical Caleb, getting into trouble and then running away, leaving him holding the bag.

"Half-brother, actually. And you are?"

The woman continued to study him. Simba tried not to look at Trisha, to give away the depth of his terror at what might happen to her if this was who he thought it probably was. Once Caleb realized they had unwanted visitors, he'd sneak away and never return, leaving them to face the wrath of his gang.

The woman dropped her hand and stepped back, satisfied. "I'm Madam Zahir. Now, *where's Caleb?*"

## Chapter Forty-One

"AND THIS IS WHY I LEFT THE FARM." CALEB PAUSED and lowered the bucket to his feet. Water sloshed over the edge and pattered on his shoes. He scowled at his damp sneakers and kicked at the bucket. "That, and my father. Drunken bastard. Only good thing about him was his collection of Disney movies. All pirated, of course. He was a fan. Of Disney, not pirates."

He glanced up into Celine's calm eyes. She was as unimpressed with his cussing as she was with everything else. He wasn't used to such a quiet child, but he liked how she didn't react to his stupidity or judge him. At least, not that he knew.

Now that he thought about it, she was the only one who accepted him as he was, dreadlocks, drugs and all. Simba was always telling him to get a haircut and sober up. He'd been sober on a few occasions and it was supremely overrated.

He winked at her with a grin. She tilted her head slightly to the side, then turned to face the horse trailer. He couldn't see the Reptar, but could certainly hear its rumbling snores and the occasional purr.

Caleb grunted and lifted the bucket, hoping Spot would stay asleep longer. Who knew how the creature would react once the drugs wore off.

"Ready?"

Celine nodded and stood on her tiptoes, helping him open the back gate. Caleb pushed the bucket inside, withdrew his hands before he lost them, then eased it closed.

He dramatically wiped a hand across his brow and exhaled heavily. "Close one. Am I right?"

Celine stared at him without expression.

"Yeah, you're probably right. I'm full of crap, but at least it's funny crap. Not like my brother. Now that's a guy who really is a pain in the …" He glanced at the house, almost expecting Trisha to storm out. If she caught him talking to her daughter in any way that resembled vulgarity …

Caleb crossed his arms and leaned against the trailer. "I'm not that bad of an influence. Am I?" He scratched between his dreadlocks. "If not for my joint, Spot here would've shredded us to pieces."

He straightened, pulling back his shoulders and puffing out his chest. "One day, they'll make a movie out of me. You just watch, kid. Stick close and I'll make sure you're in it. Well, not *you*, specifically. But someone will play your part. Although I'll probably make her talk. A character who never talks doesn't really work in a movie. You need dialogue and witty repartee. Nothing personal. Maybe the actor will be closer to my age. Romance always sells. Or is it sex?"

He shrugged and started to meander toward the house. "Anyway, I'll make sure it's at least PG-13, so you can watch it."

Something brushed by his hand. When he looked down, Celine slipped her hand into his.

"Cool. So you agree. But there won't be a Simba in my movie. Or if there is, he's the villain. A pompous, arrogant and really stupid bad guy."

Celine smiled, and somehow, that made Caleb feel that the world was maybe not quite so bad after all.

He was still feeling good about himself as he strolled into the house, hand in hand with Celine. All was right with the world until he heard a scarily familiar voice.

"I'm Madam Zahir," it said. "Now, *where's Caleb?*"

## Chapter Forty-Two

*WE'RE ALL GOING TO DIE.*

Mama Noah eyed the machete hovering near her throat, held by a man with blackened teeth. His vicious grin was enough to keep her quiet and in a submissive posture. She couldn't bring herself to meet his yellowed eyes for more than a second. The alien creature hadn't scared her nearly as much.

But animals didn't strip a woman with its eyes the way this thug was doing.

A second man gripped her arm. While she wasn't short, the hulk looming by her side made her feel small in more ways than one.

Disturbing as those two were, they only inspired fear rather than limb-quaking terror. That honor was reserved for the gang's leader now stalking the kitchen.

Mama Noah glanced sideways at Trisha. The white woman was in shock, her mouth agape, eyes glazed as she stared at the gun-wielding thug. Three other men lounged against the counters, casually flicking their weapons this way and that.

In contrast, the leader, Madam Zahir, held no weapon. And yet, Mama Noah felt in the core of her being that this was the truly dangerous one in the group. She could tell by the predatory eyes, her swagger, the total lack of humanity in her pudgy face, the general vibe wafting from her pores. Mama Noah had seen that exact set of features only once in her life, tucked inside a memory the Elders had shared with her, and she prayed daily to never see them again.

*It seems God isn't answering prayers today. We should have left when the ships arrived.*

Why had she waited? Why had she listened to the mzungu and her foolish zombie theory?

Her chin fell to her chest as Zahir strolled up to Mama Noah. Her nose wrinkled with the other woman's scent, a harsh mixture of kerosene, sweat and copper. Her eyes twitched from side to side, searching for the weapon that Zahir must surely have, probably a knife dripping with the blood of her most recent victim.

There was no weapon, no blood, just the overwhelming presence of a woman not to be trifled with.

"Where is Caleb?"

Mama Noah swallowed hard. Where, indeed? She'd known he was trouble from the moment she saw his dreadlocks and bloodshot eyes. A more pressing question weighed on her, though. Where was Celine? And although she thought Caleb would be the world's worst guardian, she silently prayed Celine was with him, hopefully running away.

"There is nowhere he can run."

Gasping, Mama Noah dared to look up into Madam Zahir's cold, hard gaze.

She smiled and somehow twisted her softness into a lethal expression. "We found him here. We will find him again. But surely, he wouldn't abandon his family." She swiveled to face Simba, now kneeling on the floor. "Or would he?"

Simba coughed, a bloody welt forming on the side of his head. "Oh yes, he would."

Zahir's laugh was gilded with the joy of bloodlust. The sound caused every hair on Mama Noah's neck to quiver.

"Hmm. That doesn't surprise me much. He's a runner." Zahir

drifted away. "Hyena, leave that woman alone. *She's* not a runner. She can barely walk."

The yellow-eyed man lowered his machete with a cackle and took a step back. Mama Noah exhaled and sagged against the fridge door, although it was hard to say which was more a relief: not having a blade to her neck or not having the madam so close.

Zahir tapped her nails against the island counter. "I do like a hunt, though. This should be fun." Her fingers brushed over Celine's drawings, and she paused.

In morbid fascination, Mama Noah watched as, for the briefest of moments, Zahir's expression flickered between surprise, curiosity and unease.

*It's just the doodles of a child*, Mama Noah thought, but her fear for Celine deepened with every passing second Zahir remained fixated on the drawings.

When Zahir lifted one of the papers and studied it intently, Mama Noah's breathing became more erratic. If a heart could gasp, hers was definitely panting.

Sweat trickled between her breasts. She wanted to scream, "Stay away from that child. She's just a little girl, no matter how strange." But her tongue was heavy and swollen in her mouth. Her throat parched.

Zahir sifted through the papers and retrieved one covered with dots and circles. She slowly spun in a circle, holding the drawing aloft. "Who drew this?"

Her black eyes cut sideways to where Simba knelt, then dismissed him immediately. She half-turned to stare at Mama Noah. "You?" She scoffed. "No, of course not. I doubt you have the creativity or insight to select a crayon, never mind draw this."

Wishing she was back in the cornfield with lions and aliens, Mama Noah's eyes betrayed them all, cutting sideways to Trisha. Then her head fell and she stared at the tiles.

Too late. Zahir spun around and stared at Trisha. "I don't see you as the artistic type. Who else is here?"

Trisha swallowed hard, and Mama Noah could hear the gulp, an admission of knowledge or guilt to any ear.

Zahir stepped toward Trisha with a smile. "I'm not a patient woman. Who drew this?"

The fridge hummed, and the living room clock kept ticking the seconds.

*Tick ... Tock ... Tick ... Tock ... Ti—*

The heavy slap of skin meeting skin cracked the silence. Mama Noah watched as Trisha stumbled to the side, gripping the counter for balance.

"Leave her alone!" Simba was abruptly cut off by Hyena, who punched him in the throat, then kicked him to the floor, all while grinning like a maniac.

Trisha straightened up and wiped a hand across her mouth, clearing the drop of blood that had formed at the corner. "She's not here."

Mama Noah sharply shook her head at Trisha, silently willing her to say nothing. Did Trisha believe Caleb could keep the girl safe? Mama Noah could smell the danger oozing off this group. And that woman, Zahir, she wouldn't stop because of Celine's tender age. The gang wouldn't be satisfied, no matter what Trisha gave them.

She blinked her eyes, trying to get Trisha's attention. Why couldn't the foolish woman see? It didn't matter if they answered all of Zahir's questions and gave her whatever she asked for. Mama Noah had stared into the gangster's eyes and seen their future.

*We're all dead. Let the girl survive, even if she's raised by a drug head.*

Madam Zahir stepped into Trisha's space, looming over her, staring until Trisha flinched and looked away. Her back was against the counter next to the sink, with no place to go.

Zahir's voice lowered into a purr. "Tell me more."

Trisha stuttered, "She's not here. She traveled with her father to Geneva."

The lie twanged in the room so loudly that Zahir actually

laughed. She held aloft an index finger and wagged it back and forth. "Tsk, tsk, tsk. No. I don't think so. Your child drew these? How old?"

On the floor on the other side of the counter, Simba grunted. The top of his head appeared as he tried to stand. The thug behind him, a hard-looking youth with an abstract tattoo on the side of his neck, slapped him down and pressed a gun to the back of his head.

"Young, is she?" Zahir asked, still not moving from her position in front of Trisha. "She must be. Interesting." Zahir stepped back and spun on her heel, sauntering toward Simba. "As fascinating as this is—" she held up the piece of paper with the dots and circles, "—I'm much more interested in Caleb."

Simba spat. Mama Noah wrinkled her face in disgust. Then again, they'd be lucky if his saliva was the only substance hitting the floor today.

"What do you want with him?"

Zahir stared down at Simba, her profile revealing nothing. "He stole something from me. No one steals from me."

Mama Noah closed her eyes and cursed the minute Caleb had pushed his way inside. She'd known. The dreadlocks, the bloodshot eyes, the whiff of drugs …

In the stillness between an inhale and an exhale, between the tick and the tock of the living room clock, a distant squeak scraped against the air.

Zahir's head jerked up, and she stared out the kitchen entrance toward the living room. Tilting her head to the side, she stared at the tattooed man with the gun.

"That sounds like a gate. Why, Samuel, I believe we've found Caleb."

## Chapter Forty-Three

*"I'M MADAM ZAHIR. NOW WHERE'S CALEB?"*

Caleb pressed his back against the wall, certain they could hear him. His heartbeat galloped between his ears like a stampeding wildebeest, his breath coming in constricted wheezes.

A little hand squeezed his fingers. He glanced down to see Celine standing in the middle of the hallway. A small crease between her fair eyebrows the only indication she was aware there might be something wrong. But in her face, the subtle change was enough.

*Thank God she's mute.*

He pulled her into his embrace, not because he thought she needed a hug but to get her out of sight. Trying not to breathe too loudly, he sidled toward the door, pulling the little girl with him.

She didn't resist; neither did she attempt to stay out of sight. Fortunately, no one bothered to poke a head out of the kitchen doorway to check on his drumming heart. If they had, they would've seen him, and Caleb knew what he would do if that happened. He wasn't proud about it, but then again, he had done nothing in his life to make anyone proud, least of all himself.

He'd drop Celine and run.

Maybe they'd go easy on her. Maybe not. But no way would he allow someone else's kid to slow him down.

When he was certain no one could see them, he pushed away from the wall and scurried to the doorway. He was about to leave, but his eyes fell on a key hanging on a hook near the door. For the Land Cruiser.

He rolled his eyes heavenward, silently thanking whatever God looked after intoxicated fools, palmed the key and stepped outside.

He stared between the Land Cruiser and the gate. Would they hear the vehicle's alarm if he pressed the button to unlock the doors? Or should he open the gate first? Since Spot had broken one of the swinging arms, he'd have to do it manually and hope the squeaky hinge wasn't as loud as he remembered it to be. On the other hand, the Land Cruiser sounded like a cranky old man belching out a hacking cough caused by too many years of chain-smoking.

He approached the driver's side and eyed the distance to the gate. The driveway wasn't long, but somehow, the gate seemed far away.

"Crap." Caleb rubbed a hand over his head. He squeezed his eyes half-shut and pressed the vehicle's button.

In the silence, the sound of the alarm disengaging and the door locks clicking open crashed against him.

His back tensed in anticipation. At any minute, Zahir's thugs would charge out of the house, guns blazing. They'd tackle him to the ground, truss him up like a pig and slowly roast him over a fire.

Nothing happened.

"Thank the god of fools," he whispered and scooped Celine into his arms. He opened the door and pushed her across the front seat to the passenger side. He hesitated next to the vehicle.

The Land Cruiser was an antique, with an internal combustion engine and a manual drive. And while self-driving, automatic, automated, talkative vehicles had taken over the streets of urban centers around the world, Kenya still hosted a large fleet of belching, polluting, ancient vehicles that still required a driver. Where else would

Europe and North America dump their unwanted cars before upgrading to the latest and greatest?

And for this, Caleb was grateful.

Leaning into the vehicle, he disengaged the handbrake, checked that the vehicle was in neutral, and pushed it toward the gate. Counting on more luck, he hoped the heavy beast would roll down the slight, sloping incline.

A few steps later, the vehicle's weight began to work with him, rather than against him. He pulled himself into the driver's seat and braked when the back of the trailer nearly touched the gate. Engaging the handbrake, he exhaled. His eyes flicked up to the rearview, but all he saw was the horse trailer. A small window was cut into the trailer so he could see the top of Spot's back. The spine moved slightly as the alien continued to enjoy a drug-induced sleep.

"Stay here."

He stepped out and peered back toward the house. No thugs ran out. No guns blazed. Just another normal day in post-invasion suburbia.

He tiptoed to the gate and disengaged the latches of the swinging arms. Caleb expected a bullet to thud into his back at any moment, but he pushed one side of the gate outward anyway. He remembered the lions and Reptars. Those beasts would be easier to handle than Madam Zahir.

But fortune still smiled on him; the dirt road was empty of other lifeforms.

With one side of the gate opened completely, he returned to the center and started on the other side. Every few heartbeats, he glanced compulsively toward the house. The doorway yawned open, showing only darkness. Three more steps, two more steps …

The gate squealed in protest as he pushed it into its final resting place. With shaking hands, Caleb trotted to the driver side of the Land Cruiser.

Maybe this would work. Maybe he could get away. And Trisha would thank him for looking after Celine, for saving her child from

Madam Zahir. Heck, he was practically the hero in the situation. Again.

If he wasn't so sick with anxiety, his stomach burping bile into his throat, he would've smiled. As it was, he allowed himself to breathe deeply, until he saw Samuel exit the house.

Breathless, Caleb met Samuel's calculating stare. Time shifted and slowed. Samuel's mouth opened with exaggerated slowness, a distorted word rolling out of his mouth. His arm lifted, a handgun at the end of it.

Caleb's legs felt heavy and rooted to the ground. Ignoring them, he grabbed the steering wheel with both hands and forced his eyes to look anywhere but at the gun drifting his way.

Freedom beckoned outside the gate. *So* close. He could taste it in his mouth, feel it in his hands.

Bellowing wordlessly, he pulled himself up and slid his butt onto the seat. Risking his arm, he reached out and yanked the door closed. He knew what awaited him if he failed.

Samuel ran toward him, gun now fully lifted and trained on his body. Madam Zahir appeared behind him, dark eyes glowing with the malevolence only she could produce.

His sideview mirror exploded. Shards of glass tinkled against the window.

Fumbling with the key, Caleb finally managed to push it in. "Please work, please work, please work."

You never knew with these antiques. They were glorious when they worked and a death trap when they didn't.

The engine turned, coughing and spluttering in protest at the urgency of his foot mashing down on the pedals. He released the handbrake, pushed the vehicle into reverse, and slammed on the accelerator.

His head jerked forward as the vehicle shot back through the gate with a fishtailing trailer. He pushed into first and pressed again on the pedal. Maybe he'd never stopped. The vehicle's slug-gishness reminded him they were pulling a lot of weight behind them. The horse trailer with the sleeping Reptar resisted the need for speed.

Cursing his luck — it was usually terrible — Caleb yanked on the wheel and straightened the tires. As the Land Cruiser rolled forward, the side window faced the driveway. Samuel was almost at the gate, aiming his gun at him.

"Heads down," Caleb shouted and led by example. The gun fired, but miraculously, Samuel missed.

Second gear.

The old diesel engine revved, and the Land Cruiser picked up speed despite its weight. Caleb's brain went into monkey mode, jumping from thought to thought.

How did Madam Zahir find out where he was? Where were her vehicles? How many people did she have? How long before they would chase after him, never giving up until they caught him?

*Go back.*

"Not going to happen." He glanced at Celine, who was huddled against the passenger door, staring at him, mouth open in a parody of shock. "Put your seatbelt on, kid. Didn't your mother teach you anything?"

Third gear.

*Go back.*

More gunshots snapped around them. But something else larger roared immediately behind him.

He glanced up at the rearview mirror and met Spot's dazed but hostile gaze.

## Chapter Forty-Four

"STOP SCREAMING IN MY HEAD!" CALEB YELLED AS THE REPTAR snarled.

*Go back. Go back. Go. Back!*

Except the voice in his head wasn't exactly using words; it was more sensations of outrage, fear, desperation and the image of a stop sign. Caleb had actually never seen a stop sign in Nairobi, and he assumed Celine was pushing a memory from some other part of the world.

Like a leaping antelope, the trailer bucked behind the Land Cruiser, bouncing up and down, then from one side to the other as Spot the Reptar went ballistic.

Gritting his teeth, Caleb hunched over the steering wheel as if expecting a large, claw-tipped paw to burst through the back window at any second and swipe off his head. Maybe a bullet would pierce through the layers of metal to thud into his back.

And if none of those things happened? Celine was definitely going to detonate his mind, leaving his head like an overly ripe papaya on the side of the road. Maybe roadkill was more apt, with all the gooey liquids.

A bullet pinged off the side of his door, and he instinctively checked the sideview mirror. The tattered remains reminded him there was no mirror to look at. He glanced up at the rearview and met Spot's furious, bright-blue glare.

"God, why me?" he wailed.

Spot hissed and slammed her head against the narrow opening at the front of the trailer. Despite having the length of the Land Cruiser and a couple layers of metal between him and the alien, Caleb didn't feel particularly safe.

He titled his head to the other side and stared at the sideview mirror closest to Celine. A motorcycle zoomed into view, one of those fancy new ones that all but floated above the ground and could almost drive themselves. Silent, electric, and far faster than a Land Cruiser hauling a trailer weighted down with God knows how many tons of furious alien.

Groaning, Caleb faced forward. "I'm dead, I'm dead. I'm *definitely* going to die today."

*Way to go with the positive self talk, Caleb.*

His inner voice sounded suspiciously like Simba giving him a lecture. "I'm fine. Bugger off."

Celine's voice, accompanied by flashing images, wailed in his head. His vision blurred for a moment as the potholed road turned and sloped downhill.

He blindly reached an arm across and smacked at where he thought her face was. His palm brushed her nose, then slid over her mouth. "Quiet, kid. For a mute retard, you sure are loud."

Another roar filled the vehicle, and his head ached with the effort of staying on the road. That was another option: death by car accident.

"Yeah, and if I'm really lucky, the engine will explode, and we'll all die instantly."

But Caleb knew he wasn't *that* lucky.

The start of a headache needled at him. He scowled, squinting at the road. "Where's a joint when you need it? Am I right?"

Celine continued to mind-scream, from hers into his.

He took the curve down the steep hill, and glanced at the far rearview. The trailer wasn't following the curve. Instead, it glided toward the far side of the road, threatening to tip them all over.

Cursing in Swahili — only because he really didn't know any good swearwords in English, if there even was such a thing — Caleb fought with the steering wheel and prayed to the god of idiots and thieves to protect him.

A second motorcycle whispered up to the driver's side, and the rider lifted a gun. But the nozzle wasn't aimed at Caleb's head. Instead, the rider was pointing at the tire.

*She wants me alive.*

The thought brought zero relief. Instead, cold terror chilled the blood in his veins, oozing through him like iced sludge. His stomach clenched, pushing up acidic bile that burned his throat.

Without thinking — *Hey, what else is new?* — Caleb veered the Land Cruiser toward the motorcycle, ignoring the screeching tires as the trailer tried to keep up.

He met the rider's wide eyes. The man's mouth opened in warning, but size won the day. The motorcycle went flying off the road and into the bushes.

Wrenching the wheel again, Caleb straightened the Land Cruiser and stared at the rapidly approaching bottom of the hill. The road curved sharply around and upward. They would only make it to the top of the hill with momentum. That meant no slowing down, and definitely no stopping.

"Guess that means no running anyone over," he reminded himself. "Because that would definitely slow us down."

Celine kicked her little shoes against the dashboard.

A swarm of bullets. A volley of outraged roars. More shaking and bouncing. Screams filled his head, and not just Celine's.

Caleb snapped his mouth shut so hard, he bit the tip of his tongue. More curses.

He pushed his foot on the accelerator, and the engine whined with the effort of keeping up.

Fifth gear. Finally.

And then, the inevitable happened.

Spot must have realized the horse trailer's back gate only covered two-thirds of the opening. With a final snarl, she twirled around and all Caleb could see in the rearview was the beast's backside as she attempted to push herself between the top of the gate and the roof.

His eyes cut sideways and met Celine's frown. "I blame this on you. Just so you know, kid. This is all on you. You're welcome."

The Land Cruiser picked up speed, its frame vibrating with every bump, hole and stone on the rough road. He had no idea if the antique was supposed to be driven so fast. The technology was ancient, outdated and explosive compared to modern options.

Clinging to the wheel and hoping he wasn't about to get swallowed in bullets or flames, Caleb steered the Land Cruiser toward the curve and eyed the top of the hill, willing the wheels to maintain their momentum. His eyes twitched up at the rearview mirror.

The trailer was empty.

"Where'd she go? Celine, where's Spot? Where—"

Spot's paw punched through the window in the back of the Land Cruiser, raining glass along the luggage compartment and back seat. The force of the attack loosened the door which swung open to a mass of inky black fury with blue light glowing between the scales. Claws sprouted out of her oversized paws, limbs coiled in on themselves.

The hissing Reptar squeezed into the luggage compartment, half her body draped over the back seat, and stretched a limb toward Caleb's head.

Glancing at Celine, he shouted, "Hey, we're friends. Remember? Control your pet. I mean, who's gonna give you your first joint if I'm dead? You owe me. Am I right? Damn it, kid!"

Hot breath hissed against the back of Caleb's head and neck.

Tears coursed down his cheeks, mingling with sweat and snot. He didn't bother trying to wipe any of it off. What was the point?

*This is it. This is how the great Caleb dies. Man, all I wanted was a quiet room and a lifetime supply of pot. Is that too much to ask?*

Celine's soft mind-voice murmured, *It's okay.*

"It bloody well isn't, Celine! It's as far from okay as we can get right now, and that's pretty damn far. In fact, on a scale of one to ten, one being hell and ten being angelic hosts and harp crap, this would be a negative one hundred, Celine. You'd literally freeze. It's that cold. And I may be an idiot from the slums, but I know about cold. I was once locked inside a freezer. So no, Celine. It definitely is *not* okay."

Pouting, Celine squirmed against her seatbelt and reached out a hand to latch onto Spot. Its purr was a death rattle. But the Reptar withdrew its claws, so that was progress.

The front tires hit a speed bump near the bottom of the hill. Momentum and oversized tires kept the antique from losing its chassis.

*Who the hell puts speed bumps on a road like this?* Caleb thought just as the trailer, practically weightless now, went airborne. It crashed back down, then lurched forward and trembled, its frame shaking with the effort of holding itself together.

As the road curved, Caleb willed the vehicle to … Not. Flip. Over.

Groaning, the antique strained to round the curve, and Caleb's cheek pressed against the window while he glared at the upcoming hill. He swore he felt one side of the vehicle lift, but not enough to tip them. They rounded the curve, all four wheels still on the ground.

The trailer wasn't so fortunate.

With a loud squealing of metal and rubber, the trailer twisted to the side and yanked hard on its tether to the Land Cruiser.

Caleb's head jerked back and forth, but he didn't lift his foot from the accelerator. They couldn't afford to slow down.

*Damn antique.*

*Damn trailer.*

*Damn everything.*

Another motorcycle zoomed up to Celine's window. Or was it the first rider? How many did Zahir bring?

Another one snuck up on his side and veered toward him, the black-toothed grin widening. Cackling his hyena laugh, Hyena lifted a crowbar and smacked the driver window.

Caleb howled. "Serious?"

A web of cracks spiked across the window as Hyena continued to pummel the glass.

On the other side, the rider's expression was wary, as if expecting Caleb to swerve toward the bike. Maybe he should. But he couldn't take out both. Besides, momentum.

Running over bodies would slow them down.

"Right," he said between wheezing breaths. "So don't slow down."

He gulped down air, wondering why he was panting by just sitting there. He floored the accelerator and aimed for the hilltop. He'd be thrilled to reach it in one piece.

And if they managed to make the ninety-degree left at the top of the hill, he'd give his second-to-last pouch of pot to Celine and Spot.

Or maybe they all could share it.

He could give them a few puffs. That was still generous.

Spot's rattling intake of breath reminded Caleb he was one claw away from decapitation.

The hissing Reptar withdrew until her toothy snout was no longer right behind his head. In one smooth, slinking move, she retreated, turned and clambered out of the opening in the back. A breath later, the vehicle shuddered as something landed on the roof.

Without thinking, his eyes rolled up to the ceiling, and he swore he saw the roof bend in slightly from the weight of some impossible creature clinging to the top. "Serious?"

The side window crackled in warning before breaking into chunks of glass. Caleb took his eyes off the road and met Hyena's yellow stare.

"You're dead, Caleb," Hyena shouted against the wind and grinned wide to show his blackened teeth.

"And you're ugly, but eh! I don't hold that against you."

*Hey, fake it 'til you make it. Am I right?*

Hyena's grin turned into a snarl, and he fumbled with his crowbar.

Caleb fought with the steering wheel as the vibrations of the antique and the rough road made control that much harder. He didn't dare try to swerve into the bike. The movement was as likely to send them off the road as anything else. Besides, he couldn't afford to slow down. They had to reach the top, then figure out his next move once he got there.

Cackling and sounding very much like the animal he'd been named after, Hyena lifted the crowbar. "Nighty night, Caleb. Oh, Madam Zahir is going to—"

Caleb never found out what Madam Zahir had planned, because Hyena was rudely interrupted. In between one word and the next, his head landed in Caleb's lap.

Caleb stared down at the blackened teeth, yellowed eyes, and leering grin that still lingered on the decapitated head. A scream filled the Land Cruiser, and when Caleb realized it was his, he didn't have the wherewithal to stop.

The motorcycle continued to keep pace for a few moments while the headless body gripped the handholds as if it hadn't quite realized that its control center had been brutally removed. Then, as if grudgingly admitting to the truth, the body sagged.

The bike tilted to one side and collapsed.

"Oh God, oh God, oh God," Caleb stuttered, his gaze locked onto Hyena's as blood dribbled out of the tattered neck and onto his pants.

Spot stuck her snout through the broken window and snarled.

Adrenaline dumped into Caleb's system, and he jerked his head up, staring straight ahead at anything but the head in his lap.

"Dammit, Spot. Now there's blood all over the leather. Do you know who's going to have to clean that up? Take a wild guess."

Spot hissed, then pulled away. A couple of thumps echoed from above. Long claws dug into the window frames on either side, a reminder of exactly who was in charge here.

Wearily, Caleb dropped his chin down and to the side to make sure Celine was still in one piece.

She stared back at him and shrugged.

The remaining rider gawked at Hyena's head before braking hard and disappearing from view.

A moment later, they summited the hill.

## Chapter Forty-Five

THE WOMEN WERE EASY TO HANDLE. THE MAN WAS ANOTHER story.

Madam Zahir was wary as she studied him. Even on his knees, there was an indomitable force about him, a ferocity he disguised with a façade of calm, detached coolness.

But Zahir saw through those kinds of masks because energy couldn't be so easily hidden. The man was a dangerous warrior. Even if he didn't want to embrace this truth about himself, she could see it.

Satisfied that Samuel could manage the man for now, she gazed around the kitchen, her nostrils flaring. The Kenyan woman — most likely the maid, judging from her modest clothes and humble demeanor — hadn't moved an inch. She huddled in front of the fridge, her posture screaming surrender.

The white woman wasn't as easy to fathom. Shocked, probably. Afraid, definitely. But there was a determined light in her eyes, one that could only come from the love of a mother for her child.

Timothy, the great hulking brute with no brains, stood between the two of them, staring idly around the room. Zahir snorted to herself. He was such a stereotype.

Despite the urgent need to find Caleb — a task Hyena and his posse would accomplish or suffer her wrath — Zahir couldn't resist the lure of the drawings. Who had drawn them?

Not wanting to admit, even to herself, just how important they may be, Zahir paced around the island counter. Despite her best intentions, her gaze continued to betray her, cutting sideways to the drawing of the dots and circles.

*How is this possible?*

The question plucked at her nerves and thrummed through her mind. As far as she knew, there were only two types of people who knew enough to draw that exact configuration. The one type had forgotten about her; the other type no longer existed.

But that was all about to change, now that the aliens had returned. There'd be a new wave. And when that happened …

They'd come for her.

But without her pendant …

Suppressing a shudder and pointedly ignoring Samuel's questioning expression, Zahir forced herself to move past the island to the far end of the kitchen.

Her back tingled from all those staring eyes.

She swiveled around and leaned against a closet door to strike a casual pose. Now she could see everyone at once, the frozen tableau of shock, fear, determination, potential violence.

She inhaled these emotions as if they were the elixir of life. And for her, they were.

Smiling, knowing full well how others perceived that harsh, predatory quirk of her mouth, Zahir dramatically sighed. "Cozy, isn't it? So where shall we begin? Names. I've introduced myself. Now it's your turn."

An engine revved out on the road, tires squealing in the effort to escape. As much as she despised the little thief, she grudgingly admired Caleb. Who else would have the balls to steal from her?

*Or perhaps the lack of brains to know better.*

That was more like it.

She stared down at the warrior, seeing the potential for violence lurking beneath his calm disposition. "Do they know?"

That got everyone's attention. The white woman jerked her head up and gave Zahir a hard stare, as if trying to penetrate the true meaning of her words.

Zahir almost laughed. But that would've really terrified everyone, so she held it back. Terror had its place, but right now she wanted to learn.

The warrior eyed her, his features revealing glimpses of inner conflict.

"Don't be shy. Tell them," Zahir cooed, waving an arm to encompass the kitchen. "Tell them what you really are, and what you're truly capable of doing."

The white woman cleared her throat. "Simba, what is she talking about?"

"Does it matter?" Simba retorted, his eyes narrowing as he continued to hold Zahir's stare. "Maybe we should be asking why she's here, and what she plans to do to Caleb and ..."

He was smart enough to bite the end of his sentence.

Zahir smiled at the white woman. "Did Caleb take your child?"

Eyes widened as the woman gulped. That unique blend of fear and determination came back into her eyes. "She's a little girl. Please, take what you want but leave her alone."

*So predictable.*

This was exactly why Zahir had never allowed herself to breed. Offspring encouraged weakness in the parents, particularly the mothers who developed an unhealthy attachment to their ungrateful spawn. She'd seen it repeatedly. It created a predictable pattern of behavior and sentimentality.

Such a weakness, and one she intended to exploit.

"And it ... she drew these?" Zahir couldn't stop. Her attention was back on the drawings.

She could feel confusion from both the mother and the warrior. But the maid seemed to understand.

*Interesting.*

"Yes," the mother finally admitted, her reluctance and her desire to protect at odds with each other. "Celine. Her name is Celine, and she's only six years old, and—"

Simba hissed, and Zahir held up her hand to interrupt the deluge of emotionality.

"Celine." Zahir smiled at the sweet relief the mother's answer offered her.

Six years old? Then it couldn't be one of *those* two types of people. But if not, then how had the child drawn what it had? Coincidence?

She shook her head, ignoring the confused gazes. She'd lived too long to believe in coincidence. And there was no chance that a little child with no prior alien knowledge could coincidentally draw this exact image. If the Celine creature wasn't … well, one of *those*, what was it?

The answer was not forthcoming, but Zahir wasn't concerned. She had three victims from whom she could extract information, and the time and skills with which to do it.

And when Hyena brought her Caleb …

Zahir allowed herself a wide smile.

*Then the fun begins.*

## Chapter Forty-Six

CALEB DROVE AS LONG AS HE COULD TOLERATE THE BLOOD pooling in his lap.

But there came a time in everyone's life when a person had to get rid of his enemy's decapitated head.

Caleb had reached that point a few minutes after turning at the hilltop. He removed his foot from the accelerator, shifted into neutral, and let the old Land Cruiser rumble slowly to a stop. He turned the key and sagged against the seat.

The soft ticking of the engine blended with the twitters and chirps of insects and birds. To one side was a tall wall of a secured housing compound; on the other, an open field. A couple of horses grazed nearby.

For a few more heartbeats, Caleb sat with his hands gripping the steering wheel, his eyes unfocused yet somehow aware of the peaceful surroundings. No bullets flew by him. No alien attempted to rip off his head. And Celine, mercifully, was no longer mind-shouting. She sat slumped in her corner, sulking.

Caleb dropped his chin forward to meet Hyena's vacant stare. "Man, you look as ugly in death as you did in life."

Figuring that was as good a eulogy as any, Caleb reached over and pawed at the door handle. When it clicked, he leaned against the door. It swung open with a metal squeak.

Grimacing with every move, he picked up Hyena's head, pretending it was a football without the patches.

*Yeah. That's all this is. A really grungy, dirty, blood-soaked ball that kinda looks like a man's head.*

Just thinking about kicking the head into the goal yanked a startled, high-pitched laugh from inside him. The sound quickly morphed into a convulsive dry heave.

Slipping out of the vehicle, he stumbled and fell against the Land Cruiser, his vision blurring.

His knees quivered and threatened to collapse under the weight of a life not especially well-lived.

Gulping acidic bile, Caleb held the ball — no, the head — away from him. He pushed himself and staggered toward the side of the road. Several birds swarmed up from the tall grass, their wings fluttering like rapid heartbeats mirroring his own.

One of the horses lifted its head and gazed at him with brown, liquid eyes. Unfazed by invading spaceships, decapitated bodies, alien lizards sitting atop antique cars, and mute, mind-screwing little girls. The horse was oblivious to it all and happier for the ignorance. Its jaw methodically chewed at the clump of grass while looking at Caleb.

Still clutching Hyena's head, Caleb grinned. "I know, I know. Me, I've never looked better. Am I right?"

He hiccupped. It transformed into a sob, then a wail, and finally a scream. Straightening up and lifting his arms, he tossed the head — no, the ball, it was just like a football. Whatever was in his hands, he threw it away and down the road.

The whatever rolled several times before falling into the grass-clogged ditch.

He stood in front of the oblivious horses with his hands bloodied, and his jeans a gory mess.

As his knees began to buckle, he flung his head back and

screamed at the world, at Madam Zahir, at his drunken father and Simba and everyone else who'd pushed him into this moment.

Even as he suspected he was only screaming at himself, Caleb continued.

Off to the side, Spot hissed, a growling purr rattling up her throat. Turning to face the Reptar, Caleb roared back, all the horror and terror of the past few minutes, hours, days gushing forth in a riot of angry sounds.

Spot reared up, sitting almost like a dog on top of the Land Cruiser, her yellow eyes blinking several times. Then, snorting and shaking her head, she flopped back down on the roof and placed her muzzle on her front paws.

Caleb's roar hiccupped into a subdued murmur, then a whimper. His knees finally surrendered to gravity, and he fell to the ground.

In an attempt to rub off the blood, he pressed his palms onto the road and dug his fingers into the dirt. A part of him relished the sensation of sharp bits of stone scraping against his skin. But some of the gore had already dried and hardened under his nails and in the lines of his palms. His arm hairs seemed permanently stained. And his pants …

If he had worn anything under them, he would've stripped his jeans and tossed them after the whatever. Despite the absence of underwear, he was tempted to do so until two small shoes appeared in his vision.

He sat back on his heels and tilted his head back. His eyes briefly met Celine's before rolling farther back and staring up at the sky. "What now? Eh? Whatcha want from me?"

Something softly brushed over the top of his head, the side of his face, his shoulder. A caress more tender than he deserved.

*It's okay.*

The words were accompanied by both image and sensation. For a moment, Caleb wasn't a broken failure of a man caught between hopeless and helpless.

Instead, he was clean and pure and wrapped in the softest of blankets. Arms cradled his little body. They were the arms of the only person who had ever truly loved him. He stared up at her. The softness of his mother's gaze embraced him as much as her arms did.

"Welcome home, my baby boy. My darling Caleb."

His mother's love whispered around him, her face still gentle and clear, untainted by the abuse and the addictions which were still to come. In that moment, it was just the two of them, safe and happy.

Smiling, she stroked his cheek. "I love you so much."

"I … Me, I …" The words tripped over his thick tongue. *I love you, too.*

Still smiling at him, his mother retreated into the past. Her image faded, but the sensation did not. Someone, somewhere, somewhen, loved him, valued him, *believed* in him.

His shoulders shook as sobs shuddered through him. He closed his eyes and let the emotions stream out in tears and wails. When his body finally stopped mourning, he gasped, then inhaled loudly through his nose, snorting in the final few unshed tears.

Once he was still, simultaneously exhausted and energized by the emotional purge, Caleb flopped his head forward and stared into Celine's unearthly blue eyes.

"We're going back, aren't we?"

Celine smiled.

## Chapter Forty-Seven

"DID YOU SAY SOMETHING?"

At first, Simba was silent, but Trisha felt his back muscles flex as if he was still attempting to yank free from the zap straps tied around their wrists. She would have offered to chew his free, but they were bound at the waist, back to back.

Even if they could somehow wiggle out of the ties, Samuel, the dangerous-looking tattooed thug, was on the other side of the door, armed and more than eager to prove his loyalty.

Simba cleared his throat and stopped struggling. "No." A pause, as if he wondered what to say next. "What did you hear?"

Trisha sighed, tilted her head, then quickly yanked it forward when she brushed against Simba's head. She pulled her knees closer and tried to get comfortable. Her backside ached from sitting on the cold tiles of the downstairs bathroom. And with her wrists bound, and her back pressed against Simba's, she was unable to wiggle in any direction.

She gazed at the small window above her. It was big enough for her to crawl through, if she could untie herself and then magically remove the security bars. Now like prison bars for them.

*How poetic.*

"Nothing." She laughed softly. "Wishful thinking, I guess."

Wishful, indeed. Because for the briefest of moments, she'd imagined Celine's voice whispering …

But it was impossible. Even in imagination.

And yet, how often had she tried to imagine the sound of her daughter's voice, picturing the moment Celine finally bothered to use it?

"How's your head?"

"Fine." He answered too quickly, his tone sharp.

She didn't argue. At least Samuel hadn't knocked him unconscious or shot the guy. Her mind fluttered away from the image of their pain. Then to a seemingly random topic like a wayward butterfly. "What did she mean? That … That woman. What did she mean about who you really are?"

He hesitated, and silence slithered around them. "I was in the army."

She rolled her eyes. "Obviously. That's why she called you a warrior. But is that all she meant?"

His whole body sighed. "Caleb must've told her."

"Told her what?"

This time, she *felt* his hesitation as a physical sensation, her body curling away from the truth.

No, not her body. His.

She frowned and rubbed her forehead against her knees.

"Why do you think Mr. Walker hired me?"

The question stabbed at her mind, sending freezing pangs of nervous energy through her body. Her lungs felt heavy. Forcing an inhale, she held her breath before letting the words out. "Because I can't drive an antique, and he knows it. Probably why he bought it in the first place."

Simba leaned against her. Was he trying to warm her, reassure her, protect her? "I'm a bodyguard."

The heaviness returned, this time adding an anchor to everything. She shivered. "Why?"

"You'll have to ask him."

She huffed a laugh. "Yeah, because that's easy enough to do."

A fist thudded against the bathroom door. "Keep it down in there," Samuel shouted.

Why would Jake ever think she needed a bodyguard?

Not willing or able to dwell on Jake, his motivation and his absence, she again veered mentally toward another topic, hopefully safer. "Who really gave you your nickname?"

"You don't like it?" Simba's tone hinted at a smile, as if the whole thing were a joke.

Behind the jovial tone, she heard ... No, she *felt* his relief. He didn't want to dwell on his role in her life any more than she did.

*Don't think I'm dropping this indefinitely, Mr. Bodyguard.*

She snickered, not caring if it would insult him or not. "Well, it's definitely not a typical name, unless you're a Disney character."

Simba tilted his head back and laughed. The warm overture of joy made her smile. He should laugh more. It suited him.

"Actually, it's not a nickname. It's my middle name. My father was drunk when I was born, and he thought ..."

He paused, and she could imagine his eyes narrowing, then looking away. "Well, I'm not really sure what he thought. Let's just say he was a Disney fan. He had this huge collection of pirated DVDs. Caleb's middle name is Aladdin, so it seems he had a theme. When I was in the army, and the guys heard my full name, they latched onto Simba, and it stuck."

She'd never been a fan of army guys. They were definitely a *type*. But now, at the possible end of the world, she found it reassuring to know he could handle himself.

*Too bad he's tied to you. In more ways than one, it seems.*

"So I guess you aren't particularly close to your father?"

Simba huffed, and Trisha could feel his hands tensing into fists before loosening up. "Hmm. We're not on friendly terms. I only see him when I absolutely have to. My mother ..." His voice hitched before he resumed with forced detachment. "She always sent me back to the farm during the long school break. She wanted me to know my ancestral home. But I always hated those visits."

Trisha rolled her shoulders, awkward as the positioning was. She tilted her head from side to side, trying to loosen the knots and tension caused from sitting too long in such an unnatural position. "And Caleb? Was he always so … well, *Caleb*?"

"Annoying, you mean?" Simba laughed. "Yeah. He's always been like this. Trouble. I think both our mothers hoped I'd be a good influence on him. But good behavior seldom rubs off. More like he always got me into more trouble."

*Look up.*

The voice was so clear, Trisha obeyed without thinking and gasped.

"What is it?" Simba craned around to see over his shoulder, but succeeded only in bumping his head against hers.

"Celine," Trisha hissed. "Go away."

Celine pressed her face against the security bars, gripping one while slipping her small hand in between two others. She tapped on the glass.

Caleb's face appeared next to Celine's. He jerked her away and shushed her, eyebrows scrunched together.

Simba gave up on looking over his shoulder. "What are they doing?"

Trisha shrugged. "Being stupid? No, wait!"

It was too late. Caleb and Celine disappeared from view.

"I swear I heard her speak."

"Who? Celine?"

Trisha nodded. "I know. It's impossible."

Simba chuckled. "Maybe a little. Or crazy."

"Thanks. Now I'm crazy, too."

*Not crazy.*

Trisha straightened up, searching for the source of the impossible voice.

Simba shifted. "I really hope Caleb doesn't do anything stupid."

"What are the chances he won't?"

His sigh reverberated through her. "Pretty low."

As if to prove the point, their guard shouted and shuffled away from the door. Something clicked — the gun's safety sliding off?

Trisha closed her eyes and listened to his footsteps pounding down the hallway, away from them, toward the back door.

"Oh, Caleb." Simba spoke the name like a curse.

The back door slammed shut, and silence settled around them.

"Where's Celine?"

"She's gone, too." Trisha shook her head, staring at the small bathroom window and the vertical bars separating them from freedom. She blinked away tears, praying to any possible god that her daughter wasn't really back here, in the same house as a gang of dangerous criminals.

Hinges creaked.

Simba exhaled heavily. "Hello, Celine."

*Hello.*

*I'm going crazy*, Trisha decided.

Because who in their right mind hears voices in their head, apart from writers and other neurotics? And she wasn't either of those. She was solid, clearheaded, not crazy. Even if the world was rapidly descending into madness and chaos, she still had a grip on reality.

*Don't I?*

A small hand brushed across her arm and wiggled between her and Simba.

"Be careful with that, Celine."

Before Trisha could ask what he meant, her bonds snapped, followed by the rope connecting her to Simba.

She let her arms fall forward with a groan and began massaging her wrists. "Celine?" She spun around in time to see Simba scooping her daughter into his arms.

He stared at Trisha and reached down a hand to help her up. "No time. We need to go."

She gulped at the short, wickedly sharp blade in Celine's hand. "Is he mad? Giving a child—"

"Trisha."

Frowning, she dragged her gaze away from her little girl holding a weapon like a toy. She reached up, accepted his hand, and allowed him to pull her into a standing position.

Simba turned and peered out the bathroom, still gripping her hand. Celine wrapped her arms around his neck and stared at Trisha, the knife still locked in her grip.

"What about Mama Noah?"

Simba hesitated, and she saw his decision warring with his conscience. Part of her rebelled against the notion of leaving any one of them behind; another part felt warm and fuzzy that he was thinking about her and Celine first, above and beyond all others.

*My bodyguard, indeed.*

A small frown formed between Celine's eyebrows. She rested a hand against Simba's cheek and leaned her forehead against his temple.

Simba nodded, and his eyes cut sideways to Trisha. "Good point. Let's go get Mama Noah."

# Chapter Forty-Eight

"YOU'RE DEAD. HEAR ME, CALEB? DEAD!"

He huddled behind the tool shed, staring at the brick wall. Caleb was tempted — oh, *so* tempted — to tell Samuel about Hyena. How he had also threatened Caleb with imminent pain and ultimate demise.

But he didn't. Somehow, Caleb restrained himself. Not that he was above gloating, but he was definitely above giving his hiding place away. Then again, his location wasn't exactly genius. It wouldn't take long for Samuel to find him.

*Getting warmer.*

He remembered a game from his childhood, one he used to force his unwilling brother to play by stealing something from him.

"Where is it?" Simba had yelled at him, face darkening with outrage as he searched for his book.

Caleb had skipped around their shared room during school holidays, thrilled to have his older brother's attention, at last. "Keep looking. You're getting warmer."

A plastic door opened and rattled shut, snapping Caleb into the present. The door to the greenhouse. As if he would hide among tomatoes and lettuce. Who ate that rabbit food, anyway? Only mzungus who gave up tasty meat for leafy weeds which any sane person would give to the rabbits.

The thin plastic door opened again, its squeak subtly different from the screen door at the back of the house. Funny, how after only a few days in the Walker household, Caleb could already distinguish between the different doors, floorboards and cupboards. Which made noise, which were silent, and which hid a bit of wealth he could tuck away for the future.

*Yeah, some future,* he thought, and longed for a joint. *Because that's what I need right now. Clearheaded is overrated. Am I right?*

Caleb almost laughed. The hysteria bubbled up his throat and crackled in his mouth. He squashed his lips together, determined not to fail this one time. Celine only needed a few minutes. She, her mother, Simba, they could escape. They didn't need to be a part of this.

*Well, look who's got all high and noble on us. Well, maybe not* high, *high. Not this time.*

Caleb shuddered, wondering how he would handle torture while sober.

Legs brushed by long grass. The soft rustling boomed in his ears. *Swish, swish.*

"Hey, Caleb. Here, boy. Come on." Samuel's oily laugh slithered across the airwaves, coating them with foul intention. "You and me, we're going to have some fun, boy. At least I will. You know what Zahir is planning to do? You know what I'm going to do to your friends? Especially that delicious-looking one. *Yum, yum.* You have the hots for her, Caleb? Or you prefer the little girl?" The oily laugh again. "That's probably it. You always were the weird one."

Caleb's hands clenched into fists.

*He's just taunting you. Trying to lure you out.*

It almost worked.

*Swish, swish.*

"You know fear has a smell, Caleb?" Samuel loudly inhaled to illustrate his point. His voice drifted closer. "Madam Zahir taught me that. She knows things, Caleb, things no one else knows. I'm learning a lot." Another loud inhale. "And I smell your fear."

Caleb rubbed the heel of his hand against his forehead. Maybe he should've hidden in the tool shed, where there were lots of interesting options for weapons. Instead, he was huddled in the weeds between the metal shed and a stone wall, with nowhere to go.

*Swish, swish.*

Long grass parted before the approaching legs.

Without anyone to mow the lawn or trim the plants, the garden had already developed a wild, untamed look. In less than two weeks. If the aliens sucked up every single human, it wouldn't be long before nature reclaimed what had always been hers.

Looking at the long grass, the explosion of weeds and vines already snaking up the wall, Caleb figured that within a few years, all traces of human beings would be covered in a veil of green.

*Swish, swish.*

And if in the far future, aliens visited Earth again, what would they find of humanity and all its civilized greatness? Nothing but strangely shaped, green humps dotting the landscape.

*Yup,* Caleb decided as an insect scuttled across his sneakers. *The cockroaches shall inherit the earth, not the meek.*

He thumped his head gently against the tool shed. Kind of fitting that they would all disappear without much of a trace. Sad but appropriate. And good luck to the cockroaches. He couldn't imagine the alien ships sucking up any of those.

Metal tapped against metal. Caleb's eyes widened. He hadn't even realized he'd closed them.

Something clicked. A gun, ready for action.

"You in here, Caleb?"

The metal door swung open, clanging against the tool shed wall. Caleb felt the vibrations in his back.

"Nope. Guess you're not that stupid after all," Samuel muttered, then snickered.

Caleb eased himself upright, listening carefully. Samuel was now on the part of the concrete platform that protruded outside of the shed. His expensive leather loafers — the ones stolen off the feet of a dying man — gave him away.

Those shiny, brown shoes created a different noise, a soft squeak with every step pressed into the concrete. Caleb pictured the leather bending across the top of Samuel's feet. He held his breath and honed in on that leathery squeak. Coming from his right.

On the balls of his feet, Caleb tiptoed around the left side of the tool shed, listening to Samuel's shoes bend, squeak and straighten. Bend, squeak and straighten.

"She'll find you, Caleb. You know she will. She is one seriously creepy whore, but she knows how to find people. It's a skill, boy. And you know what she does to those who mess with her."

Oh, did he ever.

Bend, squeak and straighten.

The sound of creaking leather seemed almost deafening in the lazy heat of late morning. The pace picked up. Samuel reached the far end of the tool shed and Caleb tensed, his eyes on the side door to the kitchen.

By now, Simba, Trisha and Celine were gone. He hadn't heard the rev of the Land Cruiser's engine, but knew Simba well enough. His brother would figure out some way to sneak out of the compound. He was probably rolling the vehicle down the steep hill, getting some distance before switching it on.

Maybe they would pass Hyena's decapitated body, sprawled in the ditch. He hoped Trisha would cover Celine's eyes, just in case she was on that side of the vehicle.

Everything was always such a mess.

His gaze fell to his pants, stiff with coagulated gore.

*Yup. A bloody mess.*

Would Simba take Spot with him? The Reptar was on top of the Land Cruiser, sleeping. Compared to the alien, Samuel didn't seem like too big of a threat. Then again, Spot was sleeping; Samuel was stalking him with a gun.

He sucked in a lungful of air, then released the tension in his muscles and sprang forward. With his eyes on the prize, he sprinted toward the house, sneakers pounding on the grass.

Samuel shouted in frustration behind him, but Caleb kept his focus on the kitchen's side door. His arms pumped, legs churned, stomach heaved. He swallowed the bile. At this moment, there was only one goal.

Get inside the house.

*But Zahir is in there.*

That realization hit him too late. He leapt onto the paved area in front of the kitchen door and ducked under damp clothes drying on a line. A shirt slapped his back.

"Caleb, I'm going to …"

His loud breathing drowned out Samuel's useless threat. Jogging up to the kitchen door, he yanked it open, slipping inside in time to see Simba slide in from the hallway.

He stumbled back, ignoring the question on Simba's face. He spun around and pushed the bolt across, locking the door. He pressed his face to the small window, watching Samuel get tangled in a bed sheet.

He glanced over his shoulder and frowned at Simba. "Whatcha still doing here?"

Simba gestured to Mama Noah standing by the stove. "Rescuing the maid. You?"

Caleb stared around the kitchen and groaned. Trisha and Celine were also there. The kid waved at him.

"Serious?"

Mama Noah pointed toward the pantry. "I'm cooking for him."

A large hulk stepped out of the pantry, a clear plastic bag of mini marshmallows in one hand and a machete in the other. Thickheaded Timothy held up his machete, unconcerned by the odds.

He dropped the bag, pushed the pantry door closed with a large, meaty hand, and pointed the machete toward Caleb.

"Rice, Timothy. I asked for a bag of rice, not marshmallows."

Tossing a spatula onto the counter, Mama Noah picked up her pan and stomped toward the pantry. She ignored Timothy, rolling her eyes skyward and silently mouthing something.

A prayer? Probably, knowing her. If it was up to Caleb, he'd be mouthing something a lot less saintly.

"Caleb." Timothy's voice was rumbling and uncertain.

"Hey, Timothy, old pal." Caleb tried to smile even as he caught a flicker of motion from the corner of his eye. Samuel's face appeared in the small window of the side door, his features twisted with frustration and fury.

Mama Noah huffed and yanked open the pantry door. "Idiot men."

"You wanna come with us?" Caleb offered, wondering how long the door would hold if Samuel decided to shoot at the lock. The door was metal, but certainly not bulletproof. Or maybe he would circle around and come in through the front door.

"Oh, enough of this." Mama Noah lifted her cast-iron frying pan and smashed it down on the back of Timothy's head with an audible THUNK!

For a moment, Timothy blinked at Caleb, his expression blank and eyes dazed.

Scowling, Mama Noah lifted up the pan and brought it back down. Timothy staggered to his knees, then collapsed. A trickle of blood leaked out from under his hair. A soft snore filled the stunned silence.

Mama Noah wheezed, staring at Timothy's body before facing Trisha. "See? These frying pans, they are *much* better than your new-age, lightweight junk."

Trisha gulped loud enough for everyone to hear.

"Well noted," Simba said, stooping to snatch up the machete. "Time to go."

Caleb turned to face Samuel who, remarkably, was still standing outside and glaring at him. Shouting obscenities, Samuel turned and ran toward the front of the house.

"Damn it!" Caleb dashed for the front door. It was a race, and no way was he going to be last. He veered into the hall, staring through the open door to freedom.

Simba's heavy boots thudded behind him, and he could only assume the women were in hot pursuit. In any other circumstance, he would have found that thought highly entertaining. Him and his brother, chased by a posse of women.

But he was only concerned with one woman right now, and she was standing in the driveway, pointing a gun at them. Her red lipstick and perfectly matched red fingernails were bright against her dark skin.

She watched his reaction, her dark eyes glittering, much as Spot's had. He preferred the Reptar.

Caleb stumbled to a halt. His mind garbled his thoughts into a knotted mess.

The woman lifted a plump hand. Her index finger tilted back and forth like the arm of a metronome.

*Tick, tock. Tick, tock. Tick, tock.*

Counting down the final seconds of his life.

"Tsk, tsk, tsk. Caleb, my dear boy. You are such a disappointment."

The pendant's weight seemed to increase, or perhaps that was his guilt. Because nobody stole from the Rat Queen. Nobody.

As if smelling his terror, Madam Zahir smiled.

## Chapter Forty-Nine

HER FIRST INSTINCT WAS TO SHOOT THEM ALL. NOT a lethal shot, of course. Maybe in the kneecaps or …

*The stomach.*

She smiled. A stomach wound resulted in a prolonged and painful demise. They deserved nothing less.

Zahir restrained herself, barely, and then wondered why. She wasn't one for second-guessing herself; her impulse to spare them was unusual. She had no use for any of them. Even Caleb was dispensable once her pendant had been retrieved. Not that she intended to let him die so easily.

But the others? Their continued existence was totally unnecessary.

"Caleb, Caleb, Caleb. My dear boy." Her smile widened at the sight of his grimace.

"Eh, Madam Zahir." He half-waved at her. "Funny thing. I was just on my way to see you."

Pounding feet momentarily distracted her. Samuel rounded the corner and almost collided with the warrior. Huffing, he stepped back and palmed his gun. His wheezing grated on her nerves.

"Have a nice jog, Samuel?" Without waiting for his response,

Zahir looked past Caleb, bemused as her gaze traveled over the group of captives. Despite the impossibility of their circumstance, they all wore a determined expression, as if they expected to triumph over her.

They'd be lucky if she let them crawl away alive, with their skin still attached to their broken bodies.

Zahir paused as she noticed the child, staring back at her with serious intent. That in itself struck her as odd. Children and animals shared a common reaction to her: neither liked her. They'd turn and run or cry or piss over themselves. Sometimes all of the above.

But this one had no fear at all.

Zahir sniffed disdainfully and tried to ignore the squirmy reaction the child's presence left in the pit of her stomach. "So this is our little artist."

She was pleased with her cavalier tone, effectively burying the tumult of foreign emotions wrestling for dominance. She forced her lungs to breathe, slowly and deeply, resisting the urge to wipe at the sudden dampness settling across her forehead and under her armpits.

And since when did her shoulders tense in anticipation of danger?

*It's only a little girl,* she reminded herself even as her pulse quickened.

Little, yes, but so much more than just a girl. And the drawings …

The white woman placed a protective arm around the child's shoulders and pulled it to her side. Simba ignored Samuel's threatening scowl and gun to step in front of the mother-child duo, as if his very bulk could protect them from what was to come.

"No, really. Madam Zahir." Caleb held out his arms to placate her, even though she'd momentarily forgotten about him. "Me, I was just telling my bro that I needed to get back to my people. And good news. They said I could borrow their vehicle. Imagine! So, here I am, and here you are. Let's go." He raised his fist to punctuate the thought.

Samuel's gun shifted toward him.

Zahir ignored Caleb's false bravado. She slowed her breathing and let her eyes slightly unfocus. She loosened her shoulders and studied the group's body language, physical placement, and energy. All of that and more. She read them as others might read a book. The story was obvious and inflexible. She might be able to forcibly take back her pendant — over Caleb's dead body, if necessary — but she would not have such an easy time extracting the child.

And, oh yes, she would have it. Zahir wanted to study the child, understand how it was able to draw those images, learn what it was and how its existence connected with hers. More than that, Zahir needed to understand the meaning of the drawings.

"Take what you came for, and leave." Simba's voice was low and steady with the heavy current of a threat.

Samuel gripped his gun, as if preparing to shoot.

"Where's Timothy? And Hyena? And his two useless sidekicks? I send them out for a simple mission, and they disappear."

Useless was a term she could easily apply to all her minions.

The maid clutched something to her chest. Zahir stared at the item, then laughed, her belly bouncing in unexpected humor. "Really? A frying pan? How ingenious of you."

Caleb shifted, too subtly for others to notice. But Zahir was not like any other. She narrowed her eyes at her former employee, eyebrow raised. "Where's Hyena?"

Caleb rubbed the back of his neck, probably in anticipation for what she intended to do with it once she had her item back.

"Him, he didn't quite survive our encounter."

Silence. A dog barked in the distance, answered by the cough of a nearby lion. Far above, a silent observer to all that was and would be, the spaceship lurked. Zahir felt its presence in the tension across her shoulders, and the prickling of her neck hairs. The ship was watching, waiting.

Zahir cleared her throat and tilted her gun to the side. "I am disappointed."

Hyena and Timothy were rare among her minions. Not many were faithful and followed her orders without any thoughts of disobedience or ever going behind her back.

"Well, then."

Movement caught her attention. She frowned at Samuel who, oblivious to her attention, was leering at the white woman. "That will be all, Samuel."

Simba stepped forward to Caleb's side. His lack of concern for his safety reminded her that Samuel wasn't this tableau's only unpredictable element.

"Give her what she wants, Caleb. Even if that means you." Simba spoke to his brother, but his attention was fixed on her, his gaze fearless and unflinching.

*Well, not entirely fearless*, Zahir thought as she reflected on the threads that bound these people together. *Fearless only when it comes to his own well-being.*

*But when it comes to others …*

She shifted her gaze to the mother and child. Simba's fists tensed, and Zahir smiled.

Samuel lined up his gun with Simba's head. "We don't need him alive. Or the maid, either."

The child pouted, her eyes sparkling with an unspoken tantrum.

Zahir saw the reaction and knew Samuel was wrong. Very wrong, on so many levels.

Samuel licked his lips and slid closer to the white woman. While Zahir had no issue giving him what he wanted, her mouth still curled in disgust. He was no better than a dog around a female in heat.

Struggling out of its mother's embrace, the child kicked Samuel in the shin. Swearing, he lifted a hand and cuffed the girl across the face, knocking it … no, *her* … to the ground.

*It's a female*, Zahir reminded herself and watched in a distracted fashion as her free hand rose to stop Samuel from going any farther in his anger.

*People are particular about gender pronouns.*

Several things happened at once.

A shout echoed from inside the house, and lumbering steps fell heavily along the hallway toward the front door.

Samuel spun around, gun raised, safety clicking off as Timothy lurched into view.

Simba capitalized on the distraction and swept past the woman and child. He shouted something at them and then lunged at Samuel, tackling him to the ground.

Caleb remained frozen, meeting her astonished gaze with a more astounded expression.

Timothy launched himself on top of Simba.

Zahir smirked, wondering if Samuel was still breathing under all of that weight.

Timothy pulled Simba upright, yelling, and wrapped his thick arms around the other man's neck.

Samuel groaned and pushed himself onto his knees. Somehow, despite the tackle and dog pile, he'd managed to keep his gun.

He clasped it in both hands, snarling.

The screaming mother dragged her child over to where the maid stood in shock. The little female offspring wriggled against the confining embrace, but it — *she* — wasn't staring at the pending execution. The young child's eyes fixed themselves on Zahir. Pale blue, like untainted firestone.

Still caught in Timothy's grip, Simba bent over as a gun fired. The explosion of sound caused birds in a nearby tree to flock upward.

Timothy dropped his arms, gasping, his expression blank. He stumbled around, showing his back and the hole of spurting blood. He sank to the ground with a groan and leaned against the wall, eyes fluttering, mouth gulping at air like a fish on the sidewalk.

Zahir watched and waited.

Chest heaving, Simba pressed his fists against his knees and stared at the women clustered together. "Why are you still here?"

Zahir scoffed. "And where do you expect them to go?"

What had he hoped to achieve? Because of him, yet another of her faithful but inept minions was now dead.

Eyes glazed over with rage, Samuel raised his quivering arms and pointed his gun at Simba.

Even before she felt the message, Zahir knew what she had to do.

*Stop.*

Accompanying the mind-word she felt an aching desire to end the violence and eliminate the threat. If Zahir didn't stop this, she would have no chance to learn the truth about those drawings.

They were as important as her pendant, maybe even more so.

"Samuel, don't." Her voice snapped like a whip.

This time, her employee didn't so much as flinch. He cocked the hammer of his gun and sneered at Simba.

Not surprised or even disappointed, Zahir lifted her gun and aimed.

## Chapter Fifty

*SO PREDICTABLE.*

That was Madam Zahir's only thought as the inevitable presented itself. Samuel realized his error and raised his hands in surrender, but her finger had already started to squeeze the trigger.

Her hand remained unmoved by the slight jerk of the gun as a bullet rocketed across the driveway.

Samuel staggered back before the sound registered. A crimson stain blossomed across his shirt. His eyes widened in a parody of astonishment before he collapsed, his eyes glazing over as they stared vacantly in the direction of her shoes.

The maid shrieked and dropped the pan to cover her mouth. The white woman whimpered but didn't scream or protest or do any of those other typically civilian reactions to violence and death.

Zahir lowered her revolver and smiled at Caleb. "Now, I believe you have something of mine." She lifted a hand, palm up, and wiggled her fingers at him.

Caleb's mouth worked, but no words came out.

*Dumbstruck. There's always a first time for everything.*

"Give it to her." Simba nudged his brother with an elbow, then limped toward the women. He wrapped an arm around the slim pale woman with a reassuring murmur. She looked up at him wide-eyed, mouth agape.

Caleb reluctantly tugged a black string over his head and lifted it until the pendant slid into view.

Eagerly licking her lips, Zahir stepped forward and reached out her arm. "Hurry."

Caleb narrowed his eyes. "Why is this so important? What is it?"

Zahir strode forward with a growl and yanked the string from his hand. "It's a firestone. A family memento and no longer any of your concern."

"What's a firestone?"

She dangled the pendant in front of her face. "*This.*"

That wasn't the full truth, but Zahir had no intention of explaining anything to them. She held the stone, admiring the ocean blue color. Darker than an unaltered firestone and, in her eyes, far more beautiful and useful. Barely more than a shard the length and width of her thumb. To this day, she regretted not managing to salvage more than a sliver, but it was enough to serve her purpose.

It pulsed a warning.

A familiar rattling purred behind her before she could react. Hot breath huffed across her back.

She lifted her gaze to meet Caleb's and found him smirking. "You let one of those things come *in here?*"

Caleb stepped back and shrugged. "I told her to stay outside, but she ain't housebroken yet." He reached down and took the child's hand. "Besides, she's the kid's pet. You can't separate a kid from her pet. Am I right?"

"You fool." Zahir cringed, clutching the shard to her chest, waiting for the inevitable death snarl before her head or limbs went flying. "They're demons, not pets."

The shard pulsed more fiercely, its light sneaking through her fingers. Her hands glowed blue.

Caleb laughed at her — *laughed!*

"It's actually a Reptar. But I can see why someone might call it a demon."

Simba's eyes cut to his brother. "Enough."

"What?" Caleb said. "It's true."

The girl brushed its … No, it brushed *her* free hand down *her* pants and straightened. Looking over Zahir's shoulder, it … she, the child, frowned ever so slightly while shaking her head.

Zahir held her breath as the creature inhaled with its rattle. The demon scuttled around her, black limbs twitching in blurred lunges interspersed with pauses. A lion-sized cockroach.

More than anything, it reminded Zahir of a past she had left behind her.

Zahir slipped the cord over her neck and tucked the shard between her ample breasts. She studied the beast as it approached the girl, prepared to leap away at the first sign of aggression.

Something was off about its behavior.

"It's not connected."

The whispered words slipped out before she was aware of their truth. Only the warrior heard her. His sharp gaze met hers.

She snapped, "Keep that demon Reptar away from me."

"She has a name, you know. Spot." Caleb pointed at the gray splotch just visible on the contorting surface of the leg. "See the spot?"

She gaped at him. "You *named* it?"

A whining distracted her, and Zahir shifted her stare. The white woman covered her mouth with her hands as if to block the inevitable scream or whatever other drivel might spill out. She was still staring at the dead men.

Samuel had served his purpose until he hadn't. There was no point in keeping anyone around once they passed their expiration date. Timothy's demise … an inconvenience, to be sure.

The Reptar padded up to the girl, nudging her with its toothy snout. Blue energy pulsed between its inky black scales, same shade as the altered firestone pulsing in time to her heartbeat.

Coincidence? Perhaps.

But Zahir knew there was no such thing. Not in the grand scheme of the universe. Everything was connected, like it or not — and she truly didn't.

Zahir was connected with Caleb, his adopted crew and their demonic pet. For now.

*That can always change,* she thought with a smile.

## Chapter Fifty-One

"WHY DON'T I JUST SHOOT YOU NOW?"

"Shoot her." Caleb thumped Simba on the back. "Serious. Just shoot her."

Trisha stared up at Simba. He could sense her anxiety and the question she didn't want to ask.

*Would he shoot someone in cold blood?*

He hoped she never learned the honest answer.

Zahir sighed, then smiled. "You always were hasty, Caleb. Act first, and never think."

Simba snorted a short laugh, then cleared his throat.

"There will be no shooting." Trisha's eyes flicked to the Reptar sniffing at a weedy flower. "Well, at least not any humans."

Caleb sulked, kicking at a tuft of grass. "She's barely human."

Mama Noah clucked her tongue and muttered the Lord's prayer.

Zahir chuckled, her chin wobbling as if they were discussing an amusing movie instead of her possible execution.

Trisha hissed, angling her head so she could stare at Simba's profile. "That's not what we do."

Despite her agitation and the sudden stiffness of her body beside his, Simba felt an unexpected warmth. She'd said *we*. *We* don't do this. And even though she was wrong — that maybe *we* didn't, but *he* definitely did — he still nodded and squeezed her shoulder in response.

Madam Zahir was unmoved by his implicit threat. She met his gaze, eyes half-lidded and almost bored. "That's utterly unnecessary, Simba. We are now on the same team."

Caleb coughed loudly on his other side, barely masking the curse he tucked inside his exaggerated hacking.

Simba widened his stance as he straightened. "Since when did that happen?"

Zahir stared at her henchmen's bodies before gazing up at the darkened sky. "Since we share the same goal."

Trisha stepped away from Simba, shivering.

He felt her absence acutely. Not only the lack of warmth pressed close to him, but something else. An undertone of emotion murmuring through him. It sounded ridiculous even in his own head, but Simba knew it was true. He was experiencing her emotions in sensation and images. Her entire being was focused on Celine, on protecting her child.

He could help her. Simba was her bodyguard, after all.

Caleb flicked a hand back and forth, indicating first himself, then Zahir. "Us, we ain't on the same team." He puffed out his chest, cocky and confident with the gang members dead on the driveway or somewhere out on the road.

Spot hissed, then issued a rattling growl.

Despite Simba's apprehension around the alien's presence, he allowed himself to gloat at the glimmer of concern in Zahir's eyes and even wished it was more. Why wasn't she terrified that an alien killer was only a few paces away? Sure, Spot was a six-year-old's companion, but the creature was on their side, not hers.

*So why is Zahir so calm?*

It didn't matter. She was defenseless and on her own, and maybe that caused her to capitulate.

"Actually, you're wrong. On all fronts." Zahir's eyes flicked up to meet Simba's gaze. "Let's not be coy, shall we? You're feeling it just as I am."

Trisha looked up from where she crouched next to Celine. "Feeling what?"

Spot flopped next to Celine with a snarl and sprawled by her side. Strikingly similar to any pet dog.

*Except it is no pet. It's a human killer.*

What the hell was keeping it restrained?

Why were any of them still standing, breathing, free?

"We won't be for long." Zahir chuckled. "Not if we stick around here."

That caught Simba's attention. He didn't question how she'd heard him. Trisha might be in denial, but he was well beyond that. "What do you know that we don't?"

Zahir's gaze was on Celine. He watched her tongue slide across her plump lips. "I know what they want. And why they're here."

Simba tilted his head upward to stare at the underbelly of the large silver disc. "Please, enlighten us."

"They'll be looking for anomalies like her." Zahir pointed a pudgy finger at Celine. "She's different. They like that. They like to learn, to probe, to experiment. They'll want her. The rest of you are expendable."

Trisha pulled Celine into her arms. The girl frowned, then pulled at a weedy flower. She began plucking petals off. One petal. A second petal. Each of them floated slowly to the ground. Spot nipped at them, sharp teeth clicking in warning.

Caleb squatted next to Samuel and removed his brown loafers. Kicking off his battered sneakers, he slipped on the leather shoes with a grin, then began patting at the dead man's pockets. "And why would they want her? She's just a little girl." He slid out a knife from a back pocket and a gun from a side holster.

Simba exhaled.

*Great. He's stupid, impulsive and armed. This should go well.*

Zahir shrugged and turned toward the ship. She shuddered, and the first real taste of fear floated off her and washed over him. "She may be little, but they'll still be curious about her—"

"Because she's different," Caleb finished her sentence, then snorted in disbelief.

The moment he stood, Simba grabbed his brother's arm, and in a quick maneuver, relieved him of his weapon. Caleb yanked himself free, then scowled and marched over to Timothy.

Simba tucked the gun into his back pocket, then crossed his arms. "And now you're on our team?"

"So it would seem."

Simba smiled without humor. He held out a hand, making a *come-hither* gesture with his fingers. "Your gun, please. As a token of good faith, since you're on our team."

Zahir didn't hesitate. She stepped forward, holding the gun by its muzzle, and slapped the handle on Simba's open palm. "I don't need it."

"No. You don't." And although Simba was tempted to pull back the safety and shoot the woman in the head, he restrained himself. Not because she deserved to live. Nor did he believe for one second that she was on any team apart from her own.

He held back for Trisha's sake. If she saw his other side, the one he kept tucked in a dark corner like soiled laundry, she would never let him near her again. Nor would she lean into his embrace, her mind whispering relief and gratitude that she'd found a man to protect her.

He cleared his throat, forcing himself to stop thinking about Trisha before his thoughts took a different turn, one in which he wasn't just the hired help.

"And how is it that you know so much about our visitors?"

Zahir's eyes became cloudy, her attention suddenly somewhere else. She rolled her shoulders, clutching hands over her chest and the strange glowing pendant, staring up at the spaceship dominating the sky. "There are those who have not forgotten."

Trisha stood, her features calm and eyes no longer glazed by horror and shock now that her daughter was safe. She kept her chin up and averted her gaze from the bodies. She glowered at Zahir. "Do go on."

Zahir smiled and tilted her head. "One day, I just might. But for now, there's only one thing you need to know."

Simba's eyebrows rose before he could stop them. "Yes?"

She lowered her chin and stared at him. "Nairobi is about to face the wrath of its creators. We must leave if you wish to escape."

Caleb opened his mouth, but Trisha talked over him. "And go where?"

"I know a safe place." Zahir looked at Spot, now snuffling at a large beetle crawling across Celine's shoe. "A secret place the demons cannot find."

Caleb clenched his fists and swaggered forward, ignoring Simba's warning hiss. "Oh yeah? And where is this safe place?"

Zahir eyed him, her upper lip peeling back in a disgusted sneer. "It's a secret. That's why it's safe."

Simba yanked Caleb by the scruff of his collar and pulled him out of the way. He searched Zahir's expression for any indication of a lie. But again, he felt more than knew that she was telling the truth. Regardless of what this woman was — a ruthless crime lord whose only interest was self-preservation — she was now their best chance at a future.

"And whereabouts is this secret, safe place?"

Zahir looked at her chest. A soft blue glow pulsed through the black fabric of her shirt. She placed one hand over the glow and peered up at him.

"One of only three places on this continent they'd never destroy," Zahir said. "Mount Kenya."

## Chapter Fifty-Two

"LET'S JUST FORCE HER TO TELL US, THEN SHOOT HER."

Trisha slapped Caleb on the arm before Simba could react, wishing she knew how to punch. "No shooting."

Caleb shrugged and raised his hands in surrender. "Kidding. No shooting. Or how about no shoot to kill? What about just shooting a kneecap? No? Torture? Just a small amount. Threatening to torture?"

Trisha scowled and he threw up his arms. "Fine. Have it your way, boss lady. But no reason to take her with us. We can leave her for the lions and aliens to finish off."

Trisha's stomach turned, and bile scorched her throat. Simba had dragged the two dead gang members around the side of the house — for her benefit, no doubt — but the blood stains remained. She lifted her gaze to avoid that gory reminder and the alien ship came into view.

*What a mess.*

The trio was standing in the entranceway, trying to decide their next move. Everyone seemed to agree they had to leave. But when, how, and with whom still remained to be answered.

As if her fate wasn't in their hands, Zahir remained on the driveway, legs planted shoulder width apart, her head flung back and eyes fixed on the ship. Spot prowled nearby, growling and hissing, its rattling inhale audible from a distance. Despite the creature's animosity, it never approached Zahir close enough to do anything more than threaten.

Trisha stared over her shoulder at the kitchen doorway. Celine was inside with Mama Noah. "Why her?"

Caleb scratched between his dreadlocks. "Because Zahir's mean and ugly. If we leave her here, and the lions eat her, at least her life would've served a higher purpose."

"I mean Celine." Trisha huffed. "Why would the aliens be interested in my daughter?"

Caleb leaned against the doorway with a grin. "Because she's weird and cute and …" His grin faded.

Trisha pursed her lips and looked away. She knew what he was going to say.

*She talks in our heads.*

Even if the truth was impossible.

Simba cleared his throat and tilted his gun ever so slightly. He hadn't moved his eyes from Zahir, nor allowed his gun to waiver from its target. "She's telling the truth. She believes she knows a safe place. And Mama Noah has that farm on the slopes of Mount Kenya. So …"

He failed to state the obvious conclusion: *they should get out from under the shadow of the spaceship and travel to Mount Kenya with Zahir.*

Again, Trisha felt the responsibility fall to her. Did Simba want her to make the final decision? Hadn't they moved past the awkward employer-employee relationship? It seemed they had left that station a while ago. Yet here they were, back to Day One, the Kenyan staff waiting for her final call.

"And the Reptar?" She lowered her voice so Celine wouldn't hear the discussion.

Caleb frowned, watching Spot pace near the bottom of the driveway. "She comes with us, of course. Spot is part of the family now."

*Part of the family.* Is that what they were?

Trisha could feel Simba's gaze hover on her before it flitted away like a hummingbird.

Why did they have to name it? As far as she was concerned, the black, scaly alien was a nameless *it*, one of the creatures that had tattered those two men to skin and gristle before pursuing her. She wouldn't humanize the thing by giving it a name or a gender.

Besides, how did anyone know it was a she? Maybe the aliens didn't even have genders. Maybe they were like worms. Maybe they had both, or none at all.

Her stomach gurgled.

She rubbed a hand across her forehead. "We could stay here."

As soon as the words were out, she felt the wrongness of the idea. They had only escaped the spaceship's transporter beam because …

Well, she didn't *know* how they had escaped. Was it merely random selection? Had they been lucky? And how long would their fortune hold out?

And while Spot …

*No, dammit. Not Spot. It.*

While that *thing* pacing her garden wasn't going into killer mode yet, the same couldn't be said for the other Reptars. And what about the pride of lions? Who knew what else was out there, lurking in the abandoned village or the cornfield, waiting for a chance to strike.

They had to go. Mount Kenya was as good a place as any. At the very least, they could grow their own food, like Mama Noah promised.

"Mrs. Walker."

Caleb and Trisha turned to face inside the house, while Simba remained steadfastly focused on Zahir.

Mama Noah appeared in the doorway, breathless even though she had only taken a few paces from whatever she was doing at the stove. "Come see. Global News, it's back online."

That in itself was strange. Ever since the attack on Moscow, the Internet had been sketchy at best.

Leaving Simba to watch over Zahir, Trisha hurried into the kitchen with Caleb on her heels. The large juke set into the wall was on. Static marred the imagery, but it was still clear enough to see and hear. The dark-eyed announcer stared intently into the camera, her bright red lipstick a reminder that even during an alien invasion, a woman could still look her best.

"In case this broadcast goes out, this is Greta San Lucas of Global News, where we give you the latest and greatest in breaking news."

Her voice faded in and out, but the image suddenly clarified. A car-sized, crystal cube dominated the screen; it was in the midst of a crowd and pulsed with the same blue light as the spaceship's ring and Zahir's strange stone pendant. On the outskirts of the image, mobs crashed against each other. People closer to the center jostled each other to touch the cube in reverence, trembling before it.

The image shifted to another cube, this time in a much more familiar setting.

Trisha narrowed her eyes. "Is that near us?"

Caleb swallowed hard. "Yup. Kibera, at the edge nearest the city center."

"It's beginning."

Dazed, Trisha turned around so fast that her hip crashed against the island counter. Wincing at her future bruise, she stared at Zahir, then at Simba behind her.

"What's beginning?" Trisha's voice climbed an octave.

Ignoring Simba's gun and Mama Noah's frying pan, Zahir took a long step toward the juke. She pointed at the large cube and met Trisha's gaze. It was like looking into the rotten core of a dead log. She could almost feel the spiritual maggots wiggling across the woman's soul.

"Those cubes. They drop them in places where people are fighting." Zahir paused and tilted her head to the side. "They're like large bombs of light. After a couple hours, if the people don't stop fighting

…" She put her hands together, then flung them out in a parody of an explosion. "*Boom*. Everyone dies."

Trisha's breathing constricted, and her eyes cut sideways to Celine. She was almost relieved to see that her child's normal, tranquil expression had returned. If the girl was listening, she didn't seem to care or understand. Although Trisha was beginning to wonder if this was a facade, and that the real Celine was anything but placid. Perhaps she was a force of nature, capable of taming dangerous monsters and inviting the interest of aliens.

"What's the range on those things?" Simba asked.

Zahir shrugged, her attention still on the juke. Judging by the angle, the footage was shot by a drone. The cube wasn't huge, but somehow it towered above everything else.

"It depends. But it can be quite extensive. Sometimes, citywide."

"And you know this how?" Doubt laced Simba's tone.

But Trisha had no doubt. She felt again the resonance of truth in the woman's words. A brutal crime lord she may be, but Zahir hadn't lied to them yet.

"We have to leave. Now." Trisha hadn't planned on saying those words aloud, but she didn't regret it. Turning from the sight of that large ticking bomb, she met Simba's gaze over the crime lord's shoulder. "She's right. It's time."

She reluctantly met Zahir's smirking gaze and added, "We're going to Mount Kenya."

## Chapter Fifty-Three

THERE WAS NO WAY HE WAS GOING TO RETRIEVE THE bloody Land Cruiser.

Just imagining climbing back into the cab where Hyena's blood and gore still covered the driver's seat … Just thinking about it made Caleb shudder.

Instead, Simba had taken a plastic sheet and an old towel with him, after muttering irritated curses at Caleb. For a second, Caleb had felt bad. But Simba was the soldier here. He was used to seeing various fluids and body parts scattered around. But Caleb?

He shook his head. *Let's be honest*, he told himself as he watched Simba slip out of the gate. *'Cause once in a while, it's good for you to tell it like it is. You're a liar and a thief, and not a particularly great one, either. Am I right?*

The truth didn't hurt as much as it should. He was fine not being the brave hero. Cowardliness had served him well so far. And fundamentally, nothing had really changed in the world, apart from everyone receiving ultimate proof that aliens did exist.

But the humans themselves? Same species, different context.

So no, he didn't feel bad about sending his brother to take care of that mess. Although when had he stopped referring to Simba as his half-brother?

*Part of the family now.* Isn't that what he had told everyone?

Chuckling, he stared around the front yard, at the Reptar playing with the mute kid, and Zahir shackled to a waist-high, decorative garden light that didn't work. "Weirdest family ever. Am I right?"

Celine stared over at him and shrugged. Patting Spot on the snout, she sat on one of the boxes of groceries scattered around the driveway. Nearby, Zahir pointedly ignored them. The handcuffs scraped against the metal post as she shifted around. But for someone who was tied up like a goat for slaughter, Zahir didn't seem too concerned. She continued to watch the large spaceship, the one she called a mothership.

*How the hell does she know all of this?* he wondered, then huffed and dropped the box he was carrying. She was probably faking it anyway, making it up to impress them with her vital knowledge.

*Safe, secret place, my butthole.*

Slumping on the box, he nodded at Celine. "Yep. Craziest family ever."

Trisha and Mama Noah joined them a moment later, each of them dragging bulging suitcases.

Trisha looked around at the groceries, camping gear and bags of clothes filling the driveway. "I think that's it. This should keep us going for a while."

Caleb grinned and jabbed a thumb at the ex-crime lord. "Yeah, and if it doesn't, we can always eat the fat one over there."

Zahir didn't respond, her eyes still fixed on the ship looming above them, large enough to cast a long shadow over the city.

A rumbling engine ended their conversation. The Land Cruiser floated into view like the ark of salvation. Simba reversed it up the driveway, the horse trailer fishtailing, then cut the engine.

Caleb clapped his hands in the silence. "Well, our chariot awaits." He winked at Mama Noah and forced a smile. "And maybe, if you're lucky, Simba has cleaned Hyena's brains off of the seat for you."

Mama Noah narrowed her eyes and wiped both hands on her red kikoi. "I am *not* cleaning up that mess. Who do you think I am, your maid?"

Caleb's eyes flicked over to Trisha. The mzungu said nothing to contradict her former maid. That, at least, had changed. He couldn't quite identify when it had happened. When he'd first arrived a few days ago, Mama Noah didn't dare say anything in front of Trisha.

Now she said whatever she wanted to.

Smirking, he stood and stretched.

*Yup. This is going to be a fun road trip.*

Simba swaggered into view, tossing a wet, stained towel onto the grass. "Let's load up."

Before anyone could tell her otherwise, Celine skipped for the back of the trailer and pulled at one of the latches keeping the ramp up.

"You must be kidding."

Celine gazed over her shoulder at Trisha, a stubborn frown forming between her eyebrows. She stomped twice and pouted.

Caleb snickered, glad that Mama Noah wasn't the only one standing up to the boss lady. "Spot's part of our dysfunctional family, so she should come on this road trip as well."

"No one asked you," Trisha said.

Shrugging, Caleb joined Celine. "Eh! Me, I'm just speaking my truth. Besides, there's still room in here for the camping gear. Spot ain't that big."

They lowered the ramp together while Simba and Mama Noah started packing the back of the Land Cruiser.

Hissing and snarling, Spot lumbered up, twirled in place and collapsed onto the floor. The entire horse trailer shook with the movement. Celine trotted up to join her.

"No way." Trisha stepped onto the bottom of the ramp. "That thing can come, but you're not sitting back here for the ride. Understood, young lady?"

Caleb slapped a hand over his mouth, waiting for her reaction.

Celine shuffled closer to Spot until the creature's black snout rested next to her little shoes. The kid straightened up and crossed her skinny arms over her thin chest. Her hair flicked back and forth as she shook her head and refused to look at her mother.

Simba strolled around the trailer and rested a hand on Trisha's shoulder. "Trisha, let it be. Spot isn't going to hurt her."

Trisha shrugged off his hand and marched up the ramp. Spot lifted her large head and snarled, revealing rows of gleaming teeth. Blue light glowed from somewhere down her throat.

Celine slid a shoe forward, resting her hand right over those teeth, as if tempting the alien to bite her.

Spot snuffled and inhaled instead, that rattling way that brought back Caleb's memories of being trapped in the tool shed. Snapping her jaw shut, the Reptar settled her muzzle against Celine's foot. Tilting her head toward Spot, Celine lifted her hands as if to say, "See? No problem at all."

Caleb smirked. *Yeah, because there's nothing strange about a little kid riding in a horse trailer with an alien predator.*

Simba put a boot on the ramp and loosely clasped Trisha's hand. "She'll be fine."

Twirling about, Trisha strode down the ramp, her eyes glistening and jaw tense.

Before she could see his smile, Caleb lowered his head and forced a serious expression on his face. "Okay, then. Let's roll."

Simba unlocked the cuff around one of Zahir's wrists. It wasn't gentle. He yanked the woman upright and led her to the driver's seat and cuffed one hand to the wheel. "You can drive, right?"

"Like you wouldn't believe." Zahir chuckled, still acting as if she wasn't a prisoner, as if she was still in charge and the handcuffs meant nothing.

Caleb was tempted to make some inappropriate comment about owning handcuffs, but he bit off the words at the sight of Simba's scowl.

Without discussion, Trisha and Mama Noah climbed into the back seat while Simba took the front passenger side.

Caleb slouched next to Mama Noah and drilled imaginary holes into the back of Zahir's head. "Why does she get to drive? I see why you're riding shotgun, 'cause you're better with a gun than me. Get it? Shot. Gun."

"I don't want any guns in the vehicle with us." Trisha rubbed her hands down her thighs. "What if it goes off and hits one of us?"

Simba reached up and tilted the rearview. "The gun can't go off unless I pull the trigger."

Caleb rolled his eyes and leaned against the window. "Yeah, I think she knows how a gun works, genius."

Simba ignored him, probably too busy admiring Trisha in the mirror. Mama Noah pulled out a set of prayer beads and started muttering invocations for protection. Zahir revved the engine a few times before allowing the Land Cruiser to lurch forward. Behind them, Spot roared once.

Caleb laughed and closed his eyes. "This is gonna be the *best* family vacation ever."

## Chapter Fifty-Four

IMAGES FLICKER ACROSS HER CLOSED EYELIDS, LIKE A MOVIE ON the juke. Silent and stilted, as if someone keeps pressing *Start* and *Pause* in rapid succession. Bursts of images appear, one frame at a time. Disconnected yet somehow part of a larger story.

A room, white on all surfaces.

Unadorned walls infused with soft light that glows from a hidden source.

A powdery white face with familiar eyes stares back at her.

Her planet, viewed from a distance, a pearl in a sea of nothing.

Emotions leak through the images: curiosity, anticipation, disappointment, and something that feels like a toxic mixture of love and anger.

A village — not Kinanda Village, something more rural — fills the screen of her inner vision. She's striding through the narrow dirt paths between huts, searching, always searching.

The perspective shifts, descending as if she is collapsing on all fours.

And now, the images come faster.

A mountain topped with a glacier and ringed by forests is bathed in unnatural light.

The savanna stretches out in front of her as she races to meet the others.

Two men stand next to a tall wall, stalking prey. But now, they are the prey, *her* prey.

As she sprints toward them, she feels nothing. No thrill of the hunt, no bloodlust. A job that must be done.

She chases them through an abandoned village and removes the threat.

Finally, darkness and silence. Fear mingles with a familiar coppery scent, saturating the stillness. But none of it is hers, not the emotions nor the images.

Gasping, she jerks upright from the dream state she had slipped into. Around her, the vehicle creaks, quivers and shakes as it bounces over the rough road leading away from home, away from the village, away from death.

A purring sound pulls her farther into the moment and away from the residual emotions.

Pushing away from the metal wall against her back, she crawls toward the agitated creature.

Spot blinks, eyes pulsing, flickering between blue and yellow.

At an instinctual level, Celine understands what would happen if the eyes stay blue. More screams, more blood flowing, more heads rolling.

Tenderly, she clasps her small hands on either side of Spot's head. Just the way her mommy does for Celine after her nightmares.

Spot has one now, a bad dream, and Celine has to be the mommy.

Gazing into her friend's eyes, she sees the flicker of doubt and despair. Those are the emotions which soak through the final image Spot gives her: a spaceship, a smaller version of the one hovering above Nairobi, floats after them, searching for them both.

Celine rests her forehead against Spot's and strokes the creature's neck. The scales seem warmer, softer. Gradually, the Reptar's trembling eases away, and the purring quiets into something more gentle. The sound reminds her of a kitten.

Sinking back onto her heels, she lifts Spot's chin until they are again staring into each other's eyes and souls. She shares hers, and so does Spot.

Celine nods and waits until Spot's heartbeat finally slows. Then, once she's certain her words will be heard, she says the only thing that matters.

"It's okay. I'll protect you."

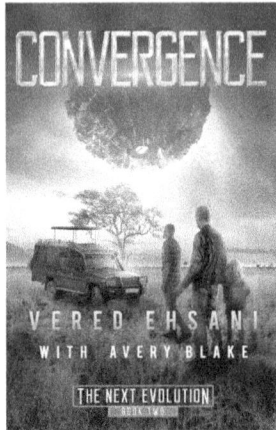

**Convergence**

Want more of The Next Evolution in your life and on your reading device? The adventure continues in Convergence!

Get Convergence

## A quick favor...

Thank you for reading *Transition*.

If you enjoyed this book, please consider writing a review of it on your favorite bookseller site so other readers might enjoy it too. Just a couple of sentences would mean a lot to me.

Thank you!

Vered Ehsani

## About the Author

**Avery Blake** doesn't want you to know where she lives, or what she does. She travels the world, moving from place to place quickly to ensure she can't be tracked. It's safer that way.

When she's not looking over her shoulder, you can find her in the corner of a cafe, facing the exit, typing as fast as she can.

~

**Vered Ehsani** has been a writer since she could hold pen to paper, which is a *lot* longer than she cares to admit. Her work in engineering, environmental management and with the United Nations has taken her around the world. She lives in Kenya with her family and various other animals.

The monkeys in her backyard inspire Vered to create fun, upbeat adventures with a supernatural twist. She enjoys playing with quirky, witty characters who don't quite fit the template for 'normal' despite their best efforts. She's perfectly comfortable exploring the brighter side of human nature.

Are you looking for a mind-refreshing dip into a charming, fanciful world? Then welcome. Sit down with a cup of tea and prepare to be reminded that life can be a delightful place.

Write to Vered (vered@sterlingandstone.net) — she loves connecting with her readers!

Lightning Source UK Ltd.
Milton Keynes UK
UKHW010844070223
416609UK00003B/1007